THE RESIDENT

K.J. KALIS

Copyright © 2025 KJ Kalis, BDM LLC

eISBN 978-1-955990-75-2

ISBN 978-1-955990-76-9

Published by:

BDM, LLC

ALSO BY K.J. KALIS

New titles released regularly!

If you'd like to join my mailing list and be the first to get updates on new books and exclusive sales, giveaways and releases, click here! I'll send you a prequel to the next series FREE!

OR

Visit my Amazon page to see a full list of current titles.

OR

Visit my website:

www.kjkalis.com

1

It's always the best dreams that get interrupted.

"Mac, we need you!" I lurch upright, my pulse hammering in my head.

By the harsh tone of Tamia's voice, I know she must have yelled for me more than once, trying to get me to wake up. Lately, it's taken her more tries than ever to rouse me from sleep. I roll over, every joint in my body aching enough to make me groan, then I absentmindedly sniff my armpit. Not bad. I'll give it a three out of ten on the stink meter, which isn't terrible given the fact that I'm on hour twelve of what looks like it's gonna be a nearly twenty-hour shift.

That's if I'm lucky.

I swallow and blink a couple times, then rub my eyes as I try to stand up, straightening the dark blue scrub top I have on so my sports bra doesn't peek out from under the collar. My eyes still bleary, I pat the lower bunk in the dimly lit on-call room where I've been sleeping, feeling around for my stethoscope, finding it coiled under my pillow like a snake. I must have been holding it when I fell asleep. "What is it?" I mumble as I take a couple of hesitant steps toward the door, waiting for the brain fog to lift.

What I really meant was, "Why are you waking me up already?"

Tamia hands me a cold energy drink — Monster brand. It's morning, or at least it seems like it is, so she went with the Java Monster flavor. For afternoons, I'm a white pineapple girl all the way.

I pop the top, chugging half of it a few steps into the brightly lit hallway. During the first twelve hours of the shift, I usually exist on coffee. The last twelve, the coffee doesn't help. I go right for the high-test energy drinks. They give me heart palpitations and occasionally the sweats, but I don't care. I gotta be ready. Always. All the time.

"Car accident. Multiple victims. Riley is sending a doc down to help."

It strikes me as strange, but I ignore it. Dr. Riley is gonna do what he's gonna do.

Yeah, he's that way.

I loop my stethoscope around the back of my neck and take a couple more sips of my energy drink as I follow Tamia back to the nurses' station. "Any idea how many victims?" I ask. As the chief resident, it's my job to dole out the precious and limited resources that we have in the Emergency Department at Liberty Hill Medical Center. I thought I was lucky when I got this residency placement right out of medical school. I'd always wanted to be a trauma doc, and Philly is one of the best places to learn the ropes.

But given how I feel at this moment, I'm not sure.

I chug the rest of the Java Monster drink, tossing the can in the trash as the first gurney makes its way through the door. I grab a set of gloves and try to judge by the look on the paramedic's faces how bad things are. I can usually tell. Sometimes

I think they know before I do whether a patient has any hope of making it or not.

"Morning, Doc," the first paramedic starts, dark circles under his eyes telling me he's been up all night just like I have.

"Is it?" I give him a lopsided grin.

"Well, the sun's up." He cocks his head to the side.

Working the overnight float does crazy things to a person. "What you got?" I pause. As the resident in charge of the ED, I stand at the door when traumas come in, listen to the report, and get them handed off to our staff for treatment. It's a little like being a traffic cop, if you know what I mean.

As I survey the patient, he gives me the rundown. "Twenty-nine-year-old female, vitals stable, appears to have a fractured right arm. Was conscious and responsive at the scene, though she's got a nasty bump on her head."

Got it. Sounds like orthopedics and neurology. "Bay six is open. Roll her over there." I give Jamir Lopez, a third-year resident just like me, a nod. He follows the gurney to get things started, a bounce to his step. Unlike me, it doesn't matter what time it is, night or day, Jamir always looks like he's just come in from a week on the beach in his native country of Guatemala, happy and rested.

It's not fair.

Dr. Randy Riley appears a second later, his white lab coat swishing around the backs of his calves. Unlike me, Dr. Riley, the head of the Liberty Hill Emergency Department, doesn't wear scrubs. He's old-fashioned like that and stands a little bit shorter than me. Then again, I'm not all that tall. If I'm five foot six, he's probably five foot five. It wouldn't surprise me if he was the kind of guy that wore lifts in his shoes. He's wearing his normal uniform — a white starched shirt, dark pants with a belt tight across his paunch, and an ugly tie. From what Tamia and I can tell, the ties seem to be on a regular rotation —

Monday, red stripe; Tuesday, yellow polka dots; Wednesday, navy.

And yes, people make fun of his name. I mean, who would name their child Randy Riley? Every time I think about it, I can hear the mean kids on the school bus or at recess running by him, rolling their R's feverishly or making engine revving noises.

"You have this handled, Forbes?" he barks.

Dr. Riley never calls me by my first name, which is McKenna. Most people call me Mac. He doesn't even have the courtesy to call me Dr. Forbes. He just uses my last name.

It bugs me.

"Yep," I answer, stepping away for a second as the next gurney comes rolling in from the car accident. It's the morning rush, as Tamia, one of my best friends in the hospital and the charge nurse for Liberty Hill's ED says. People are in a hurry to get to work or get their kids to school and then they make dumb decisions, usually ones that land them up square in front of me. I stop, walking over to the gurney and quickly getting the run down as I lift up a few of the sterile gauze pads that are covering the victim. It's not too bad. Probably just cleaning and sutures.

I return to Dr. Riley after I send the paramedics and Dr. Hudson to bay three, "Yeah, the first victim is in bay six with Dr. Lopez, and this one looks like they have some lacerations that need to be stitched up."

I glance over Riley's shoulder as he's staring at me with his buggy eyes through glasses that seemed to be perpetually smeared with some sort of grease. How he can see through them, I'm not exactly sure. Tamia signals me behind Riley's back. She holds one finger up. "We have one more victim on the way in." Tamia makes a cutting motion across her neck. "From the reports, it's not looking good for the third victim, but

I'll be able to give you a better assessment as soon as they arrive."

Out of the corner of my eye, I see the elevator doors open. A dark-haired physician wearing scrubs and a white coat emerges. Inside I groan. Does Riley really think I need more people to manage? I look back at Dr. Riley. "Tamia said you were having another doc come down to help? I really think we're fine." I'm trying to tell him that I've got it handled. Knowing Riley, he'll totally miss the point. That's why I'm here, right? I'm supposed to be getting experience running the ED.

Riley narrows his eyes. The move gives him a distinctly frog-like expression as his eyelids slide over his bulging eyeballs. "Well, Forbes, as you know, this is *my* ED. I'm responsible for it and I think you need more help, so Dr. Shaw can assist. As you know, I have *other* responsibilities as the head of the Emergency Department. I can't be down here holding your hand all the time."

Holding my hand? You're hardly ever here.

"And as you know, pursuant to your residency stipulations, there needs to be an attending on duty at all times."

I nod blankly. I've heard this spiel a million times, and who uses the word *pursuant* in a sentence anyway?

I keep trying, but every time, I come to the same conclusion: there's no point in arguing. "Absolutely, Dr. Riley. Thanks."

The last thing I wanna do on no sleep is to break in a new attending.

I'd seen Dr. Jonathan Shaw on and off in the Emergency Department. Since he started at Liberty, he seemed to spend more time on medical-surgical cases upstairs. Until that moment, I wasn't clear that he was going to be assigned to the Emergency Department.

Typical.

I take two steps to go deal with the lacerations, sending them to bay five, and then look over my shoulder when Tamia whistles. She and I have developed a whole a series of hand gestures and whistles to get through the day. It's like our own personal language. When you're working as many hours as I am, sometimes even words are exhausting. Mostly, we use them to circumvent people like Dr. Riley. She said it on my first day at Liberty — the less time I spend with him, the better. At first, I thought she was crazy, just a nurse with an overblown ego who was trying to trip me up.

I learned very quickly that I was wrong. Really, really wrong.

Tamia Pitts might be a nurse, but she has more medical knowledge in her pinky than I have in my entire body after finishing four years of medical school and almost three full years of my Emergency Medicine/Trauma residency. She knows more than most attendings and, even better, makes a wicked daiquiri.

Her whistle alerts me to the fact that the last victim from the car wreck, the one with the most serious injuries, was approaching the door. I glance over my shoulder and see a nurse disappear in with the laceration victim. Jamir comes out of bay six. I wave to him, holding five fingers up. He gives me a salute and disappears behind the curtain where the laceration victim is waiting. As I turn back to the door, Dr. Shaw appears.

"Morning," he says, a grin tugging at the corner of his cheek.

"Morning," I mumble, absent-mindedly pushing a strand of hair that desperately needed to be washed behind my ear, hoping he doesn't notice the growing body odor that is emanating from me.

Given the way that Dr. Shaw looked, it was a miracle that any female in the Emergency Department could concentrate. He had the cut jaw and green eyes of a bare-chested man on the cover of a romance novel. Add to that his dark, nearly black hair and the muscles I could practically see rippling underneath his scrub shirt. Dr. Shaw left most of the women in the Emergency Department stumbling for words.

But not me, of course. I'm a cool customer. And I'm at Liberty Hill to learn, right? Not to drool over a handsome attending.

After trying to avoid breathing in the pleasant scent of Shaw's cologne, I look at him. "This one's supposed to be bad."

He arches an eyebrow. "We won't know until we take a look, now will we, Mac?"

I like the way that he says my name, even though I shouldn't. If my boyfriend, Donovan Keller, could hear the thoughts in my head he would worry about our relationship. Then again, I'm exhausted. My defenses are down. I straighten, taking a step back from the whiff of cologne I'm enjoying.

I'm a pro.

The last victim from the car wreck comes in. Dr. Shaw was right. It isn't as bad as we think it's gonna be. The two of us stand, our eyes scanning the man in front of us as we listen to the rundown from the paramedics. From the damage to his face and arms it looks like he wasn't wearing his seat belt but the airbags deployed. Nasty business. Why people think the airbags would protect them on their own, I'll never know. Shaw looks at me, as unaffected as if he's surveying brands of bread at the local grocery store. "I've got this one. You go handle the other patients."

I give a nod, trying hard not to look too relieved. Everyone warns you about how hard residency is — how grueling and tiring it is, how many hours you're locked inside the hospital where there is no night and no day — but the reality of it is sometimes far worse than anyone ever described. It's not just the long hours; it's the expectations of people like Dr. Randy Riley and the myriad of things that could go wrong at any given moment.

The challenge is trying to prevent all those things under stress and with little rest.

So yeah, I'm relieved as Shaw follows the paramedics with the final victim. I frown. I bite the inside of my lip. As I turn away, I realize there's something about Dr. Jonathan Shaw I'm not sure about.

Was this a test? Was I supposed to tell him, "Oh no, Dr. Shaw, I'll take this one!" like an eager kid on the first day of summer camp until he realizes how bad the food is?

Just as I take a couple steps forward, Tamia appears at my side, her brown eyes glinting against her mocha skin. "He took the patient for you?" she asks conspiratorially.

I nod. "Yeah."

She tilts her chin down. "He must like you. I haven't seen him do that for anyone else."

I believe that about as much as I believe the sky is yellow. No, I have the sinking feeling I've just failed a test.

A big one.

2

The next hour flew by. I spent it darting from room to room, doing exactly what Dr. Shaw asked me to — taking care of patients. I first checked on Jamir, who was handling the victim with a broken leg and a probable concussion. (Right on both counts.) Most of the time I spend with one of the other nurses, a tall, lanky dude named Mark who helped me take the glass and shattered plastic out of one of the other victims and then get him X-rayed and stitched up.

As an aside, no matter what anyone tells you, sewing up people's skin isn't that much fun. It's painstaking work. Sometimes I feel like Betsy Ross. I remember learning about her in second grade. She made a whole flag or something.

Sewing isn't my thing.

Anyway, I sneak a glance down the hallway a couple of times. From what I can tell, Shaw is still in working on the final crash victim. He seemed to keep a similar cadence to the rest of us. He'd pop into a room, handle a few things and then pop back to the nurses' station letting Tamia play traffic cop and guide him to what needed to get done next — who needed their discharge papers, who needed orders to be admitted upstairs, and which of the residents needed to have orders or lab results double checked.

About an hour later, our department is finally in a lull, I wander off to the break room, grabbing a bottle of water from the refrigerator, and sit down, putting my feet up. In the midst of the chaos, I notice that I missed a call from Donovan. Leaning back in my chair, I rub my forehead and groan. Trying to get a hold of him has been a real pain. He's in tech sales and travels around the world hawking some sort of super-secret tracking software that a lot of the largest companies and governments want to buy.

It sounds like a cool job, at least what I know of it.

But then again, since it's so super-secret, he can't tell me much.

I'm just about to call him back when I realize that there's a phone call from my mother coming in.

Ignore. *It's not a good time for a chat, Mom.*

It's not that I don't want to talk to her. I do. It's just that when she calls it ends up being a little, how should I say?, involved?

Honestly, it hasn't been a good time for a while. Things have been a little strained in my family, if you know what I mean. I know every family goes through stuff. I guess it's my turn.

I quickly try to call Donovan back, paranoid that as soon as I dial, we'll get a rush of patients. I check the time on my watch. It seems like every time Donovan tried to call me, I'm in with a patient, dealing with Riley, or trying to get a precious few hours of sleep.

Just the thought of it made me yawn.

Sleep. What a beautiful thing.

I quickly write a text to Donovan. "Are you around? Sorry I missed your call earlier. Car crash."

I wait for a second, hoping to see the little bubbles working on the other side of the world. I imagine Donovan holding his phone in his hand, excited to see my message, happy I reached back out to him.

Truth be told, I never thought I would be able to grab the attention of a guy like Donovan. He's smart, he's got a great career, and he's cute — maybe not hot like Shaw, but cute, nonetheless. He's got a runner's build, tall and lanky, which I'm into, brown hair, and soft brown eyes. It doesn't surprise me that he's good at sales. He can sweet-talk me into doing just about anything.

Well, maybe not *anything*. Just most things.

I wait for a second. No bubbles.

Thinking about Donovan reminds me that there are still unpacked boxes in the extra bedroom in my apartment from when he moved in. Donovan's been traveling so much that he and I decided that maybe it was a good time for us to move in together. His lease was up, and his company put him on notice that he'd be traveling probably three out of four weeks every single month. Any normal couple would have hated that, but Donovan and me, we're not exactly normal with our crazy careers.

Sitting in the break room, I think about when he brought it up. We were relaxing on the couch in my apartment, a movie playing in the background. Donovan had his arm around me. I was resting my head against his chest after yet another long shift. I had been hoping for some alone time with him, if you know what I mean, but my body was so tired that anything other than sleep didn't sound good. You know, that old "the spirit is willing, but the body is weak," thing from the Bible. When I was just about to nod off, I felt his warm fingers underneath my chin. For a second I thought he was lifting my face to his so he could kiss me. Instead, when I opened my eyes, he had a frown on his face. He looked so serious I jerked my head back. "What's wrong?"

"I need to ask you something."

Are you breaking up with me?

My heart skipped a beat. "Sure." I'm almost a real doctor so I pride myself on being able to keep my cool. "Anything." I stopped using my physician lingo. My most common catch phrase is: "What seems to be the trouble?" I thought that might be a little ridiculous given the situation.

Donovan slipped his arm out from behind my shoulders and scooted back on the couch, angling his body towards me but pulling away.

Uh oh. He's gaining personal distance. This can't be good.

"My boss called me today."

He's lost his job and is moving to Mumbai.

"Really?" I tried to stay as calm as possible.

He winces, then shifts in his seat as if he just discovered he was sitting on a pile of tacks. "Yeah. They've got a lot of travel coming up for me. Probably going to last at least six months." Donovan shrugged. "Knowing them, could be the next year or two for all I know."

I press my lips together, pushing them out far enough they touch the bottom of my nose. Donovan calls it my duck face. "And this is a problem?"

"The thing is, my lease is up. With work saying I'm going to be gone like three out of four weeks every single month, I was wondering..."

Are you about to get down on one knee? I glance at the pockets of his pants. There's no bulge. No, not that kind of bulge. A bulge for a ring box.

"What are you asking me, Donovan?"

He looked away, then back at me, letting out a long sigh. "What would you think about me moving in with you? I mean, you're never here and I won't be here much either. I could help take care of Snort. At least it would be easier to see each other when I am home."

As if on cue, my gray, fuzzy cat, Snort, appeared on the back of the couch, emitting one of his sinusy noises from his adorable pushed-in face. I swear, sometimes I think he's half pug with all the commotion he makes.

I reach up and pull Snort down onto my lap, stroking his back. He darts away after a second, shooting me a disdainful look.

Very on brand for Snort.

"So, you wanna move in?"

Donovan nodded. "You have crazy hours. So do I. Why should both of us pay for apartments that neither of us gets to spend any time in?"

Very Donovan. Very logical. The girly part of me would have liked a bit more romance added to the mix. A little, "I can't live for another moment without you. Let's move in together right now," would have been good, but that's not Donovan.

"Sure," I say cheerfully. "I think that sounds like a great idea."

Donovan nodded, his expression brightening. "And I'll pay half the rent and half the utilities. I don't want to be a freeloader."

Still no romance, but okay. "That sounds great."

To date, Donovan has spent eight days in the apartment.

3

After waiting for another five minutes, my feet up on one of the chairs in the break room, I see Dr. Randy Riley saunter by. Any hope I had of taking a longer break just ended. If there's one thing that Riley hates more than anything, it seems to be seeing his residents trying to catch their breath. I check my armpits again. I am quickly approaching a four out of ten on the stink level, despite the gobs of deodorant on my pits, and I'm being generous. Glancing at my locker, I wonder if I have a second to apply yet another coat, but then I see Riley circling the nurses' station. A healthy dose of paranoia starts running up my spine. He is probably looking for me. As chief resident, he expects me to be accessible to him at all times, whether I was at the hospital, or at home trying to catch up on sleep, or curled up in front of the television with Snort.

I wince. Curling up with Donovan would have been better, but like I said, he's hardly ever home.

The urge to put more deodorant on subsided with the over-arching paranoia I'm feeling. At this rate, with the amount of it caked underneath my armpits, I was going to have to take a palette knife to my skin to scrape it off.

My paranoia grows. All that aluminum couldn't be healthy, could it?

I make a mental note to research the effects of aluminum toxicity on the body in my free time, then chuckled out loud.

Free time? What was that? Even when I was off, all I wanted to do was sleep.

As I make my way out to the nurses' station, I check my phone again. Still nothing from Donovan.

Come on, text bubbles. Just a quick message back would be so nice.

"There you are," Riley says in a way that only he could muster. No matter what he says, his words come off as cutting, like he's better than anyone he's talking to

I try to look innocent. "Were you looking for me?"

"Yes, Forbes. I came down to see the status of the department."

Isn't that what Dr. Shaw is for? I keep my commentary to myself. "Everything seems to be fine. We had a little lull, so I was taking a break."

Riley narrowed his bulgy eyes at me. "Then why weren't you updating your charts?"

Perhaps because I needed five minutes to myself in this overly long shift? Technically, I'm only supposed to work twelve hours, but that's where I was when Tamia woke me up for the car accident. All of this is bonus work right now that I don't get paid for, which means the hospital pays me even less per hour than I'm supposed to make. I'm nothing but a glorified volunteer when they keep me over. It's just one of the fun parts of being a resident. "I'm sorry, I needed to use the bathroom. I've been holding it for hours."

Riley presses his thin lips together. Part of me is sure that he is currently running through all of the symptomologies for a urinary tract infection, but since I didn't tell him exactly what I needed to do when I went to the bathroom, he's probably also thinking about the implications of not allowing his residents to go number two and how much it might cost the hospital if they have to repair a bowel blockage. "Alright, Forbes, but try not to take so much personal time when you are on shift. When I come down here, I expect to find you available."

"Sure, Dr. Riley." My shoulders slump. It's just yet another correction by Riley in a long series of them since I started at Liberty Hill.

As he walks away, I'm absolutely positive that if I had not referred to him as "Dr. Riley" that he probably would have barked at me on the spot. He's a stickler for those kinds of things.

And apparently not using the bathroom.

As Riley disappears through the doors that lead out to the elevator and the rest of the hospital, I glance at Tamia. She shakes her head ever so slightly. I know that look. It's the one that means, "If only I had charge of all the residents, you all would do so much better."

She's probably right.

As I check my phone again for the millionth time to see if Donovan has responded, (he hasn't), I hear a low whistle. As I glance up, I see Tamia looking at me and then giving me a head bob. A new patient has just arrived and has been slotted into one of the rooms. I walk over to the nurses' station where she hands me a tablet. "What do we have?"

"Frequent flyer in bay two."

"Who is it?" I ask without looking at the chart.

Tamia crosses her arms in front of her chest. Her expression is somewhere between the anger of, "You're past curfew," and the excitement of, "You're not going to believe what I just found out!" I'm kind of hoping it's more the latter and not the former. It's bad enough being on thin ice with Riley. I don't need to be on thin ice with Tamia too, especially given the fact she's one of my few friends here at the hospital.

"It's Bill Palmer again."

I close my eyes and sigh, my back very professionally turned toward the bay where the intake nurse, Rosemary, was getting him settled into his bed.

"Are you kidding me? I think he was here like two days ago, wasn't he?"

Tamia shakes her head. "No. That was just yesterday."

I squint, looking up at the ceiling. "That was yesterday?"

When I look back at Tamia, she is full-on shaking her head. "Yeah, Mac. That was just yesterday. How many more hours do you have on this shift?"

"The better question is how many hours I put into the shift already."

"The answer?"

"Fourteen."

"I thought they were only supposed to keep you for twelve hours at a time."

I shrug. It's a conversation we have regularly. Tamia wants me to push back at Riley about it, but I'm concerned he'd strangle me with one of his ugly ties if I even broached the subject. I feel a knot in my gut just thinking about it. As the Director of the Emergency Department and my residency coordinator, he holds my entire career in his small hands. "I guess that's technically true, but tell Riley about that while he's home sleeping in his bed."

Tamia looks conspiratorially at me. "You know he's one of those guys that wears actual pajamas, don't you?"

"Seriously, you think?"

She nods.

I shake my head. "I'm not gonna be able to get that visual out of my head."

Tamia looks toward the back of the ED where Dr. Shaw had

just emerged from one of the bays. I could see her eyes lock on him. Shaw stops to talk to one of the techs from upstairs. I think she's a respiratory therapist named Sarah. The girl's attention was locked on Shaw, her eyes wide, her lips parted. I try not to roll my eyes. Just the expression on her face reads like a Hallmark movie.

Tamia broke off her gaze at them and looked back at me. "Maybe you should talk to Dr. Shaw about your hours? He seems to like you."

I shake my head. "I'm sure that would get me in Riley's good graces. First, he'd be mad at me for asking, then he'd be mad at me for asking Shaw and not him."

Tamia laughs. "The classic Riley two-step. Can't win with him and can't win without him," we say in unison. She hands me the tablet. "Go get it done."

Grudgingly, I accept the tablet from her and step away from the chat we were having. Literally, these little snippets of conversation I have with people like her and Jamir and some of the other staff is the only real life I get to ever experience. By the time my shifts are over I'm so exhausted that I can barely form a sentence, let alone offer a reasonable diagnosis on a complicated case. Even though I'm in my third year of residency, I still can't quite understand why the medical system treats residents like this. Wouldn't you want your people awake, well-fed and well-rested in order to teach them how to save people's lives?

It's these kinds of questions that I'm sure would keep me awake if I could ever manage to catch up on my sleep.

As I approach Bill Palmer's bay, I stop and use the hand sanitizer foam that's stationed outside of every room, rubbing the stuff on my hands. Per usual, it burns, probably because I have used so much of it. Looking down at my red, angry cuticles and the splotches on the backs of my hands, I'm pretty sure

I have developed contact dermatitis from it but ignore the stinging and push the curtain aside.

I make a mental note. Maybe I can get Shaw or Riley to prescribe me some hydrocortisone cream before I go home?

Bill Palmer is someone whose story I pretty much know by heart. We see him nearly every week. "Well, hey, Mr. Palmer, how are you doing today?"

"Oh, good, it's you, Dr. Forbes. I'm really glad that you're working today. I was worried it would be someone else."

I don't want to get into a long conversation with Bill. He's nice enough, but if he's coming to the ED for social time, he's missed the point. I deploy my catch phrase. "What seems to be the problem?" I ask, but don't look up. I'm busily rereading the notes I had put in apparently the day before. Luckily, what I wrote actually halfway makes sense.

He points down to his foot. I can't see it. It's covered by the sheet. "The foot again, Doc. I just don't understand. I took all the medication that you told me to get, just like it said. But it's not getting any better. It really hurts."

Pulling a set of blue latex gloves from the box mounted to the wall, I snap them over my wrist. "Let's take a look and see what we can figure out."

As soon as I lift the sheet, I fight to stifle a gasp. Bill's foot, which according to my notes had been slightly red the day before, was now black. How did this happen so fast? His foot isn't just slightly black, but black-black, like it had been run over by a car. There is a rotting smell coming from a sore on the top of his foot, an open lesion, the edges gooey with greenish-yellow pus. As soon as I put my fingers near his ankle, I can feel the heat coming off of it. The pulse was still there, but barely. The infection had eaten away at the blood supply to the rest of the tissue. I blink, quickly covering up his foot and pulling off my gloves, using the hand sanitizer, this time a large amount of it on my hands, grateful for the sting, hoping the bacteria that is eating his toes isn't eating at my fingers. "All right, it seems that the infection has gotten worse. I think we're going to have to put you on some IV antibiotics and then figure out what to do next. How does that sound?"

Bill winces. "Good. Could I have something for the pain, please? It really hurts."

I have no doubt it does. "Of course. Let me write up the orders and we'll get some pain medication and an IV started for you in just a minute. You just stay put, all right?"

Not that he was going anywhere with his foot like that.

As I'mm walking out of the room, frowning at my tablet, Dr. Shaw comes out of the bay next to me. I had no idea he was working so close by. He lifts his chin. "What you got in there?" He bobs his head toward Bill Palmer's room.

I shake my head, trying to conceal how freaked out I am about the fact that Bill's foot went from red to black in about twenty-four hours. I'm not just a resident, I remind myself. I'm the Chief Resident. "Just a frequent flyer. He's got an infected foot. Not looking good."

I see a flicker of concern on Shaw's face. He holds out his hand for my tablet. "Let me see."

I hand the tablet over, trying to avoid brushing my fingers against his. All the other girls might be oohing and aahing over him, but I'm not. We're colleagues. And I'm a pro. But now I'm beginning to wonder. Am I a pro? Do I know what I'm doing? Is Shaw gonna call me out as a fraud? I might deserve it. I push the thought away. Every resident goes through the mind game of being an imposter. I'm no different.

I refocus on Bill. His foot looks like it belongs to a cadaver, and I have no idea how Shaw is going to react.

By the look on his face, I'm not going to like it.

I think my day is just about to go from bad to worse.

4

___

Shaw's tanned fingers end up brushing against mine as I hand him the tablet with Mr. Palmer's records, setting off a flutter of butterflies in my stomach. I follow him into the room. Once again, we spray our hands with more of the hand sanitizer. This time it stings even more than before. I look down, noticing how red my hands are and then shove them in the pockets of my scrub pants. The last thing I want is for Shaw to see my hands peeling and chapped. I look like I spent the winter digging the snow out of my driveway with my fingers.

Not a good look.

Maybe I'll ask Riley for that hydrocortisone. With any luck he'll send me home so I can sleep while it works.

Embarrassed that I'm so worried about what Shaw thinks, I pull my hands out of my pockets. What am I doing? I don't need a boyfriend. I just need Donovan to be home. That's all.

I sigh.

Maybe the Shaw-mania is contagious.

There's a rattle of thoughts in the back of my head that sound surprisingly like my mother. It's like her voice pops up in my head every time I do something stupid, which seems to be happening more and more frequently. I know it's just the lack of sleep talking. Or at least I hope that's the case.

Shaw introduces himself. "Hey, Mr. Palmer. I'm Dr. Shaw. I just wanted to stop in and take a look at your foot."

Mr. Palmer eyes up the two of us like there's either a conspiracy against him or a blooming romance, as if Shaw is riding in to rescue me from his gross, black foot. Mr. Palmer waves Shaw off. "It's just my foot. Hurts a little, that's all." The speed of his hand moving through the air lifts the nest of thin strands of hair left on the top of his head. It reminds me of an empty plastic bag caught up in a breeze. "Dr. Forbes says she has it under control. She's always good to me."

See, Shaw. I've got it under control.

Undeterred, Shaw sets the tablet down on the edge of the bed and puts on a pair of blue gloves, frowning. I grab gloves as well, just in case. Not sure I need them, but I guess it's just so ingrained to have my gloves on and ready that I feel a twinge of panic without them. Shaw looks up at me. "There's no notes in here from today yet?"

My face reddens. "I literally just walked out of the room when I found you outside."

Lame excuse, but true.

"Okay." The words come out slowly, like he's not sure it's an excuse.

As soon as Shaw lifts the sheet, I can tell by his expression there's trouble. Shaw goes through basically the same exam that I just did, examining the wound then checking for distal pulses. The only difference is I can see a flicker of a muscle tightening across his jaw.

That's never a good sign.

After being at Liberty Hill for a while, I've become a master at interpreting all forms of communication from the attendings, both verbal and nonverbal. Believe me, they make no bones about letting you know when they're unhappy about something, surprised, disgusted, frustrated or otherwise.

Shaw is clearly unhappy.

Lucky for me, he's not making a big fuss about it in front of Mr. Palmer. Then again, that's probably because the poor man's foot is black.

What I didn't say to Mr. Palmer was that given the way his foot looks, amputation is probably now on the possibility list. I probably should have, but I didn't have the heart. My stomach tightens into something that feels about the size of a pebble and just as hard. I glance at the tablet. Shaw's still holding it. I fight the urge to snatch it out of his hands. Given how bad Mr. Palmer's foot looks, it's hard for me to believe that only twenty-four hours have gone by.

Lucky for Mr. Palmer, Shaw keeps his cool. He gives me a sideways glance that tells me I'm in for a conversation outside the room, one I might not like. I try not to shrink at the thought. Shaw gives Mr. Palmer a nod. "All right, Bill, I'm going to go out and have a chat with Dr. Forbes, and we're going to put together a treatment plan for you. I'll be back in a couple of minutes to chat with you about what we're gonna do next."

The way he says, "*I'll* be back in," sends a chill down my spine.

Shaw doesn't exactly shove me out of the bay, but I can feel the heat of his body pushing me forward like an invisible force field. As we walk into the hallway, he closes the curtain then the door, stopping to squirt his hand with a giant-sized ball of foamy hand sanitizer again, the tablet locked underneath his arm. It's a testament to how decayed Mr. Palmer's foot is. Shaw waves me over to an unoccupied corner of the nurses' station. I can see Tamia, who's at the other end, glance my way and then turn in the other direction. I wince. Even she doesn't want to witness what's about to happen. Shaw pushes the tablet toward me. He points to the screen.

"Okay, Dr. Forbes, tell me how Mr. Palmer's foot looked yesterday."

It wasn't exactly a question; it was more of a command. His tone bordered on accusation. "Well, it looked like I described in the notes. It was red, with a small wound on the top. I asked him about it. He said he was in the kitchen and dropped a mug. It hit the top of his foot and the skin split. I noted in here that he said it had been red for a few days before he came in. I prescribed him the standard Amoxicillin-Clavulanate treatment that Dr. Riley recommends, plus told him to use Ibuprofen as needed for pain and inflammation." I point toward the notes. "See, I even put in here that he should follow up with his primary care physician, a podiatrist or an orthopedic."

Shaw furrowed his perfect eyebrows. "Who signed off on this?"

My face reddened. I flip back through the notes, dragging my finger across the screen. My chapped skin stings every time I change the page. I had submitted my orders for approval, hadn't I?

Shaw doesn't give me a chance to answer. He grabs for my tablet, nearly ripping it out of my hands. "I'm not sure exactly what happened here, but the infection is clearly out of control. You see that, don't you?"

My face goes from slightly red to beet red. My cheeks are so hot that I imagine that every capillary is bursting, leaving me with a permanent set of spiderwebs on either side of my nose. "Yes, of course. I mean, his foot's black." I quickly try to cover my tracks. "But it wasn't when I saw him before."

Tamia shoots me a look. My voice must have been louder than I thought.

My face gets even hotter. I suddenly remembered the line from *Hamlet* —" The lady doth protest too much, methinks."

I am doth protesting.

When I look back at Shaw, his face is calm, almost too calm. "This time, instead of referring him to an orthopedic, we're gonna admit him to the medical surgical floor. He needs to get seen by an orthopedic right away. They're going to have to make a decision about whether they can try to treat that foot or whether they're going to have to take it off."

I shift uncomfortably and look away. I know that Mr. Palmer lives alone. "If you do that, he's going to have to go to rehab. He might never walk again."

Shaw shrugs. "I don't know what you want me to say, Dr. Forbes. When he came in yesterday, if his foot was as you described it and we had put him on IV antibiotics right away, he probably wouldn't be in this position. You are aware that the tibial pulses in both ankles are low, aren't you?"

I frown. "No. I just checked the one on the infected foot. I expected it to be low with the inflammation."

Shaw nods once, as if he were Sherlock Holmes and had just solved a case. "If you had taken a minute to check the other one, you would have realized that he has some obvious circulation issues. Also, the tips of his fingers have a slightly bluish cast. Nothing that normally would be a cause for alarm, but with an infection like that it can make it very difficult to treat."

My head begins to swim. Whether that was a consequence of all the energy drinks I had consumed, the lack of sleep or the fact that Shaw was three steps ahead of me, I wasn't sure. When exactly had he checked the other pulse? I only looked away for a second when we were in the exam room.

Shaw doesn't give me an opportunity to answer. He moves to the nurses' station, sets the tablet down and submits a set of orders, ones I'm sure aren't anything like what I planned on doing. He looks at me, his expression a handsome mix of surprise and disappointment. "I'm going to go in and talk to Mr. Palmer about his foot and what we're facing. There is a real possibility if we can't get that infection under control and he decides to keep that foot, that he could become septic. What I need you to do is walk upstairs and make sure that they have the orders and that they have a bed for him. The sooner we get him up there, the better."

"But you just sent the orders? They'll get them. Probably have them already." Was Shaw that new to Liberty Hill that he thought we had to send our orders upstairs by carrier pigeon?

His face tightened, the muscles flickering over his sculpted jaw. "Dr. Forbes, with a patient like Bill Palmer, we can't take a risk of any communication error. Go upstairs, tell the intake nurse I'm asking her to get this one moving quickly." The words come out calm, almost too calm. I can tell that Shaw isn't happy with the situation, but the way he says it is strange. I pause, my lips parting slightly. Something seems off. He didn't seem to be completely unhappy with me. That's a first. Usually, the attendings tend to make things personal and dump the blame on the nearest resident.

Which was usually me.

"Sure." I'm humbled at the lack of personal attack. I take a half a step back, realizing that waiting for Shaw to make his judgement had made me sweat. If I had been a four on the stink scale before, I knew I was probably at least a six by now.

As Shaw turns away to go talk to Mr. Palmer, I start toward the elevators, glancing at the locker room. I could just run in for a second, strip off my scrubs and put on a fresh set and a new coat of deodorant, bringing me back from the deep abyss of body odor, but then I glance at the elevator doors. I've already screwed up once. It probably isn't a good idea to make any detours, not after how calmly Shaw had dealt with me, especially given the fact that he was new. For all intents and purposes, as an attending, he was my boss.

And one that was very easy on the eyes, even if he didn't like how I've dealt with Mr. Palmer.

Maybe I was wrong about Shaw. Maybe he'll work out to be okay after all.

Stepping into the elevator, I move to the far side, not wanting to expose anyone else in the small space to the rank smell I'm sure is following me like a cloud. I tap my fingers on the handrail. If it had been Riley who had found out about Mr. Palmer's foot, I was sure that he would have read me the riot act. But Shaw hadn't. He'd been calm, nice about it, even though Mr. Palmer's foot was clearly in an almost fully necrotic state.

As I step out of the elevator and start wandering around on the medical-surgical floor, trying to find Marcus to tell him what Dr. Shaw had said, my mind reeled. How could Palmer's foot have gotten that bad so fast? Shaw had clearly been unhappy with the fact that my orders hadn't been approved, but what was I supposed to do? I thought I hit send. I must have because Tamia had discharged him, complete with his prescriptions. If Dr. Riley hadn't looked at it, that wasn't my fault.

I stop in the middle of the hallway, nearly running into one of the nurses. The answer comes to me suddenly. I know what happened.

Bill Palmer probably hadn't filled his prescriptions, figuring he didn't need them. It happened all the time. People decide they feel better, don't want to pay for their meds, or decide we are wrong and ignore the advice they've been given.

A little ray of sunshine poked out of my dark heart. It wasn't my fault after all.

See?

The revelation helped my gut to settle. I adopted my best stern physician face. Clearly, I needed to communicate better with patients about the risks they would be taking if they didn't take the medication I prescribed. I suck in a deep breath. Even in my exhausted state, I could take criticism, especially if it came that nicely. I would definitely work on my patient communication skills. I would talk to Marcus, get Mr. Palmer all set in medical-surgical, then tell Shaw about my revelation and commit to better patient communication skills.

All would be well again.

Wouldn't it?

A cloud covers my newly bright heart. It might not be if Mr. Palmer didn't survive.

5

After searching every nook and crevice of the medical-surgical for ten minutes, I ended up having a somewhat terse conversation with the intake nurse, Alexey, a bald Russian who has taken over for Marcus. Unfortunately, Marcus, who was exceedingly easy-going, had taken the day off. Alexey wasn't tuned up the same. I can tell from the moment I arrived on the floor that it isn't a good idea. He took exception with the fact that I felt the need to come up personally. I try to make it seem like I'm just double-checking. "I know, Alexey. You always get it done."

I can tell by his expression that he's not buying my explanation. "A new doc on the floor sent me up here. Sorry to bother you."

There's nothing more formidable than a charge nurse.

Alexey narrows his eyes at me. "We will handle it. No need to come here and bother me. I read my orders."

Told ya, Shaw.

As I step into the elevator, my phone rings. I pull it out of my pocket in time to see it is Donovan.

Thank God.

"Hey!" I answer, hoping there's a signal in the small space. I look around apologetically at the other people in the elevator who probably don't want to hear me talk to my boyfriend in this small space, but they don't understand. We've hardly talked.

I wait. There's no response.

"Donovan?" I ask as the doors open. I'mtrying to keep my voice low, but once again, I must have been louder than I thought I. The other people on the elevator give me a strange look as I step out, as if I've lost my mind.

Instead of going right back to work, I turn left, slipping into a dark shadow that's between the elevators and the entrance to the Emergency Department door. I haven't had more than about a five-minute break in hours, not since Tamia had woken me up for the car wreck victims. I decided I was entitled to a break, even if it is just a couple of minutes with Donovan. I mean, who could blame me? We hardly ever get to talk with his travel schedule. Maybe I could tell him what happened with Shaw. He'd tell me everything was fine and then I could get back to work.

I'm not that lucky.

The phone crackless in my ear as if Donovan is trying to talk but the connection iss bad. I hold the phone away from my face and look at it. The screen look like we're still connected. "Donovan? Are you there?"

Nothing.

A second later, the call ends. I check my service. I only have one bar. My skin prickles. Am I not on the hospital Wi-Fi? I look again and the bars all of a sudden perk up, giving me a full array of signal.

I sigh. Just my luck, Donovan calls right when I 'm in the elevator. I try dialing him back really quick now that my signal is better, but all I get is more static.

"Donovan? Donovan?"

Then it occurs to me. Maybe it was at his end and not mine. If that was the case, I could call all I want and I won't be able to talk to him.

Bummer.

Feeling sullen, I walk slowly back into the emergency department, the wide gray metal double doors opening as soon as I hit the button on the wall. I'm staring at my phone when I walk back into the ED, not really paying attention to where I'm going. I feel a warm hand on my shoulder. Tamia. She steers me toward the break room. Closing the door behind me, she stares. I know that look. The Inquisition has begun. "What was that with Shaw?"

My face twists. "What are you talking about?" I know Tamia is protective of the people in her department and Shaw is new, but our conversation was pretty cordial given how Riley usually treats me. Then it occurs to me — I bet she's just pumping me for information since Shaw's the new hot commodity in the department. I know Tamia's not in the market. She already has a boyfriend. I figure she's asking for someone else.

"It looked like he was reading you the riot act."

"It wasn't that way. He was just asking me questions."

"About Palmer's black foot."

Man, news travels fast. The only thing that she didn't say was, "How did you miss that?"

My chest tightens. Who is she to ask questions? Where was this coming from?

She's just a nurse.

The minute the thought flickers in my head, I don't like it. Tamia is my friend and has gotten me out of more scrapes than I can count with Riley. She's the den-mother, mama bear, and troop leader of the ED. I suck in a deep breath, glad it was just a thought, and my lack of filter mouth actually worked like it should for once. We're a team in the ED. We have to work together. I give myself a pass. This is just a lack of sleep issue.

"Yeah. I think he was just trying to figure out how it got so bad so fast." I test out my theory on Tamia. "I think Mr. Palmer didn't fill his prescriptions."

She shrugs in a way that tells me she thinks I'm wrong. I fidget with the end of my stethoscope. "Maybe I should have gone with an IV option when he first came in."

Tamia doesn't say a word. She has no mercy.

A split second later, she changes the subject. "When is Shaw gonna let you go home?"

I glance down the hallway. As much as I want to go home and be done with this excruciating shift, after what just happened with Bill, I'm not sure now is the time to inquire. "No idea."

"You could ask."

I frown. "Why would I ask him? Wouldn't I just ask Riley like normal?"

Tamia arches an eyebrow, like I missed something that was as big as a tractor-trailer parked in the middle of the hospital. "I don't think so, Mac. Rumor has it that Riley's gonna stay the department head, but that he's gonna spend more time in administration. Looks like they're grooming Shaw to take over the actual day-to-day operations."

I throw my hands in the air. "Well, that's just great. The first case I work with him, and I totally screw it up."

Tamia narrows her eyes. "Yeah, that's not like you."

Again, no mercy.

My gut feels like it's being squeezed by a giant boa constrictor. "I don't need this right now, Tam. Seriously. I sent him home with the prescriptions, and if he never filled them, there's nothing I can do." I hold my hands up and shake my head, my expression slack. She's not actually accusing me of anything, is she? My eyes widen and my head pounds. I'm about to lose my cool.

It would be a hard argument for Tamia to counter. Patient

compliance was always a problem. People come into the emergency room time after time with the same problems — panic attacks that feel like a heart attack, seizures that aren't being adequately managed, even folks who are looking for narcotics. We tell them over and over again what to do, and they won't do it.

"You know how it is. Think of all the times we get somebody in here who's in a diabetic crisis because they just won't control what they're eating or their insulin."

Tamia didn't say anything, her arms crossed in front of her chest. With her dark eyes, she is the kind of person who could just stare right through you.

She did it to me regularly. I'd like to say I was immune to its effects, but that would be a lie.

She blinked. "You seriously think that Mr. Palmer didn't take his medication? Is that what you're saying?"

All I can do is shrug. "I have no idea, Tam. I remember doing the discharge paperwork, printing off the prescriptions, and handing them to him. I told him to follow up with his primary care doc, a podiatrist or an orthopedic."

Tamia's questions cause my knotted stomach to flutter. Did I?

My mind starts to swim. My shifts are starting to become one big blur. What if I forgot to give Mr. Palmer his prescriptions? He wouldn't have left the hospital without asking for them, would he?

My face gets hot again. It stings almost as much as my hands do when I use that sanitizing foam. Tamia has a tablet in her hand. "Let me see that for a second."

Tamia shoots me a look as if she's enjoying watching me squirm.

I hold my hand out. I guess I didn't use the magic word. She stares at me. "Please?"

Honestly, sometimes she acts like my mother.

After handing it over, I thumb through the records again. I slide over next to her, careful not to get too close, given how badly I need a shower. I point, my stomach twisting into a knot. "*See*. I put the prescriptions in. It even shows that I printed them off. Isn't there a way you can check and find out if they were filled?"

Tamia holds out her hand, a withering look on her face as if she doesn't believe me.

A second later, her face relaxes, her mouth hanging open. "Look. He never filled them."

I throw my hands in the air. "See! I can't control that. Shaw can get mad at me all he wants, but if Mr. Palmer doesn't go and get his prescriptions filled, there's nothing I can do."

Feeling vindicated, I glance out into the ED. I can see Shaw's having a conversation at the nurses' station with a cute, strawberry blonde respiratory therapist named Emma. Dagger glances are coming from a couple of the other nurses as they watch the two of them together. If Shaw and Emma are just standing around shooting the breeze, that means that the department's quiet for the moment. I look at Tamia, my eyes wide and hopeful. "You think I can run down and get a sandwich really quick? I don't think I've eaten since I got here yesterday."

Tamia scans the Emergency Department like a general taking stock of their soldiers. "Yeah. But make it fast. You know how things go. One minute nothing's happening and the next minute we're slammed."

I stride toward the door of the break room, a grin on my face. "Just page me if you need me back in a hurry." Not that I won't hurry anyway, but at least I won't have to sprint back if nothing's going on.

"I will."

But, like Tamia says, nothing stays quiet in the ED for long.

6

The second I get to the cafeteria, which is on the other side of the hospital, my pager goes off. There's a message flashing across the screen. It's from Shaw. "Palmer. Upstairs. Did you tell them?"

Shoot. I totally forgot to talk to Shaw when I got back from going upstairs. I'd gotten so distracted by the almost phone call from Donovan and talking to Tamia that I didn't check in with him. I press my lips together. There's no way to respond over the paging system. It was meant to call people back to their departments with a short message, not send a reply, and I don't have his cell number yet. I have to get back. Shaw's waiting for me.

My eyes dart around the cafeteria as my stomach grumbles, I snag a turkey wrap and another energy drink. Across the dining hall, I feel someone watching me. It's my friend Marshall. He works in security. He's sitting with another guy and just gives me a casual wave. I wave back and stride to the checkout. As much as I'd like to have a minute to say hello, I gotta go.

I drum my fingers on the conveyor belt at the checkout as I

stand and wait for the woman in front of me. Bless her heart, she's an older lady with an overflowing plate of roast chicken, mashed potatoes, green beans, a salad, and an orange, and even a bowl of red Jell-O along with two chocolate milks. There's even a chocolate chip cookie on her tray. Was she eating for twelve? Most of it looks really heavy, but as I wait for her to dig through her purse for loose change (who even carries cash anymore?), I look over my shoulder, eyeing up the bakery display.

I shouldn't.

Most of the food at the cafeteria is iffy at best. I think they work under the philosophy that if it is basically nutritious, and the doctors and nurses are hungry, the taste doesn't matter.

They are kinda right.

But the chocolate chip cookies at the Liberty Hill cafeteria are good. I look away. A couple of them would taste really good, but I don't have time. I feel perspiration gather at the back of my neck. Shaw is waiting.

I shift from side to side and inch forward. Maybe if she knows I'm waiting — I mean, how can she not? — she'll hurry it up. I feel the tick-tock, tick-tock of expectation thrumming in my head. When I'm just about to abandon my sandwich, the woman in front of me finishes paying, but not before shooting me a nasty glare.

I feel bad for being impatient, but c'mon. Why don't they have a lane for hospital personnel in a hurry?

I quickly scan my Liberty Hill employee badge to pay and do my best walk-jog toward the other side of the hospital. I'm sure I look like one of those ridiculous speed walkers in the Olympics, but I don't want to outright run to the ED and risk knocking someone over.

As I make the third turn of what I know to be eleven zigzag turns to get back, I pull my phone out, pulling up Tamia's contact information and sending her a voice text. "Shaw just paged me. I forgot to tell him I went upstairs. Tell him that Alexey said that there's no beds but that there should be one in a few hours. I'm on my way back now."

A second later I got a thumbs up from Tamia.

I slow down to a reasonable pace. Crisis averted.

By the time I get back to the Emergency Department, I've chugged down half of the energy drink. I accidentally grabbed the peaches 'n' crème instead of the white pineapple. It tastes bad, but I chug it anyway. I hear my mom's voice chirping in my head, "No reason to waste, Mac!"

I wince. I just want a normal relationship with my mom.

Shaw's standing at the desk when I got back, a frown on his face. He looks up as I approach. My face reddens. Again. "Dr. Shaw," I use the Dr. part for good measure. I adopt my best contrite expression. "I'm so sorry. I was down at the cafeteria trying to grab something to eat really quick when you paged." I hold up the sandwich for emphasis. It's a good touch and proves I was actually in the cafeteria and not dawdling. "I don't know if Tamia told you, but yes, I talked to Alexey upstairs. There'll be a bed available in a few hours. I also put in a request for orthopedics and wound care to come down and take a look at Mr. Palmer's foot."

He looks at me, not saying anything for a second. The waiting is horrible. I feel a bead of perspiration run down my back from just under my ponytail from my semi-sprint back to the ED. I'm frozen. What is he gonna do?

The silence lasts for another second then his face softens. "Thanks for handling that. Why don't you go eat your sandwich? Next time, just remember to get me the information first, okay?"

"Sure."

I have to admit I'm surprised at how calm he is. Riley would have used my failure as an opportunity to make a scene. I'd seen him do it before a million times, not only with the residents, but with the interns, the medical students, and even the nursing staff. Lucky for the nurses, they have Tamia. After Dr. Randy Riley decided to get his tie in a knot one time too many with the nursing staff, Tamia had it out with Riley. She'd backed him down with her steely eyes and sharp tongue. Riley hadn't messed with any of the nurses since.

See why I'm friends with Tamia? She's a good person to have in your corner.

I'm just about to turn and head for the break room when I stop to look at Shaw. He's already staring back at the tablet, his broad back arching over the nurses' station like he's Samson. Should I press my luck?

Why not? I mean, I'm already under the microscope with what happened to Mr. Palmer. What's a little more pressure?

"Dr. Shaw, one more thing if you don't mind?" Again, I go for uber polite. My mom, the kind of person who is filled with all sorts of sayings that don't mean anything, used to always say, "You get more flies with honey than with vinegar." I'm not exactly sure what that means but it seems to apply. I'm from a smallish city in Ohio — Youngstown. Maybe it's a Midwest thing.

"Mac?"

I tingle. It's the first time he's used my first name. It makes me feel warm inside, like the first time the most popular guy at school walks past your locker. I swallow.

Donovan. Remember, Donovan is your boyfriend.

Avoiding Shaw's gaze, I look in his general direction without meeting his eyes. "I was just wondering how much longer you might need me? I was supposed to be off about three hours ago."

When I finally look, I notice that Shaw has raised his eyebrows. "Really? No one told me that."

I nodded. "Yeah. I'm working an overnight float right now, but that ends at seven AM."

His jaw stiffens. "I know when it ends, Dr. Forbes."

Back to Dr. Forbes. Oops.

He looks at his tablet and then back at me, pressing his lips together. "I can probably get you out of here in the next couple of hours. Why don't you go eat your sandwich and put your feet up? Take five minutes and then we'll see if we can get some of these patients moved out of here so you can go home. All right?"

"Sure. Thanks." Only five minutes to eat and catch my breath after the sprint back from the cafeteria? I walk away, my stomach sinking. I really want to go home. I want to see Snort and try to call Donovan again. I can't help but wonder where he is, the thought sending a tingle down my back. I glance over my shoulder at Shaw. He's heading to another exam room. As he ducks inside, he looks at me, lifting his chin as if he's wondering why I'm watching him. I turn away, feeling my stomach knot. Shaw was so nice about Mr. Palmer, but now he's stalling about letting me go home. Maybe I'm just tired, but something seems off.

He almost seems too nice.

Still, something about that moment sticks with me, though I can't say why.

At least not yet.

7

The sandwich didn't do much to make me feel any better after all of the energy drinks I'd consumed in the last few hours. From the staff refrigerator I grab a bottle of water and then a second, chugging them both down. I can only hope that the influx of fluids will tame the caffeine that was coursing through my veins. No one wants a doctor with trembling hands, right?

As soon as I toss the second bottle in the trash, I regret my hydration plan. I should have just sucked it up and let my hands shake. If I get stuck with patients, there's no telling when I'll have a minute to run off and use the bathroom. My stomach rumbles. Whether it is from eating the sandwich too fast or guzzling all that water, I have no idea.

All I know is it feels like a distinct warning sign.

I'm just about to walk back out on the floor and check in with Tamia when I notice she and Shaw seem to be happily camping out at the nurses' station. Maybe my paranoia was unwarranted? If they are chatting, then maybe I will get to go home soon. My spirits lift. I start making my way to hang out with them when my phone rings. Hopeful, I look down. Is it Donovan?

The brief joy I felt evaporates as fast as a gob of spit on a hot sidewalk.

Julia.

I groan but paste a smile on my face, determined to not let her derail my momentary peace.

"Hey, Jules, I'm at work." I try to say with lightness in my voice. It's a preemptive strike designed to keep the conversation short. Not sure it's gonna work though.

"Oh, I know, I know, Mac. You're *always* at work. But the bride has a question!" Julia sounded like she was doing her best impression of Reese Witherspoon in *Legally Blonde*. Why she keeps referring to herself in the third person, I'll never know.

"Well," I pause, feeling the sandwich curdle in my stomach. I feel like Alice peering down the rabbit hole. "I just have a minute."

"The bride would like to know if the maid of honor could come into town a week before the wedding. You know, there's so much to handle, lots of little details that only the maid of honor can take care of before the big day."

Oh boy. The big day.

Julia Forbes is my younger sister. For some reason she feels like the entire world needs to come to a complete standstill for a twenty-minute ceremony and a couple hours of a party afterward while she dances around in a white dress. I foolishly agreed to be the maid of honor when she got engaged the year before, not fully considering how much time Julia would want me to help her with the wedding.

I should have known better. This is my sister, after all.

I press my lips together. *Helping* her isn't what she's going after. Julia has every detail of the wedding planned, including how much air we're allowed to breathe as we walk down the aisle. As far as I know, the only thing she still wants is for the

skies to part and the angels to come down in heavenly exalta-
tion when she walks down the aisle.

Still not sure we're going to be able to pull that off.

"I don't know," I say cautiously. "I've already requested a
couple of days off, but we're pretty short-handed. I'm not sure I
can stay for an entire week. You remember your wedding
happens at exactly the same time I'm finishing up my residency
and trying to get ready for my new job, right?"

I ask it as a question, though it's more of a statement than
anything else. My comment about the new job is largely aspi-
rational. I have a job offer, but the HR department over at
Schuylkill Valley Hospital won't sign off on my contract until
I finish my residency. I've got two months to go. And of
course, Julia, in her wisdom, decided to plan her wedding for
the week before I finish it out, even though she knew I'd have
to be in Philadelphia. I'm not saying that Julia should have
scheduled her wedding around my residency, but a little flexi-
bility given the fact that I have to be here would be nice,
especially given my performance this morning with Mr.
Palmer.

Julia huffed. "Are you *kidding* me, Mac? When is this residency stuff ever going to end?"

"Two more months," I grunt.

"Why can't you just take the week off? Don't they
understand?"

*No, Julia, they don't. What they understand is that they are
training me to save people's lives.*

That's what I would really like to say, but the fact is that
Julia would never understand that line of argument. She and I
are about as opposite as they come.

Everything.

I have average-looking brown hair and average-looking
brown eyes. I wear my hair in a ponytail most days because I'm
a resident and the idea of styling it, even if I could, given how

limp it is, is just ridiculous. Looking bedraggled is part of the job.

Julia, on the other hand, is five-one, a full five inches shorter than I am, with crystal clear blue eyes, a mane of shiny blonde hair, and the hard, petite body of a cheerleader. As my mother says, she got all of the beauty, and I got all of the brains.

There are days I wish that things had been doled out a little bit more evenly.

I decide to take another tact.

I glance toward the nurses' station. Shaw turns and glances at me. I know he sees me on the phone through the glass partition. I turn away, trying to hide the phone under my stringy hair, but it's too late. He already saw me. I've gotta somehow get Julia back on track and do it in about thirty seconds before Tamia walks down here and drags me out of the break room. "What exactly is it that you need me to do over during the week that I'm home before the wedding?" I'm from Youngstown, Ohio. It's a nice town, but there's not a lot going on, if you know what I mean. Maybe if I can convince Julia that there really isn't anything that needs to get done, then she won't give me a hard time about not showing up until the last second. I have this all planned. Spend my first day off sleeping so I don't look like a zombie for the wedding, then get myself back home, spending the five-hour drive to Youngstown stopping along the Turnpike and eating my favorite foods while Donovan does most of the driving. I'll show up, take a shower, drink a bunch of champagne, throw the dress on (I think it's lavender or some color like that which I look horrendous in), grab whatever twenty-five-pound bouquet that Julia is going to want me to carry down the aisle, say something nice about my sister and new brother-in-law at the reception and then get hammered.

"You know, Mac, *all* the *things*," Julia says, her tone exasperated as if she's stunned I'm even asking.

All the things. I cross one arm in front of my chest, tucking my hand into my armpit and lean against the wall, watching a group of nurses wearing scrubs with teddy bears on them pass by. "What does that mean?"

There's a pause. I can't tell if it's because Julia's annoyed that I don't know what "all the things" means or she doesn't have an example.

"You know, all the things. Like, when I get my hair done, then there's the spray tan, so I don't have lines, the manicure and pedicures and, of course, I really want you to come and hold my hand when I get my Brazilian."

Oh great, just what I wanted to do. It's been on my top ten list forever to hold my sister's hand while some person spreads wax on her nether parts and rips her hair out. "Anything else?"

Of course she has an answer.

"Well, there's the facials and the workouts. I even found someone who can meditate with me during the week so that I'm calm. The last thing I want to do is have a breakout from being stressed."

Hearing all of this, I feel more like she's preparing for a pageant than a thirty-second saunter down the aisle in a church.

"All of that sounds good, Jules, but like I said, I just don't think I'm gonna be able to get there until maybe a day or two before the wedding." I keep my back to Shaw and Tamia. Someone's eyes are boring into my back. I don't want to look.

"Are you kidding? What am I supposed to do?" Julia's voice is shrill. "My maid of honor *needs* to be there. How am I gonna get through the waxing if you're not there to supervise? What if I get some sort of a rash or an infection? What if I pass out? You're a *doctor*. That's why I want you there."

Great. Now I'm her personal physician in addition to being maid of honor. "If you are that concerned about the cleanliness of the place that you are going to or the trauma that it's going to cause to your skin," I throw in the word trauma because it's one of Julia's favorite words, "then I would suggest that you either find someplace else or cancel your appointment."

"I can't *do* that." Her voice is strained. "It's for our wedding night. I want to look pristine for Jacob."

I fight off a groan. Julia and Jacob have been dating for three years. I'm sure it's not the first time he's seen her pubic hair. Time to shift strategies again. Julia is as slippery as they get. "The other part you haven't considered is that until I complete my residency, I can't write any prescriptions without the approval of an attending physician. If you get a rash, there's nothing I'm going to be able to do about it. You'd have to go see your own doctor." Just as I look up, I can see Shaw staring at me, his lips parted. It's not the look that I'm hoping for. It's more a, "get off the phone because we have work to do and I'm sorry I gave you a break," look. I've got to wrap this up. "Listen, I'm sorry, Jules. I've really gotta go. We've got patients coming in. I'll do what I can, but I don't think I'm going to be able to get there any sooner. Maybe one of your other girls can step in?" The offer sounds reasonable to me. She's got a pack of bridesmaids. Certainly, someone can step in, right?

"But they aren't my maid of honor."

"But they aren't in residency!"

I instantly regret the words as they come out of my mouth. There's silence on the other end of the phone, and then a click.

Julia hangs up on me.

As I walk out of the break room, I'm carrying a pit in my stomach the size of a basketball. I can envision the next turn of events. Julia will go running to our mother and cry foul like she has for forever. She will throw herself down on my mother's lap and cry herself a river of tears about how unfair life is, how mean Mac is, and how she's only getting married once. Mom will end up calling me at some point and trying to straighten things out, acting like the Swiss trying to broker peace between the Israelis and the Iranians.

Well, it might not be quite that dramatic. After a little time, things will settle down.

Predictable.

I stuff my phone in the back pocket of my scrub pants and walk out of the break room, realizing I still need to pee. But there's no time. Shaw has already made eye contact with me. I just hope I haven't annoyed him too much by taking a couple of extra minutes. I look at my watch.

Oops, it's been twenty, not five.

I start with an apology. "Sorry," I say as I approach the nurses' station, tucking a loose strand of brown hair behind my ear. It feels greasy. I'm sure I'm way past a six on the stink scale, but there's absolutely nothing I can do about it at the moment. Luckily, as I'm talking to Shaw, we are both enveloped in a cloud of his yummy cologne. Maybe that will help him ignore the odor coming from my body. "Dealing with some drama at home."

Shaw cocks his head to the side. "Really? What kind of drama?"

Normally I wouldn't answer that kind of question from an attending but given the fact I'm trying to get myself out of what feels like hot water I decide to break my own rule. "I'm the maid of honor in my sister's wedding. She's not happy that I'm not going to be able to get home to hold her hand through her Brazilian wax before the wedding. I just told her, work comes first." It sounds good as the words come out. Real good. Very professional and doctorly.

Shaw nods in agreement. "Yeah, families can have a hard time understanding the sacrifices that we make in order to help others."

His words carry a weight I don't understand. On the positive side, I feel like he and I are maybe building some sort of camaraderie. "I'm ready to go now. Just got a run to the bathroom really quick," I point in the direction of the ladies' room, taking a half a step.

Shaw hands me a tablet. "Go get this patient started first."

I'm about to protest that my bladder is going to explode, but I stop.

Work comes first, right?

As I walk toward the exam room, I look over my shoulder. Shaw is watching me.

And I don't know why.

8

"Samantha?" I ask as I push the curtain aside in bay four, sucking my thighs together, hoping not to spring a bladder leak.

The woman nods.

"I'm Dr. Forbes. What's going on?"

Even before she answers the question, I have part of my answer. Samantha Watkins is pale, wrapped up in a blanket on the bed, her lips devoid of color. There's a pink container next to her. I know what it is. It's the puke bucket. One of the nurses, a new gal named Jasmine, stands by. Puke is one of the many reasons I decided to become a doctor and not a nurse. As a physician, once you get through medical school and your internship, you get to, for the most part, avoid vomit. The nurses aren't so lucky.

Samantha manages to croak out a response. "I'm really not feeling good. I think I have some sort of a virus."

I squirt some more of the stinging hand sanitizer onto my hands then pull on a pair of gloves unwrapping the stethoscope from around the back of my neck. I quickly take a listen to her heart and lungs, then step back. The last thing I need is to get sick myself. Her lungs both sound clear. "How long have you been sick?"

"Three days."

I look at Jasmine. "She's running a fever."

"How high?"

"One hundred point three."

Not bad, but certainly not very comfortable. Her blood pressure is a little low too. I squeeze the tips of her fingers. The capillary refill is a little slow. Her voice sounded raspy when she was talking. All the throwing up can cause dehydration. "Have you been able to keep anything down?"

Samantha shook her head. "No." She looks away for a second. "Not really. Maybe this is just food poisoning?"

I start making notes on the tablet. "It could be. Viruses and food poisoning look almost exactly the same. It can be difficult to discern the difference, although given the fact that you're running a fever, I'm leaning more towards a virus as the cause. I'd like to draw some blood and just double-check your levels and make sure that there's not anything else going on. In the meantime, we can give you an IV to get you rehydrated and get your blood pressure up, some Zofran for the nausea, and we'll give you some Ibuprofen to see if we can get your fever down. I think once you have some more fluids in you, you'll start to feel better. How does that sound?"

When I look up, I can see Samantha fighting off another round of nausea. But she nods in agreement. "That would be great. Anything you can do to get rid of this nausea would be amazing."

Technically, I should run the diagnosis by Shaw before I do anything, but this poor woman is clearly in distress. The thing with Bill is just a hiccup. I'm the chief resident, right?

Feeling a surge of confidence, suddenly certain the whole thing with Bill isn't my fault, I look at Jasmine. "Let's go ahead and get the IV started and push the Zofran and Ibuprofen. You can draw blood for a CBC while you're at it." As I step to the foot of Samantha's bed, I look back at her. "I'll be back to check on you in just a few minutes."

After I pee.

By the time I get back from using the bathroom, there's been an influx of new patients. Shaw gives me an apologetic look. "I need you to stay a little bit longer. The next round of docs to relieve you will be here soon."

Soon, in medical terms, means in between now and when hell freezes over.

"Sure." Given the fact he's now running the ED it doesn't seem like it's worth arguing.

Especially if I want to get extra time off approved for Queen Julia's nuptials.

A half hour later, after sending a fifty-year-old woman who'd fallen off a horse at her riding lesson off to X-ray, working on a man with a splinter the size of a small car imbedded in his right butt cheek, and dealing with a standard, garden variety ear infection in a toddler who was more interested in jumping up and down on the bed then he was having his ears looked at, I stopped at the nurses' station. Tamia was there, directing traffic like usual. With her hand signals, she sent two nurses down to deal with intakes on new cases that had come in. She looked at me, pointing. It was a signal that something had come back.

"Labs?"

Tamia nodded. "Yeah. They're slow this afternoon. But they came back on the throw-up case you have. Samantha Watkins."

Setting my tablet down on the counter at the nurses' station I pull up the lab results for Samantha Watkins. Her white blood count is at seventeen thousand, right in line for what I'd expect to see. I scan the rest of the long list of labs. The CBC — a Complete Blood Count — always returns tons of data, but there are just a few I need to check. I chew on the inside of my lip, giving the list a second glance. Everything else seems to be perfectly normal. I nod, looking at Tamia. "Viral is the winner."

Tamia gets a disgusted expression on her face as she keeps staring at the patients in the waiting room. "That stuff is going around again?"

"Not a fan of the throw-up cases?"

"Not so much."

"We could send them to the clinic?" The clinic at Liberty Hill dealt with less severe cases — things like sprains and sinus infections.

"I wish. They're slammed. Had a slew of foot and mouth today."

I wince. Delightful.

I call over my shoulder as I walk away, feeling the energy come back into my body. "Does it ever stop?" I'm getting my swagger back, I think. I'm a diagnostic machine. Having a new attending isn't a problem. I've got this handled.

Tamia sucks in a breath. "It does not, Dr. Forbes."

Now that my bladder isn't screaming, I circle back to Samantha's room. She is still in bed but has pulled the covers down a little bit. Her color looks better, the pink in her cheeks returning. I check the notes Jasmine added while I was busy relieving myself. Samantha is three-quarters through her first bag of fluids. Her fever has started to come down a little bit too. "How are you feeling?"

Samantha shifts in the bed, tugging on the blanket. "Better. That medication you gave me really helped."

As I walk closer to the bed, I notice her arm. It has a bruise on it. A big one, probably four inches long on her forearm. "How did you get that?" I ask, putting on a pair of gloves.

She shrugs. "Oh, that. Yeah, I was trying to get stuff out of my car and banged my arm into the edge of the door. Just a stupid mistake."

By the yellowish cast to it, it looked like it was healing, as if it had happened a week or so before. Still, it was a big bruise. She must have hit something really hard. I frown. Dr. Riley had trained me to always follow up and ask about bruises, especially on our female patients. There were times when people who had issues at home would come to the ED just waiting for one of us to ask so that they could get some help. But it didn't seem to be the case with Samantha. I glance out of the bay. Nobody was hanging around leering at her and preventing her from telling the truth. She seemed relaxed and responded quickly about what had happened.

And after all, the only thing I can do is take somebody at their word.

I check my tablet again and then look at the IV, which is almost done. "All right. Well, this bag of fluids that you're getting should be done in the next five minutes or so. I'll go work on your discharge paperwork and be back with you in a few minutes and we'll get you out of here. I'm going to send you home with some more anti-nausea medication. Keep up the Ibuprofen to control your fever. If it doesn't go away in the next forty-eight hours, I'd recommend checking with your primary care physician. You can always come back here too. We're open twenty-four/seven."

Samantha looks relieved. "Thanks, Doc. I appreciate it."

"No problem."

I walk to the nurses' station, having sent the prescription for some Zofran to handle Samantha's nausea, and was headed back to her room when Shaw stops me. His perfect eyebrows are knitted together in concern. "What are you doing?" he practically hisses.

I kept moving. He probably has more patients for me to handle. "Discharging my patient."

"The one in bay two?" He grabs the sleeve of my scrub shirt with a tight grip. It's like having one of those dinosaurs from *Jurassic Park* get a grip on you. I'm not going anywhere.

My eyes widen as he lets go. What's going on here? "Yeah. It's clearly viral. Throwing up, fever, counts all look fine. Gave her Zofran, fluids, and Ibuprofen. Standard stuff."

At this point we're standing halfway between the nurses' station and Samantha's room. He glances over toward her room, takes two steps, and slides the glass door closed. A pit forms in my stomach. What's going on?

"She doesn't have a virus, Dr. Forbes. You can't discharge her."

"What? What are you talking about?" The words come out a little bit more clipped than I want them to.

Shaw blinks, as if he's surprised by my response. "Did you even take the time to look at her blood work?"

My face reddens. "Yeah, I sure did. Tamia said it came back in, and I stood right over there and looked at it." I pointed to where I had stood with the tablet. When I look up, Tamia turns away. That's not a good sign.

"Dr. Forbes, her blasts are at twenty percent."

That's the second time he's called me "Dr. Forbes." This can't be good. I stiffen. "No, they're not. I checked. They were at zero." I know if Samantha's blasts — the immature white blood cells — are that high, there's a problem. A big one.

My whole body tenses. I've done this diagnosis for two years now. It's a virus. Definitely a virus. I grab the tablet and look, ready to point out to Dr. Hot Stuff that he's not all that. Then I stop, my mouth falling open.

Samantha's blasts *are* at twenty percent.

"How is that possible?" I stammer. "I just looked at this a little while ago. Did the lab just update it?" I look back at the time on the report. It hadn't been updated.

"No, Dr. Forbes. It hasn't been updated." The words come slowly out of Dr. Shaw's mouth. He stares at me without blinking, his eyes boring holes into me. "Are there any other results that you would like to double-check?"

Panic fills me. I stare at the results, the numbers swimming in front of my face. How did I miss this? I would have bet Snort's life that when I looked at the report the blast levels were at zero. I refresh the screen, turned my tablet on and off and look again, but they're still the same.

Twenty percent.

Heat fills my cheeks. This is a huge error. Huge. When I look up, Shaw is still staring at me. His expression is strange, as if he's sizing me up, like I'm an opponent he's facing in an MMA match.

By his expression, I'm clearly lacking.

Any confidence I had just found evaporates. "I'm not sure what to say, Dr. Shaw. When I looked at it, I thought it read zero. I must have just missed the two." The words are so ridiculous I can't believe I'm saying them. Who mistakes zero for twenty?

I guess I do.

My mouth goes dry. It hits me. If Samantha's blasts are at twenty percent, she doesn't have a virus.

She probably has leukemia.

I start stammering. I'm not even sure what I'm saying. When I look at Shaw, he's just looking down, shaking his head, his perfectly gelled dark hair never moving out of place. He rubs some stubble that is starting to emerge along his jaw as if he's trying to figure out what to do. He looks at me. "You can't discharge her. With blast levels this high, she's going to need to be admitted so that she can have a biopsy. Right now." He looks away for a second, his expression tight. "I'm sorry, Dr. Forbes, but this is a big screw up. We'll have to talk about what happens next with Dr. Riley, but for now, let's get Samantha informed and upstairs."

My whole body starts to shake. It's like my life is flashing in front of my eyes. Bile rises in the back of my throat. What does this mean? How could this happen? First Mr. Palmer and now

Samantha? I've never had this many problems before and of course, they happen as soon as Shaw takes over as my attending.

As he turns and walks away, a sinking feeling runs through my body. I'm not sure what to say. I want to call after him, but it's pointless. He's right and I'm wrong. Again.

My stomach lurches as I follow along after him, my head hanging. If I keep making all these mistakes, I might be able to make it to Julia's wedding a week early after all.

9

For better or worse, Dr. Shaw decides to go into Samantha Watkins's room with me. Her legs are dangling over the side of the bed, a fresh Band-Aid on the spot in her arm where the IV had been pulled. Her expression brightens when she sees me. "Oh, Dr. Forbes. I'm feeling so much better. I can't thank you enough."

I feel my lips thin out on my face. I glance at Shaw, wondering if maybe he's going to rescue me from the news I have to deliver, but he doesn't. I pull out the rolling stool that's near where she's sitting and plop myself down. To her, it probably looks like I'm being relatable. As far as I'm concerned, it's a preventative measure to keep me from passing out. "Samantha," I start, setting the tablet off to the side. "This is Dr. Shaw. He's the attending in charge of the Emergency Department. He and I were reviewing your test results as I was preparing the discharge papers, and he pointed out just a little something that I missed."

A little something can't be that bad, can it?

A flash of concern runs over Samantha's face. "Something you missed? Like what?"

My face reddens. All of a sudden, I remember some of the basics I was taught by Liberty Hill's hospital administration when I started. "If you miss something, blame it on technology until you get your attending involved."

I hold my hand up, attempting to recover, glancing at Shaw for help. There's a grim expression on Shaw's face. I wonder if it's because of her diagnosis, then I realize it's me. He's upset at me. "The lab has been running slow. And when I got your initial results in, they hadn't quite finished loading all of them."

I'm sure to Shaw it was a flat-out lie, but to me, it was entirely possible. Maybe they hadn't.

"And?" Samantha asked, leaning forward.

Shaw decides at that moment to step in and save me. "Samantha, as Dr. Forbes said, I'm Dr. Shaw. It's nice to meet you. What Dr. Forbes is trying to say is that there are some irregularities in your blood work. We'd like to send you upstairs and have some further tests done."

She shifts uncomfortably in her bed, her face suddenly paling. "More tests? Why can't I have those tests done here? Do you just need to rerun my blood work?" She looks between the two of us. I look away. I can't bear to let her see the shame on my face.

Shaw shakes his head. I'm sure if I hadn't already been sitting on the stool this would have been the moment when he flipped his lab coat out from behind him and sat down on it, ready to have a heart-to-heart with Samantha. Instead, he sets his tablet down at the foot of her bed. "The irregularity that Dr. Forbes is talking about is with a type of cell in your blood called a 'blast.' We expect that those would be zero but unfortunately yours are at about twenty percent."

"Twenty percent? What does that mean? What's a blast?"

"Blasts are immature white blood cells. Given that the level is so high, it's likely there's something else going on. We need to do a biopsy."

Samantha's mouth flops open. "A biopsy? Her face froze and then her eyes widen, searching each of our faces. "Are you saying I have cancer?"

Shaw nods slowly. "With this type of lab result, we generally expect that someone has leukemia. Now the good news is that these types of leukemias are highly treatable —"

I don't hear the rest of what Shaw is saying. I'm busy looking at Samantha. She keeps glancing at me like I'm an idiot. She's gone from feeling better and ready to go home and take her Zofran and her Ibuprofen to having to face the fact that she might have cancer. I have no idea what to do. While Shaw keeps talking, I pick up the tablet and look at the test results again. How did I miss this? It was zero when I saw it.

And now I've gone from hero to zero too.

I turn back in just in time for Shaw to finish. "Our hope is that with the biopsy we'll get conclusive results."

Samantha shakes her head. "So, now you're saying you're not sure?"

I can tell that we're losing her. I look up at Shaw, who gives me a little nod. At least he was going to let me try. This is a good thing. I put my hand on her knee. "Listen, I know this is scary and not the news that you were thinking you were going to get when you walked in here today, but just let us check. Let us run the test and then we'll know for sure. If there's something there, we have great doctors here at Liberty Hill. They'll help you and you'll get through it." I was very careful about what I said. Promising a clean bill of health was yet another thing we weren't allowed to say.

Come to think of it, there are a lot of things we aren't allowed to say.

Seeing the look on Samantha's face — a mix of anger, shock, and disappointment — all I want to do is leave the room. I feel so guilty for setting her up to think that she was okay when she clearly isn't that I nearly grab her pink throw-up tub and use it myself. First Bill Palmer and now Samantha Watkins?

Worst day ever.

With the promise to get her upstairs as soon as possible, Shaw and I walk out of the room. He glances at me sideways. "You handled that pretty well."

Thank you, I think? I'm not sure what to say, so I don't say anything at all. My stomach is coiled tighter than a noose. Why am I making all these mistakes? Am I just distracted by Julia's drama? I look around the ED. From what I can tell, some new staff has come in. Shaw notices it too. He looks at me with an expression that reads pity, as if I'm one big fat failure.

It was the same expression that my gym teacher used to give me when I was the last one chosen for kickball.

He bobs his head to the side. "Why don't you get out of here, Forbes. I know today's been a rough day. Maybe it's too much pressure on you to be chief and work these long shifts. I can talk to Riley about it —"

Now he's thinking I can't handle the chief position? Are you kidding me? I mean, there's nothing really to it. I just help Tamia with getting staff organized. Riley told me he'd have me do paperwork and attend meetings, but that never materialized. My guess? He doesn't want to give up any of his own responsibility. My eyes widen. "No, I'm okay." I see a confused look on his face, then correct myself. "I mean, I'm fine in the chief role. I'm just really tired. I think I've been on for the last twenty hours."

Shaw shakes his head as if his disappointment in me has suddenly turned to pity. "Hopefully, we can get this straightened out, so you don't have to do any more twenty-hour shifts." He puts a hand on the outside of my shoulder and stares at me, leaning toward me. I feel a little tingle run down my spine as the scent of his cologne mixes with my body odor. Is this why all the girls have been oohing and ahhing over him? He gives my arm a squeeze and then lets go. "Try not to think about today. Go home, get a shower, and get some rest, and we'll try again tomorrow."

As I walk away, despite the issues with Bill and Samantha, I start to feel a little bit better about how the day went. Then I realize Shaw made a comment about showering. As I walk into the locker room, I sniff under my armpit.

I know why. We're at a level eight on the stink meter.

10

I barely make it to my car when I'm dialing Donovan.
I dial at the same time I'm trying to get away from the hospital. My aged Toyota Corolla, a car I've had since I started medical school, refuses to start and then ends up turning over as if it's holding a grudge against me. Just as the engine revs, I hear the call click in my ear.

"Donovan? Are you there?"

There is nothing that I want more at this moment than to hear Donovan's voice. It has been a horrible shift. Between Bill Palmer's necrotic foot, Samantha Watkins's virus turned leukemia, and dealing with Julia, pretty much everything that could have gone wrong did. I know Donovan. He'll calmly tell me I'm okay, to go home and get some rest, and that I'm a good doctor.

At this moment, even if he tells me all those things, I'm not sure I'll believe them, but it's worth a try.

A second later I hear his voice. "Mac? Are you there?"

"Yes, yes! I am!" I yell into the phone as if he's deaf, nearly plowing into the back of a bakery truck as I pull out of the Liberty Hill medical campus.

I'm so relieved to hear Donovan's voice I miss the first two turns on my way home and end up having to circle around and go the long way. I guess I shouldn't be surprised. Twenty hours of nearly non-stop work with barely a nap can mess with you. Like really mess you up. The only one that doesn't seem to suffer is Jamir. The rest of us always look like we've just finished the Ironman after a long day, only to slog it right back to work the next day. Hearing Donovan's voice, I fight off tears as I drive. I'm not a crier in general, but I'm exhausted and feel like an idiot. "I'm here, I'm here!"

His voice sounds concerned. "Can you hear me all right?"

I scowl and press my ear against the phone harder as if that will help. "Barely. Where are you?"

"I'm at the airport in Singapore. I'm trying to get home but the flights are all screwed up."

The fact that Donovan was trying to make his way home sent a new wave of tears running down my cheeks. All I wanted to do was take a shower and sleep and then wake up and find Donovan. I imagined the two of us sitting on the couch watching a movie and eating greasy microwave popcorn. It sounded boring but it was about all the energy I had after my shift.

"When will you get out? When will you be home?" The words come out in a mad rush.

"I don't know. Are you okay? I saw you've been trying to call me?"

"It's been a really bad day. I just got off work. Did a twenty-hour shift." I start to tell him about Bill Palmer and Samantha Watkins — not using any names of course, because God forbid I should violate their HIPAA privacy. I throw caution to the wind and only talk about first names. It's not like their names are all that unique. There are probably twenty Bill Palmers just in Philadelphia and nearly that many Samantha Watkins.

Before I get to the part about Bill's black foot, Donovan

interrupts. "Mac, can we talk about this when I get home? I can barely hear you. I'm exhausted too. The time change is killing me."

I frown. I mean, I know I'm droning on, but the time change? Yeah, Donovan has been traveling around Southeast Asia for the last three weeks, but aren't they all on the same time zone? I try to play it cool. Nobody wants a desperate, emotional girlfriend, even one who has had a *horrible* shift at work. "Yeah. Of course. Sure. We'll talk when you get home."

Whenever that is.

By the time I get back to the apartment, I realize I'm not the only thing that stinks. The smell hits me as soon as I open the door. Only one thing could be responsible for this level of desecration.

Snort.

My beloved cat apparently ate something that didn't agree with him and is now making me suffer for his gastrointestinal issues. I poke my head into the closet where we keep his litter box, then try not to gag. I'm not even going to describe it. Just imagine if Chernobyl and a septic plant had a baby and you'll get the drift. The stink is unbearable. As bad as I smell, my apartment smells even worse.

As I set my bag down, I realize my dreams of immediately hitting the shower aren't going to happen. I've gotta handle this now. For his part, Snort crosses in front of me, his nose in the air, making one of his little characteristic chuffing sounds as if he's commenting on my body odor. I look at him. "Don't be judgy. You haven't left the apartment smelling very good either, have you?"

Ten minutes later, after dealing with the litter box, I decide to turn the shower on and then run the trash down the hall, dropping it in the trash chute. I open the door, leaving it cracked and make my way down the hallway, hoping not to bump into any of my neighbors, especially Mrs. Dixon, who has the uncanny ability to want to chat after I have been up for way too many hours. To that end, I move as stealthily as possible, pretending I am a Navy SEAL on a secret mission as I drop the bag of litter down into the chute. Yes, I'm practically delusional after being up for so long. Lacking the coordination of an actual Navy SEAL, I let go of the door to the chute too fast and it slams shut. Instantly, as though Mrs. Dixon has been waiting for me, her door flies open.

"Mac!" she crows.

"Hi, Mrs. Dixon." She's really a very nice old lady, at least sometimes. I think she's just lonely and needs someone to talk to. That's what I keep telling myself, but it is strange how she always knows when I'm in the hallway. Maybe bordering on more than strange, almost creepy.

"Did you just get back from work?"

I hear the trash chute door slam.

"Do you have to *always* slam the trash door?"

I take that back. Maybe she's not so nice. I wince. Sometimes Mrs. Dixon reminds me of my mother. She likes to give me little shots about things. I mean, who cares if the chute door slams? It's not like it's super loud or anything.

"Sorry about that. I'll try to close it more gently next time."

She purses her lips. "It's nice to see you're actually home for once."

Yes, and that's exactly where I would like to be. At home, and not out in the hallway talking to you. "I'm sorry, Mrs. Dixon, I've gotta go. I left the shower running."

"You know, my daughter says the same thing to me when she doesn't want to talk."

From what I've been able to gather, Mrs. Dixon and her daughter are not on good terms, probably because Mrs. Dixon has as terrible timing with her daughter as she does with me. "I'd love to hear about it sometime, but I really do need to go."

I trot down the hallway and grab the door to my apartment

and twist the knob. It won't open. Instantly, sweat gathers on my forehead. I'm locked out. I frantically twist the doorknob. This can't be right. I left it cracked open. I bang my shoulder against it, sure Mrs. Dixon is watching my desperate attempt to get back in, cataloging it for her use later on. I've never gotten locked out before. Then I remember. I was so taken aback by the smell of the litter box when I walked through the door that I didn't turn the tab in the lock. The open window must have blown the door closed when I walked down the hallway.

And now the shower is running, and I can't get back in.

I rattle the door again, my ears starting to ring. Normally, I wouldn't care if the shower was running for just a minute. But in my apartment, the drain runs slow. I'm sure it's my fault. Donovan is never there, so it can't be him. It's probably because hair has been coming off my head like an actress ripping her extensions off at the end of a show. I keep telling myself it's stress, but if I keep losing hair at this rate, I'm gonna be completely bald for Julia's wedding.

On the bright side, it would be a lot faster to plop a wig on my head than go through the styling hell I'm sure she has planned for all of the bridesmaids.

As I jam my shoulder against the door again, I start to panic, goosebumps running up and down my arms. I hadn't had to do it in a while, but there had been times when I had to shut off the shower to let the drain catch up so that it didn't overflow. With my lack of sleep, I can't remember if the drain is clear or not. I'm running out of options. I need to get back into the apartment before there's a flood.

And there's only one person who has a key besides me, and Donovan and the super.

Mrs. Dixon.

I could risk running downstairs to see if George, the super for our building, is in, but he probably isn't. He has a day job when he's not managing the apartment building and usually doesn't get home until the evening, or at least that's typically when I see him.

With Donovan somewhere between here and Singapore, that leaves me with one option.

I walk tentatively back down the hallway, sure Mrs. Dixon is watching, but she's not. She's gonna force me to knock and beg. I know it.

I feel heat in my face, just exacerbating the body odor and cat litter smell I'm sure I'm carrying with me. All I want to do is get in the shower and sleep. What choice do I have? I've got to do something before the shower overflows.

I knock extra gently on Mrs. Dixon's door. She makes me wait a good thirty seconds before she answers it, feigning the fact that she was busy. She's wearing one of her typical outfits, a blue house dress and white slippers, her cropped hair plastered against her scalp, a dot of pink lipstick, the only makeup she wears. "Need something, dear?"

You know darn well what I need. "Um, well, the door."

She raises an eyebrow. "Did you lock yourself out?"

I nod, not able to form any other words.

As she disappears to go retrieve the extra key for my apartment, I say a silent prayer of thanks for Donovan's wisdom. When he moved in, he asked me about a spare key in case we got locked out. I had told him I never locked myself out. Never. Not once. I remember he looked at me, frowning. "Well, if you don't get locked out, then I probably will. Which one of these neighbors can we give a key to?"

The only logical answer is Mrs. Dixon. She's the only one who's home all the time. Everyone else on the floor has a day job. Nosy neighbors can become overly nosy at times. But now, I'm nothing but utterly grateful that she has a key. I stand at the doorway, suddenly realizing not only could I smell myself, but I needed to pee again, badly. Those two bottles of water and the energy drink I had consumed a couple hours before were hitting my system. Hard. I squeeze my knees together and wait for another second then lean in the doorway. "Mrs. Dixon? My shower is running. I'm getting concerned."

"Coming, coming!" she calls in a sing-songy voice.

A second later, I heard the scuffling noise of her flippers on her floor. She moves slowly toward me like she's making her way through tapioca, holding the key out in front of her like it is a nuclear bomb. Taking it, I trot back down the hallway. "You're welcome," I hear her call behind me. "Thanks, Mrs. Dixon! I'll return this back to you in a little while."

"Okay, dear. Enjoy your shower!"

It took me two tries, but I finally slid the key in the lock and got the door open. As I close it, I'm half tempted to leave the door unlocked so I don't lock myself out again, but then I realize it's not a good idea given the fact that I live by myself and was about to get into the shower. Fighting off images in my head of being attacked in my shower, I slap the key down on the counter next to my car keys. I run off to the shower, nearly tripping over Snort, who gave a yowl. "Sorry!" I call to him as I run for the bathroom. The sound of the running water really makes me want to pee. I strip off my scrub pants and sit down on the toilet, sighing. I glance at the shower. I have just seconds to shut the water off before it gushes over the lip. I stand up, tugging my scrub pants back up over my hips and shut the water off, pulling a big wad of brown hair from the drain. It gurgles appreciatively.

Crisis averted.

Starting the water again, I move more slowly, pulling off my scrub top, my sports bra, my panties, socks, and scrub pants, the combination of my body odor and Snort's litter box disaster floating on the humidity of the steam in the bathroom. My mind is empty. All I want to do is get cleaned up and relax.

Wadding up my clothes, I toss them into the hamper. Then I realize the actual clothes I'd worn to work the day before were still at work. We weren't technically supposed to wear our scrubs home. They're the property of the hospital and are supposed to stay there, plus there are always concerns about contamination. I shake my head. If Riley or Shaw had seen me leave the building wearing their scrubs, that would just add to the issues I was having at work. I feel my skin prickle. There's nothing I can do about it now. What am I gonna do, rush the scrubs back to the hospital when I finally have a chance to be home?

Nope. I'll take my chances. If they're worried about my scrubs, then I'm really in trouble.

The thought burrows deep into my mind, small but sharp, refusing to let go.

11

After the debacle with the litter box, the clogged shower, and Mrs. Dixon the night before, morning came too fast. Just as I'd been settling down to watch television, I'd gotten a text from Tamia, who had told me to show up for the day shift the following day instead of having to go right back in for the overnight float. Apparently, Shaw wanted me to have a full night off to get some rest.

Maybe he's not so bad after all.

After my shower, I ordered takeout and managed to stay awake long enough for the delivery driver to arrive, who brought me pizza and salad. Really, all I wanted was a pizza, but I am a doctor, after all. I feel like I should have at least a few bites of something green. If any of our patients knew the stuff we actually ate, they'd roll their eyes when we tell them to watch their diet.

With a full belly, I didn't last long. I sat down in front of the television and after a few minutes flopped over on my side, seeing Snort on the back of the couch. I gave him a little wave goodnight and closed my eyes. The next thing I know, my alarm is going off. It's six AM. I have to be back at the hospital in less than an hour. I never made it to bed the night before.

As I sit up and shut off my alarm, I congratulate myself. Even in the haze of the day before, I'd managed to not only get a full night of sleep, but I'd even remembered to set my alarm so I wouldn't be late to work. Today is off to a ripping good start. I do a quick stretch, then check my phone to see if there is anything from Donovan.

There isn't, but in the process, I discover there is another problem. My phone is almost dead, which means my lifeline to Donovan is almost gone. I'm down to a painful two percent. I inhale sharply. With no time to waste, I jump off the couch and plug my phone in. In response, it gives a happy little beep. I decide to take another shower, this time washing my hair twice to make sure it's squeaky clean before my shift starts. I pull on a pair of jeans and a shirt, quickly dry my hair and put it up in a clip, adding a few little touches of makeup. It's been a couple of weeks since I've been on the day shift at Liberty Hill. Maybe working a different shift would give me a different perspective and allow me to put the things that happened the day before out of my mind.

That is, until I see the scrubs I technically stole from the hospital the day before. In the spirit of putting things behind me, I grab them from the hamper, stuff them in the trash and walk to the kitchen.

I haven't technically stolen something from the hospital if they don't know the scrubs are missing, right?

I quickly make a cup of coffee in our Keurig and dump it into one of the many Philadelphia Eagles travel mugs that Donovan brought when he moved in with me. He doesn't have a lot of stuff at our apartment, but what he does have, he's got a lot of. There has to be ten travel mugs. I'd love to pitch a bunch of them, but I think he'd get annoyed.

With a last burst of energy, I clean out the litter one more time before I go. It's more of a preemptive strike against anything Snort might decide to produce while I'm gone than anything else. There's no way I want to come home to a mess like that again. I lock the door in time to see Mrs. Dixon sticking her head out, a not-so-subtle reminder that I was supposed to return the key, my key, to her the night before. In an exceedingly cheerful mood because of all the sleep I've gotten, I stride down the hallway and deposit into her hands with a cheerful, "Good morning!" before heading down the steps.

I must be on a roll. It's smooth sailing getting into work. Not only am I on time, but I'm a little early. I find a decent parking space that prevents me from having to walk five miles to get into the Emergency Department and scan my badge a full twelve minutes before my shift has started. In the locker room, I deposit my backpack into my locker, seeing my clothes from the previous thirty-six hours still hanging there. I wrinkle my nose at them the same way Snort would wrinkle his nose at me and then start to get changed. As I'm tugging the blue scrub top over my clean body and fresh sports bra, applying an extra layer of deodorant before the shift even starts, Tamia pokes her head in. "Morning. You ready?"

"I will be. My shift doesn't start for a couple of minutes yet." I reach for my stethoscope and loop it around the back of my neck.

Tamia presses her lips together. "Nope, your shift starts now. Riley needs you. Motorcycle versus truck. He needs hands."

Seriously, Tam? I could use a minute. "Um, okay. Where's everyone else?"

"Jamir and Hudson got here a couple of minutes ahead of you. They already got sucked into the fray. You're last man up."

My stomach sinks. It seems that even though I'm on time, somehow I'm late.

"I'll be out in just a second," I say, slamming the door to my locker, then realizing my ID is inside. I quickly reopen the locker and grab it, clipping my ID to the pocket on my scrub shirt.

Slamming the locker door once again, I catch myself in the mirror as I pass by. I stop for a second, something that Riley would not appreciate. I tighten my ponytail and smile at myself in the mirror. "You've got this, Mac," I whisper to myself. It's a trick my mother taught me. Supposed to give me a positive attitude.

Which reminds me, I haven't heard from anyone in Youngstown.

I make a mental note to check in with them as I walk out of the locker room. Today has to be a better day, doesn't it?

It has to be. There's no way it could get worse than yesterday.

Still, the knot in my stomach won't let me believe it.

12

I stride down the hallway toward the nurses' station, adjusting the stethoscope that's looped around the back of my neck. Tamia, who had disappeared while I was getting my ID, grabs me. "Bay one. Riley needs you. Now."

The door to bay one is wide open. That's a sure sign that somebody is in serious trouble. Before I even see what's going on, I assume it's the motorcycle driver. Jasmine, one of the nurses, is standing in the doorway, holding a filmy disposable yellow gown ready for me, her lips in a straight line, her expression stony. That can mean only one thing.

A lot of blood.

As I approach the bedside, Dr. Randy Riley looks up at me, giving his head a little shake. He'd stripped off his white lab coat in favor of a matching yellow gown to protect his starched white shirt and his tie of the day.

"Nice of you to join us."

I glance at the time, trying to ignore his sarcasm. I'm still five minutes early. What's his problem? "I'm sorry, Dr. Riley, I just got here. My shift just started."

Maybe it wasn't the most subtle way to tell him that I'm on

time and to get off my back, but I don't feel like getting pushed around. Not after what had happened the day before.

I stand off to the side, adjusting the sticky latex gloves. It didn't take a genius to see what had happened to the man in the bed. The truck had definitely gotten the better of him. Dr. Riley is working near his head and his critical organs, yelling out the names of medications and telling the staff to pull blood for tests and order X-rays. The words rattle out of his mouth like machine gun fire. I stand by, waiting.

As a resident, that's my job.

A second later, Riley looks up at me. "Forbes, handle the lower body. Call it out."

I suck in a sharp breath. I hadn't had to call out my findings since I was a first-year. My face gets red. Had Shaw already gotten to him with the report of how I screwed up the day before?

But what was I going to do? Riley is the head of the department. Whether I become an attending or not is up to him. "Of course, Dr. Riley." I start at the man's hips, double-checking to make sure they are stable. "Pelvis is normal." I double-check, just to make sure. A broken pelvis can cause a lot of bleeding. After a second push, I decide I'm right. I nod at Jasmine, who has a pair of clothing shears in her hands. She starts cutting the man's jeans off of him. Even before she gets to his legs, I can see there's a problem — blood seeping through the fabric on the lower part of his right leg. As she cuts away the fabric, I stand by, tugging at the fabric. As soon as we peel it back, I have to force myself to keep my eyes on the man's body. There are bone fragments sticking out through the skin. It's bad. Really, really bad. Not only are the two lower leg bones — the tibia and fibula — poking up through his skin like fried chicken bones on a paper plate, but there seem to be shards broken off too. My stomach sinks. It's a tremendously painful injury with a very long recovery time. "Dr. Riley, it appears we have a compound fracture about sixteen centimeters above the ankle." Jasmine hands me a pile of four-by-fours — sterile gauze — which I gently lay over the open wound. "Wound has been covered."

Riley gives a grunt. I proceed to check his left leg and the distal pulses in his extremities, calling my findings out as I go. It is kind of comforting in a weird way. I feel kind of like I'm just along for the ride, like Riley's the one driving the bus for once. It's not a bad feeling, actually. When I'm done, I look at Riley. "Dr. Riley, lower body is normal except for the compound fracture."

The man's blood pressure has started to drop. Riley yells for more medication. "Get that IV open wide, Jasmine. Push pressers. We need to get his pressure up or he's gonna code on us." Between commands, he glares at me. "Don't just stand there, Forbes, go get a splint and get that wound properly covered. Now. Before he gets an infection."

He doesn't have to tell me twice. I've seen that look from Riley before. I trot out of the trauma bay feeling like a first-year or a trained circus pony. Not sure which. I stop at the trauma cart that had been pulled out right in front of the door of the room, searching through the drawers. There was no immobilizer in there. I rummage through them again, feeling a prickly heat on the back of my neck, like I'm about to get a rash. I need a specific kind, one with an open top so that it doesn't crush the bone fragments that are loose in the wound. Compound fractures are not only excruciating, but they are fragile and prone to sepsis. I need to move fast, not only for the man, but to mitigate any damage my performance from yesterday did to my reputation. If Riley can get the man stabilized, then he would likely be off to surgery within the next few hours to get the leg put back together again.

Tamia holds her hands up as I run down toward the supply room. "Where are you going?" Her tone is only a half step less patient than Riley's.

I throw my hands up. "There's no open immobilizer on the cart. I need one. He's got a compound fracture."

Tamia waved frantically toward the supply closet, her signal for go and come back quickly.

I know, I know. Riley's on my case, not yours.

I swipe my badge at the supply room door and push my way in, turning immediately to the right where all of the immobilizers are. I know exactly what I'm looking for. Orange. Open top. Comes in four sizes, with black straps. I scan the third shelf from the bottom on the right-hand side. I'm thinking I need a large but given how things have been going with Shaw and Riley I decided to grab a medium, a large and an extra-large just in case. If I have too many I can put them back or put them in the trauma cart. Either way it was a win-win.

Right?

I go to the spot where the immobilizers had been the day before, but nothing was there. My heart skips a beat. Am I going crazy? The immobilizers were always on that shelf. Have been since I started at Liberty Hill as a resident and I'm in my third year. Instead of a pile of orange splints, it was filled with rolls of gauze and four-by-fours. I stop for a second, my mouth going dry. *Where are the immobilizers?* My eyes wide, I spin around, looking at every single shelf. No immobilizers. There are bins of needles and a bunch of different gauges, but no immobilizers. A second later, Jasmine sticks her head in the room. "Mac? Where's that immobilizer? Riley is looking for you." She's holding her hands up as if she has no idea what I'm doing.

That makes two of us.

Sweat is gathering on my forehead. "Jas, I can't find it! They were right here."

Jasmine shakes her head as if I'm an idiot. She points. "Over there, Mac. They're right in front of you."

On the other side of the room, exactly opposite where I

would have expected them to be, were the immobilizers. Grabbing what I need, I run down the hallway at nearly a full sprint, almost crashing into Shaw as he comes out of the bay next to where we're working on the man who'd met the truck in a most unfortunate way. He holds his hands up and I mumble, "I'm sorry," as I charge around the corner. Tamia gives me a look of pity as I run by. I set the medium and the extra-large on the trauma cart and walk in with the large, hoping to God I have the right size the first time.

Riley shoots me a look of disgust. "Where *were* you?"

"Just trying to find the right size, Dr. Riley. I brought extras just in case." I'm out of breath from my sprint to the storage room. If Riley had intended to make me feel like a first-year, he's succeeded. I sure do.

Riley stops what he's doing and stares at me. It's the same look he gives the medical students when he's about to hold their feet to the fire. Shaw definitely complained about me the day before. I'm sure of it. "All right, Forbes, you have a compound fracture. Tell me what medication you're gonna give him."

This is a test. I suck in a breath, my chest still heaving from the sprint from the storage room. "Normally, I would lead with 50 micrograms of fentanyl, but I'm assuming that you have already dosed him with that or something similar," I pant. "Am I correct?"

Riley gives a short nod.

I want to wipe my forehead with the sleeve of my gown, but I don't. Maybe if I just let the sweat drip in my eyes Riley won't notice that I'm totally flustered. "In that case, I'd recommend two grams of Ansoff and five milligrams of Gentamicin to stave off any infection until we can get the wound cleaned, get the leg stabilized, and get him up to orthopedics for a reduction and repair."

Riley narrows his eyes as if this is an interrogation and he's waiting for me to break. A second later, he nods at Jasmine. "Go ahead with the Ansoff and the Gentamicin. Let's get neurology down here to assess for a concussion. I don't like that he hasn't come around yet." He pivots his gaze to me. "Next time, don't take so long getting a stupid splint." He stomps out of the room.

I'm left standing there with the patient, no idea what to do next. Jasmine rolls her eyes and then shakes her head as if commiserating with me about Randy Riley.

I decide to stay in the room with the patient for the next couple of minutes, fighting off tears. The day had started off so good. I got to work on time, looked presentable, and smelled even better. Now I'm hiding in the room of a trauma victim, whose name I don't know. I had no idea that there was going to be a big accident and that someone would decide to move the splints. It's not my fault that people keep getting hurt.

I stare at a crack in the tile, trying to take a couple of deep breaths. I can hear my pulse beating in my head.

Calm down, Mac. Just try to relax.

As I look up checking the man's IV's, I realize I'm just here to try to put people back together. That's all.

But it seems like no matter how hard I try, I keep screwing up.

My dad always tells me to do my best and forget the rest.

It sounds like good advice, unless you are a doctor. There are so many things I can't forget. So much pressure, so many people depending on me.

And I'm not even a real doctor yet.

Pretending to check the monitor, I stay with the patient, who I discover is a guy named Nelson O'Hara, while I try to get myself together. I'm a third year. The chief resident. Why am I falling apart?

I double-check the patient. Whatever Riley had given him had knocked him out. Jasmine hovers near the doorway, giving me a minute and then joins me. "Neuro just called. They're going to take him upstairs for a CT scan now."

I know I didn't miss their visit. I've been standing here (hiding, really) for the last few minutes. "They aren't coming to look at him first?"

She gives a single head shake. "Nope. We told them motorcycle versus truck, and they sent an order."

Okay... efficient, I guess?

I nod. "Need help packing him up?"

Jasmine shakes her head. "No. I got it. Transport will be here in a minute."

I barely make it out of the room when Tamia meets me. "You okay? What happened? You seem like you're off your game," she whispers under her breath.

If she's whispering, I'm in real trouble. Tamia doesn't get involved unless she's hearing something from the other docs. I twist away from the view of the other medical bays, suddenly feeling like I'm being watched. The last thing I want is for Riley or Shaw to catch me whispering with Tamia, but at this moment I need a friend.

A good one.

"Riley told me to go and get a splint. I ran into the supply room because there wasn't one on the trauma cart like there should have been." I shoot her a look. It's only half accusing. It is the nursing staff's responsibility to make sure the trauma carts are restocked. "Then, when I went to get the splint from the supply closet, nothing was where it was yesterday."

Tamia looks down and shakes her head. "Mac, I'm sorry about that. Are you sure the splint wasn't there?"

I cross my arms in front of my chest. "Yes, I'm sure. I looked."

Tamia strides toward bay one where my patient had been. He's gone, but the cart is still there, housekeeping already in the room doing a preliminary clean-up. Tamia leans over and tugs open the third drawer. Sure enough, there are splints in there. I blink. "Wait, those are the ones I just put in there."

Tamia pulls three out of the drawer. "Did you put in three larges?"

"No, a medium, large, and an extra-large. I used the large on the patient."

"No medium or extra-large here, Mac. Just three larges."

I bend over, clawing through the drawer. Not only are the splints I needed right in front of me, but the ones I brought from the storage room are gone. As I stand up, I feel the blood drain from my face. I don't know what to say, so I don't say anything.

Tamia puts a hand on the outside of my arm, giving it a squeeze. It doesn't help. I still feel like an idiot. I looked in the drawer. They weren't there. Was Riley playing a game with me, trying to knock me down a peg?

Tamia looks away for a second as if she's giving me a chance to process on my own, then she says, "Shaw had us rearrange the supply closet after you left yesterday. He had some new system that he likes better, thinks it makes more sense."

Crossing my arms in front of my chest, I lift my chin. "Well, it doesn't to me. And somebody should have told me."

"We did."

What? "Nobody told me anything."

"We sent an all-hands text. You didn't get it?"

I pull my phone out of my pocket. "No," then I look. In my hurry to get out the door earlier that morning, I'd only checked for a text from Donovan, not work. It was right in front of me. My face reddens even more. "I guess I did."

"We're all allowed to have a bad day, Mac."

My shoulders sag. Tamia knows just what to say. "Thanks. I feel like I'm in hot water with Riley after yesterday."

Tamia grimaces. "Try not to worry about Randy Riley of all people. Seriously."

Easy for her to say. My whole future rides on what Randy Riley thinks of me — all the hours of classes, study groups, exams, lab hours, and internships, not to mention the cost to get here. It's all I've ever wanted to do ever since I started taking Barbies apart and putting them back together with my dad's glue and duct tape when I was five.

"It's okay, Mac. Just keep going. That's all you can do. Just like when you started. Move on to the next patient." She grabs a tablet. "Speaking of which... While you kids were having so much fun with the motorcycle and truck victims, we have a backlog of less interesting cases to handle."

Less interesting doesn't mean less problematic. I shudder, thinking about what had happened with Samantha Watkins the day before. She was supposed to be a simple case, but her viral situation had turned into something way more than that. "Sure."

Like Tamia said, all I can do is keep going.

As I walk away with a tablet in hand, reading the notes from the intake nurse on the woman in bay six who's complaining of abdominal pain, I stop to think. Everything had been going fine until Shaw showed up. First there was Mr. Palmer, then Samantha Watkins, then I end up getting embarrassed in front of Riley because Shaw decides he's gonna reorganize the supply closet and no one bothers to tell me.

Shaw might be good-looking, but underneath it, there's something else, something I can't put my finger on. Then again, everyone seems to just love him.

Maybe it's just me.

My mother's voice interjects itself in my head. I love my mom, but she can be a little stern at times. "Don't blame others for your own failings, McKenna." It's one of her favorite sayings. Maybe that's what I'm doing. Change had never been all that easy for me. That's one of the reasons I like medicine. Although the cases are always different, the procedures are all about the same. If somebody comes in with a broken arm, you stick to the script. If somebody comes in with abdominal pain, you stick to the script. There might be slight variations, but for as chaotic as it looks, working in the ED was pretty organized.

Or at least it was *supposed* to be. Lately, I felt like someone had changed all the rules to the game and hadn't bothered to tell me.

Maybe it wasn't Shaw. Maybe Riley was just testing me.

Or maybe I was slowly losing my grip.

After examining the woman with the abdominal pain and triple-checking all of the results, plus running the case by Dr. Riley, the rest of the afternoon went by without a hitch. Shaw was nowhere to be seen, probably either off or relocated to another floor while Riley was running the Emergency Department. After the dust-up over the immobilizer, Riley didn't seem to pay any attention to me at all, except I did catch him staring at me a couple of times with his buggy eyes.

Maybe things were finally back to normal.

Maybe.

13

A few hours passed but based on the knowing looks I'm getting from some of the nurses and residents, I'm still not convinced that things are back to normal. Every time I pass someone, I feel perspiration bloom on my forehead. My attempt to stay in the lower regions of the stink meter is quickly failing. I can't stop thinking about the supply room. What would possess Shaw to have the entire thing reorganized? Was it a whim? Was he trying to control the Emergency Department now that it looked like Riley was going to hand it off to him? Did Riley even know?

I shake my head. The supply room had been like that since I started at Liberty Hill. Didn't he realize that we needed to know where things were? How did I miss the text? I look up from where I'm sitting at the nurses' station, the thoughts running in my head like a herd of wild pigs. Now, granted, I've never seen wild pigs, but you get the idea. While I'm sitting here freaking out, I see the nurses flowing in and out of the rooms like parts of a symphony, everyone moving calmly, as though everything is handled.

Except for me.

Bile rises up at the back of my throat, a sour taste covering my tongue, like I'm burping up yesterday's pizza. I stop for a second, running through the possible reasons — gastritis, food poisoning, a bleeding ulcer that will lead to my untimely death from stomach cancer. I close my eyes for a second and shake my head. What am I doing? It's just stress and lack of sleep.

And probably a healthy dose of embarrassment.

Get it together, Mac. You gonna let a little immobilizer ruin your career?

I couldn't help but see the irony of an immobilizer making me immobile.

I blink, then continue with my charting. Keep moving. That's all I can do.

As I log out of the computer, I look at my phone. It would be good to talk to Donovan right now. I send him a text, saying a silent prayer that the little bubbles of a reply will pop up as soon as I hit send. "You around? Where are you?"

I wait for a second, trying to persuade the bile down in the back of my throat that it should go back where it belongs.

Nothing.

After drumming my fingers on the counter at the desk where I'm sitting, I stare at my phone again then tap the location finder. I sit and watch while it spins at the same rate as my stomach. I remember when Donovan and I decided to share our locations with each other. It seemed like such a momentous step in our relationship. That would mean that he knew where I was all the time (always the hospital) and I would know where he was.

I wait, staring at my screen, watching the little wheel grind away.

Nothing.

A second later, the app says, "Service unavailable."

Service unavailable? What does that mean?

I try reloading it, but Donovan's location still won't come up.

My Mom's location and Julia's location pop up with no problems. My Dad, not a big fan of technology, refuses to have anyone use his location finder. Doesn't even carry a phone most of the time. He's that way.

Part of me wishes I could sneak off to the break room and call my mom and tell her about the supply room fiasco, but I know what will happen — I'll get something between "You should have been better prepared," and the newest updates on Julia's wedding.

Neither of those sounded like good options. I'd rather suffer alone in my humiliation than hear about Queen Julia again.

I look around, really wanting someone to talk to, someone who understands what I'm going through, someone who understands how a simple immobilizer is ruining my life. A lump in my throat adds to the acid reflux that I'm sure is eating away at my esophagus. Paranoia is tiptoeing around the edges of my mind. I suck in a sharp breath. Had Shaw reorganized the supply room to specifically embarrass me? I know they sent a text about it, but there was a good chance I wouldn't read it given I was exhausted. I get so many of them. Was the text just a cover?

I feel myself slipping into a deep hole that could land me pink-slipped to the psych ward for a lovely vacation if I don't stop the nonsense that is churning in my head. I see Tamia walking toward me. She can help. I know it. I hop up from my desk, taking my tablet with me, hoping that if anyone sees me, it'll look like I'm consulting with our charge nurse about a patient. That's my job, after all. I'm the Chief Resident. Consulting is my gig.

I wince at the thought. I'm Chief Resident until I can't find something else that Riley needs.

As I stride over to Tamia, she arches an eyebrow at me. "You okay?"

"No. I keep thinking about the immobilizers."

I know I'm asking for it. Telling Tamia I'm ruminating about something we've already talked about is tantamount to asking for her to snap me back to reality with a bucket of cold water.

Tamia shakes her head. Her expression shifts, hardening into the expression that looks more like den mother than friend. "Come with me."

Uh oh. Suddenly, my best friend at Liberty Hill sounds a bit like my mother. I would happily take a pep talk at this point, but it doesn't sound like I'm gonna get it. "Sure," I say, adopting what I hope sounds like a cooperative attitude.

I follow her over to the bay where the accident victim had been treated. I know from checking the chart that Riley had already sent him upstairs to orthopedics. They were getting him prepped for surgery to get the fracture on his leg fixed before it got infected. The room was empty, already cleaned and ready for the next patient. The trauma cart was still sitting in the hallway. The trauma carts, filled with medication and equipment that were commonly used around the ED, had wheels. There were six of them and they tended to migrate, rolled from place to place as they were needed.

Tamia bends over, giving me a sideways glance as if she's super annoyed that we are having this conversation again. She pulls open the bottom drawer and points to a line of orange immobilizers in the bottom drawer. "I didn't want to tell you, but these were in here the whole time, Mac."

I feel my face flush so hot I'm sure someone has poured hot honey all over my skin. "I thought you said you didn't have a chance to restock the trauma cart?"

"We didn't, but after you said you couldn't find the immobilizers, I realized we didn't use the immobilizers with the last case. These were in here, Mac, I'm telling you."

I stiffen. Is someone playing a joke on me? "They weren't in there, Tam. I opened that same drawer."

She doesn't say anything, simply folding her arms across

her chest. I feel my lips twist. I open the drawer myself again, feeling like I've gotten caught in a magic trick where there are disappearing immobilizers.

They are there. All orange and pretty, wrapped in plastic and ready to go.

"This isn't the same cart, is it?" I ask, making it sound like it's a question to be nice.

Tamia raises her eyebrows. "It is."

I don't believe her. I stomp away and, acting like I'm on a vendetta, I check every single cart for immobilizers.

They *all* have them.

By the time I return to Tamia, she's shaking her head somberly.

I feel my hands start to shake just a little bit. I press my hand into my forehead. "Tam, I'm sorry. I don't know what's going on."

She shakes her head as if she's seen this before. "You're a resident at the end of your training. You're fried. You need sleep."

Thank God. She understands. I press the back of my hand against my forehead. "This job, I just don't know —" I hate the fact that at this moment I feel like I could walk out of the Emergency Department and never come back and not miss it. I've worked too hard to feel like this. Am I that thin-skinned that a few changes — Shaw joining the team and a storage room reorg — are making me feel like I'm going crazy? My breath comes in short pants. All of the hours and the studying and the money that I've put into becoming a doctor. Am I that eager to just throw it away? I close my eyes for a second. When I open them, Tamia's sizing me up. She's probably right, though. I mean, how many residents has she seen come through Liberty Hill? This is normal. If she says I'm just tired from the grind, I probably am. "Maybe you're right. I probably just need sleep. It's gotta be the switch from overnight float to days. That's all."

Tamia looks around. I know what she's doing. She's calculating the load on the staff. I hold my breath. Even though I'm the Chief Resident, the Emergency Department is Tamia's house. As the charge nurse, she ultimately makes all the calls on breaks and who's working and who's not. Surprisingly, even Riley defers to her.

Well, for the most part. Things seem to be changing now that Shaw is here.

That's what I like about Tamia. She's tough, but in the best way, like your mom or your aunt. Well, not my mom — she's got her head so far up Queen Julia's you know what about this wedding that it's a miracle that she can do anything else.

But I digress.

Tamia looks at me, her face softening. "I sent Jamir to go take a rest a little while ago."

Of course she did. Tamia has a thing going for Jamir. Everyone, save for Jamir, seems to know it, but that's very Jamir. He's the kind of guy that just floats through life without a care in the world.

She continues, "Why don't you go to the on-call room. Let's see if you can sleep for an hour or so to clear your mind. You're probably still tired from being on overnights for so long. Everything will seem better if you get a little rest."

I fight off the urge to hug Tamia. "Sure," I say, pretending that I'm good.

But I'm not. I'm utterly relieved.

I dart to the on-call room, nearly running there before someone grabs me. I charge in the door and then stop. The lights are dim, the single set of bunks only shadows in the room. It smells like a combination of lemon cleaner — like someone has just mopped the floor — and bad breath. That's probably from Hudson. I saw him come out a little while ago.

Jamir is, predictably, on the upper bunk, directly across from the shelves with the scrubs and extra linens on them. He's sound asleep, a giant set of headphones covering his ears. I can hear the faint hum of some sort of music in the background, the bass bumping. But I don't care, I'm so tired again that it doesn't matter.

The whole immobilizer drama has drained me.

As I lay down, I kind of feel bad about taking a rest this early in my shift, but if there's one thing I've learned it's when the charge nurse tells you to go lie down and take a rest, it's probably a good idea to do that. If this shift is anything like the ones I've had over the last few weeks, then I could be on well over my twelve-hour allotment.

In fact, I'm counting on it.

For some reason, it seems like the closer I get to the finish line of my training, the harder Riley is making it on me to try to get my residency done. It's like he's turned up the level of expectation on me without letting me know, as if he's moved the goal line a little bit further away each time I show up for work. I realize it's not entirely his fault that we've seen an uptick in traumas over the last few months, but my twelve-hour shifts are now regularly eighteen to twenty hours. Even if Donovan was in town, I still wouldn't be able to see him much.

Which reminds me, where's Donovan?

As I lay down on the lower bunk, I look at my phone once again. I'm trying to fight off the urge to look for him. He has to be on a plane, right? I mean, that's one of the only reasons that his location would be unavailable.

Unless he stopped sharing it with me.

The thought sends a twitter into my already upset stomach. I flip my phone to silent and curl up on my side, still wearing my lab coat, my stethoscope still around the back of my neck. The rubber hose on my stethoscope is tugging at the sensitive skin on my neck. I pull it off and set it on the pillow next to me. I pat my hip, absentmindedly, making sure my pager is attached. With any luck, the vibration will be enough to wake me up if Tamia needs me.

Relax, Mac. She knows exactly where I am.

I take a deep breath, close my eyes and try to think about nothing. It's impossible. My eyelids flip open again. Shaw's face and the immobilizers and Tamia's disappointed expression scroll through my mind like they are on a loop. I try to push the thoughts away. There's no telling whether I get paged in ten minutes or an hour, or at all, but if I'm gonna get sleep, now is the time.

I slam my eyelids closed and try not to think about anything at all. I can't start reliving the things I've done wrong. These aren't the first mistakes I've made as a resident and I'm sure they won't be the last.

Who am I kidding? First mistakes? I've been on a run lately. The faces of Bill Palmer and Samantha Watkins float in my memory.

Using the last bits of self-control I have, I force myself to keep my eyes closed. Donovan, Riley, Shaw, Tamia, the patients — I have to let it all go. I'm not going to be good for anyone if I don't sleep.

THE NEXT THING I KNOW, I feel the pager buzz on my hip. I pull it off, hearing the springs from the bunk above me squeak. Apparently, Jamir has gotten paged too. I rub my eyes and sit up on the edge of the bed as Jamir jumps down. He lands silently, like a panther, just a couple of feet in front of me. How he does it, I'm not sure. When I get stuck on the upper bunk, I have to use the little ladder, trying to feel my way in the dark. Unless I'm missing something, he was asleep, but he doesn't look like he's just waking up. He's got a big grin and a bright look in his eyes that I can see even in the dim light of the on-call room. That's Jamir — fully caffeinated and fully rested, ready for fun no matter the time of day or night.

I hate him.

I stay where I am for a second, waiting for the fog in my brain to lift, then stare at the text on my pager. It was from Tamia. It wasn't specific. We're just needed back on the floor ASAP. Most likely, they'd had a slew of cases come in and need help. I sigh, not moving.

Jamir, still right in front of me, pulls his scrub shirt off and tosses it in the hamper that's next to the door, walking over to the shelves that line the on-call room. Even in the dim light, I can see the ripples of his abs, the cut muscles of his shoulders and arms. I try to look away, but I almost can't. No wonder Tamia has a thing for him.

Part of me wonders if that's what Shaw looks like with his shirt off.

Donovan. Donovan. Kind, sweet, quiet Donovan. Remember Donovan?

I look down, staring at the pager, pretending that there's something really interesting on it and trying to sneak looks at Jamir's naturally bronzed skin while he changes. Jamir has the chest of someone that looks like he does a lot of push-ups. It's the kind of chest I'd like to lie against. I mean, Donovan's chest is okay, but he's a runner. He's tall and lanky, all arms and legs. Jamir looks like he just has more substance to him. I push the thought away. What am I doing?

Standing up, I clip the pager back on my pocket. Jamir looks at me. "You get any sleep?"

I check the time on my watch. "Maybe an hour?"

"That's all you need."

I start for the door when Jamir stops me. "Hey, you've got some blood on your shirt."

I look down, tugging the fabric away from my belly. Sure enough, there's some splatters of blood on my blue scrubs.

That's a big no-no in the hospital. Jamir and I have known each other for years, and we have seen more body parts between the two of us than I think either of us would like to recount, so I just strip off my lab coat and top right in front of him, tossing my ID, stethoscope, and pager back on the bed. I notice the covers are rumpled, like I was thrashing in my sleep. I toss my dirty scrub shirt down next to it, since Jamir is in the way. I'll put it in the hamper on the way out the door. I take a couple of steps angling for the shelf where the medium-sized woman's scrub tops are, bumping into Jamir. It's not like I'm naked, or anything. I have a sports bra on underneath my shirt. I feel the tingle of his warm skin next to mine. Our arms get tangled trying to grab for the scrub shirts that are the right sizes for each of us when the door opens. Jamir is between the door and me, so I peek around his muscled torso to see who is coming. It's Tamia. She gives us a startled look when she notices that I don't have a shirt on and neither does he. "You two coming?" Her voice is stony.

"Yeah," I stutter as I follow her eyes. They've gone from a half-naked Jamir to me in my sports bra, my scrub shirt, stethoscope, ID, and pager flung on the rumpled bed. My face reddens for about the fiftieth time that day. "We were just putting clean shirts on."

"Uh-huh," Tamia says and slams the door closed.

My day has just gone from bad to worse.

By the time I tug my shirt on, Jamir has an even wider grin on his face. He's like Teflon. Nothing bothers him. "That was hilarious." He points to me and then to himself. "You and me? Nah." He turns on his heel and walks out the door, chuckling under his breath, leaving me with my mouth hanging open.

Nah? What does that mean?

I scramble, clipping my ID badge to the pocket of my scrub shirt then looping my stethoscope around my neck. I grab the pager on my way out the door, stuffing my lab coat in the hamper too. As I stride down the hallway toward the nurses' station, I give myself a stern talk. "Self, you're here to learn. Don't pay any attention to anyone else. You gotta be like Jamir. Don't pay any attention to what anyone else is saying. Just do your job. That's how you get through this shift. One patient at a time."

Who was I kidding? Sometimes it's one minute at a time.

But this shift is gonna be very long if I can't convince Tamia that what she saw between me and Jamir was nothing.

Like he said. Nah.

14

Predictably, the rest of the shift got busy. Even though I was supposed to be off at seven PM, I didn't end up getting home until nearly two AM. Not that I went straight home. Shaw cut us all loose at eleven, but I was too wound up to go home and go to sleep. Being overtired does that to me. Feeling the need to blow off some steam, I went with Jamir, Hudson, one of the other residents named McDonald from another shift, and Tamia to a bar around the corner from the hospital called the Angry Orchard. Tamia, after finding me and Jamir half undressed in the on-call room, barely said anything to me. Against my own better judgment, I decided to join Jamir in doing a shot after each one of the three beers that I had, which Tamia dropping off my car, while Jamir followed in hers. Jamir, of course, suffered no ill effects. Has to be something in his Guatemalan heritage. Has to be.

The shrill tone of my phone alarm going off made me nearly jump out of my skin. Morning already? How did that happen? I check the time on my phone. It's five thirty AM. I have to be at work by quarter to seven for the handover. It's when the shift that's on duty gives us the information about who is in the ED and what still needs to be done. I groan, staying in bed for a second, opening my eyes and then closing them, willing the swirling of the room and the nausea in my stomach to go away.

Perhaps the shots were not my wisest move.

I sit up on the edge of the bed for a second, waiting for Snort to make his morning visit. Usually, as soon as he hears me sitting up on the edge of the bed, he comes into my room, giving a long meow, stretches, and then turns with a little snort if I don't look like I'm ready to immediately feed him. I sit on the edge of the bed for another second wondering if maybe he just didn't hear me then, looking at my cell phone, I realize I don't have time to worry about whether Snort has made his morning visit or not. I'm already a few minutes behind. I stand up, the room still spinning a little bit. Between the alcohol and only three hours of sleep, I'm really not sure how I'm gonna make it through the next shift. For a second, I consider texting Riley and calling in sick, but undoubtedly, he will call me, ask me to describe all of my symptoms in great detail, make me do a differential diagnosis on myself, and then demand that I come into work anyway.

It would be a lot of work for nothing.

Resigned, I trudge off to the shower, standing under the hot water for maybe a little longer than I should, waiting for my head to clear. I jump out, dry myself off, floss and brush my teeth, (after all, who wants to have a doctor whose breath smells like last night's shots), then pull on a pair of leggings, an oversized T-shirt I stole from Donovan, and comb my hair. Grabbing a clip from the edge of the sink, I grab it and twist it behind my head — there's no time to do anything more interesting with it — put on a coat of moisturizer for the wrinkles I'm hoping to avoid if I survive residency, add a little mascara and Chapstick, and call it a day.

The reality is, I could go to work with a full face of makeup and my hair done in perfect waves around my face, like the way my sister wears her hair, but within five minutes, someone would inevitably throw up on me, or something else would happen that would force me to go put my hair back into a ponytail and wash my face.

Why fight the inevitable? At least that's what my dad always says.

I make my way out to the kitchen, feeling only marginally better. I check my cell phone to see where Donovan is. From the location, which suddenly seems to be working again, he appears to still be in Singapore. I'm tempted to send him another text, but he still hasn't responded to the ones I sent him from the night before, which would be the day before where he is.

I shake my head. I don't know. All these time changes are too confusing, especially with how I'm feeling right now, post shots. I think about Jamir for a second. He's probably doing five hundred pushups or running a marathon before our shift. How he does it, I have no idea. I make a mental note to talk to him when I get a chance.

I pop a coffee pod into the Keurig, the extra strength kind I keep for after a long night, slamming the top closed and setting it to brew after putting a travel mug beneath it. I check my phone again, feeling my stomach knot. I thought I had plenty of time, but I must have stayed in the shower for too long. I look down, noticing Snort still needs to be fed. I quickly refill his water dish, leave a little dry cat food in the bowl, and scoop out his litter box, tying up the bag and leaving it by the door. I can walk it to the trash on my way out the door, as long as I don't run into Mrs. Dixon, which will make me even more late.

I look up, realizing I still haven't seen Snort. "Snort? Where are you? It's time to eat."

A second later, I realize Snort is nowhere to be found.

15

I am in a complete and utter panic. I have to get to work. Like I *really* have to, like if I don't leave soon, I'm gonna be late, but there's one problem.

I still can't find Snort.

I've looked everywhere, all of his normal hiding places — the closet, underneath my clothes where he likes to take naps, on the corner of the couch where all the pillows are. I even check around the boxes where Donovan still hasn't unpacked, wondering if Snort has somehow fallen in and can't get out.

No Snort.

Desperate, I run back to the bedroom, ready to start the cycle all over again when I notice something.

The window is open.

I stop, frozen, staring at it. How is the window open?

I don't open the window ever.

Never.

Well, except a couple of days ago when Snort bombed his litter box. Then I had to. I had no choice.

If there was nothing outside the window to my apartment

like every other regular building, that would be one thing. The problem is, I live in an older building in Philadelphia, one that has an iron fire escape bolted to the outside — the same kind people think of when they think of apartments in New York City.

They are kinda common in Philadelphia. Though I haven't done it in a while, I have sat on the fire escape for a little while, staring out at the street below, especially when I've had a heinous day.

I frown. Come to think of it, I only did that one time. I realized what a long drop it was down to the first floor and decided to come back in, not quite sure how solid the fire escape was. I'm sure it's solid enough if there was a major emergency, like the building was on fire. In that case, I would probably prefer to fall to my death rather than burn to my death.

I search through the apartment again. Snort wouldn't have gone outside, would he? Panic rises in my throat. I know I was a little tipsy when I came in the night before, but not so tipsy that I would have opened the window.

Would I?

My head starts to ache, like I'm wearing a hat that's two sizes too tight. I check the time again. I literally needed to be out of my apartment five minutes ago if I was hoping to get to work on time. Now I'm on the bubble. If Snort comes back in the next thirty seconds, I can slam the window closed and run out the door, hoping to sneak in just as the handoff begins before Riley catches me. The thought of Riley brings up memories from the day before, what I'm now calling "The Case of the Missing Immobilizer." I try to calm the churning of my stomach by reminding myself that people struggle from time to time, don't they?

But not everyone couldn't find an immobilizer and missed a foot that probably needs to be amputated, and a woman who I almost sent home with the flu who likely has leukemia.

And then there was the half-dressed run in with Jamir and Tamia.

Wow, I'm having a great week.

The voice of the woman from the adoption agency where I got Snort is running through my head. "Now, this kitten came from a litter that was born outside. They were wild for a little bit. I'd be very careful about leaving any windows or doors open. We've seen him try to escape already."

Cuddling my new little gray ball of fur with the pushed-in face, I promised I wouldn't.

And I haven't.

Until now.

Or did I?

I look toward the bedroom, where the bed is still rumpled, a book I've been trying to read on time management is gathering dust on the nightstand. Why would I have opened the window in the middle of the night? There was no reason to. I wasn't too hot, I wasn't too cold. I had just had fresh air on my way home in the Uber. I glance at the window, the thin drapery moving in the morning breeze. A chill runs down my spine. If Snort made it out the window, he could be anywhere. Philadelphia is a big city. It's not like I have some sort of tracker on him or something. My mind lurches. Snort could have made his way down the fire escape and wandered off, sniffing the air in the way that only he does, giving an occasional snort, looking for his long-lost family or some cute girl cat to hang out with.

I poke my head out the window, looking down at the fire escape but I don't see anything. Frantically, I run through the apartment one more time, calling and clucking like a mother hen, wishing I had spent more time watching cat videos that claim you could train your cat to come when called. I don't need a lot of commands for Snort, just teaching him to come when called would be perfect. Especially now.

I stop in the kitchen, staring at the door, seeing my work

bag ready to go, sweat collecting on my forehead. I check the time once more. I am *definitely* going to be late. Worse yet, because it's a day shift, Riley will be running the handover. He'll know that I'm not there. I'm out of time. I run back into the bedroom, planning on closing the window when all of a sudden, I hear something, a scratching sound. Snort jumps onto the windowsill. I freeze. I know if I move too suddenly, Snort is going to jump right out the window again. I need to think fast.

Treats!

"Here, kitty kitty," I call. Why am I saying this? Whoever invented that had to be an idiot. I back up slowly and then dart to the kitchen, making a lot of noise with the cabinets so he can hear me, then rustle a bag of some cat treats, his favorite ones, the Cat-Man-Do Bonito Flakes. I dart back to the bedroom and stop in the doorway. A second later, Snort jumps down from the windowsill as if nothing had ever happened, his tail high and curled in the air.

But there's one problem.

He's standing between me and the window.

I freeze, trying to calculate my options. I'm fast, but cats are faster. Especially Snort. It's like he was a sprinter in a former life.

Against my better judgment, I grab a handful of the treats out of the bag, scattering them on the floor, hoping that Snort will chase after them and be so distracted that he will have no idea what I'm up to. Luckily, he does. He trots toward me, eating the treats as fast as he can, making little grunting noises as if he hasn't eaten in a week.

It's my opening.

I sprint for the window, slamming it closed and securing the latch. I lean against the wall, panting, then double-check the latch. As I do, the thought occurs to me.

If I didn't open the window, then who did?

It obviously wasn't Snort. And Donovan's out of town.

My knees go weak. There's a downside to having a fire escape. As much as I could go down in an emergency, I realize something else.

Someone could also climb up.

16

As much as I would have liked to have made it to work on time, I didn't. That's the bad news.

The good news was that despite all of the drama with Snort, I was only twenty minutes late.

Technically, that meant I started my shift only five minutes late, though I did miss the first fifteen minutes — the handoff, which is a big deal. I had just received a text from Tamia and Riley when I rushed into the Emergency Department, flinging my bag down in the break room. As I get changed, I run through my options, perspiration collecting on my skin. I'm the Chief Resident. I'm not supposed to be late. I'm supposed to be early so I can assess the needs of the department and help Riley and Tamia make decisions.

And there's no way to hide it. I'm late.

After quickly getting changed, realizing I'd have to wear a large set of scrubs instead of a medium, I trot out onto the floor, hoping to skate by. I mean, other people are late sometimes. Like Hudson. He's always huffing and puffing in at the last second, hauling his big farm-boy body into the ED. No one ever seems to say anything to him.

Why am I any different?

I'd just made it to the nurses' station when I bump into Dr. Riley. "You're late," he says, his face reddening above his yellow polka dot tie. I haven't seen him that mad in a long time, probably not since Jamir and I were first-years and decided to race wheelchairs up and down the hallway one night. Even his jowls are shaking, like he's experiencing his own personal earthquake.

Sucking in a breath, I'm not sure what to do. I go for the truth. The truth will set you free, right? "I'm so sorry, Dr. Riley." I'm so very careful to use the Dr. part of his title. If there were other titles I could add, I would. At this point, I'm not above groveling. I'm already in trouble. I don't need to make it any worse. "I was up on time, I promise you. But my cat, Snort, somehow he —"

Tamia, who is lurking nearby, narrows her eyes. "Is Snort okay?"

I give a big sigh of relief, letting my shoulders slump, even doing a little lip quiver as if I'm thinking through the whole horrible situation, hoping that my dramatic presentation will fend off Dr. Riley's wrath. "Thank God, yes. Somehow, the window was open. He escaped and I didn't know what to do. It's not like I could just leave the window open all day."

He arches a single, bushy eyebrow. "It's not like you can leave patients just sitting in the Emergency Department all day either, now is it, Forbes?" Dr. Riley's words were cutting, mimicking what I had said.

I stare at the ground. The only thing I can do is apologize, staying just a hair away from full-on groveling, though I am really frustrated. "Again, I apologize, Dr. Riley. It was unavoidable."

As soon as the words came out of my mouth, I know I've made a huge mistake. I freeze, waiting for the wrath of Riley. All I can do is brace myself and hope.

"Oh, it was completely avoidable, Forbes. First, keep your window closed. Second, have one of your neighbors take care of your cat. The third option, and probably the best one, is to get rid of your cat. It seems you can hardly handle your responsibilities here, let alone another life, albeit an animal one."

Ouch. All I can do is stand there with my mouth open, feeling my eyes well up with tears.

With that, Riley stomps off, his white lab coat swishing and snapping behind his calves the same way that Snort's tail snaps in the air when he's unhappy. I look at Tamia, willing the tears to just go away. I point down the hallway. "Did he just —?"

Tamia's expression is hard as if she's still mad at me. Then she shakes her head. "Ignore him, Mac. Yes, he did just suggest that you should get rid of your cat, but he's in a mood today."

Underneath my breath I mutter, "When isn't he?"

Tamia ignores my comment. Normally, I feel like we'd commiserate, but she still seems a little distant after what happened with Jamir. She whistles low and shoos me away. It's my signal to get to work. There's a full waiting room, which means there's work to be done.

A lot of it.

I realize in my panic, I've forgotten my stethoscope. I made a hand motion at Tamia so she knows where I'm going. She nods, but I can tell she's getting impatient. She hates it when there's a log jam of patients waiting to be seen. It's one of the things that makes her so good at her job. Among the ED's in Philadelphia, we have the shortest waiting times anywhere in the city.

But that means we all hustle.

I jog to the locker room, take a second to put away my clothes and bag and check the shelves to see if by some miracle there are sets of medium scrubs available. Right now, I'm swimming in the ones I have on. I frown. There aren't. All I can do is tighten the strings on the pants as tight as I can and tuck my shirt in, hoping I don't look like I'm wearing a set of bed sheets. I fling my stethoscope around the back of my neck, grab my ID, and slam my locker door closed.

As I walk out of the locker room, I nearly slam into Shaw. "I was just coming to find you."

My stomach sinks. What did I do wrong now? I blink. "Um, okay. Sorry I'm late."

Shaw shakes his head, grinning at me, one of his dimples showing. As best I can tell, he has only one on his left cheek.

I blink, shoving the thought in the back of my mind, into a deep, dark closet. I don't notice these kinds of details. I can't. I have Donovan.

"I'm sure you saw that the waiting room got pretty full."

I nod. "Yeah." Just the thought of examining all those patients in the waiting room was making me tired already. It was a lot trying to see my own patients and coordinate things with Tamia.

He gives me a gentle smile, which reveals a set of perfectly white teeth that I hadn't seen before. "I'll give you a hand. We'll get through it. Don't pay attention to Riley. He's kind of a jerk sometimes."

I'm not sure what to say. Why was Shaw being so nice? Had he already figured out Riley? I pause, a little surprised. Shaw hasn't been at Liberty Hill for very long. I start to say something about Riley, but then I stop. There was one big difference between Shaw ignoring Riley's antics and me ignoring Riley. I'm a resident. Shaw's an attending. I need Riley to sign off on my residency or I don't become an attending anywhere. My career would be over before it started. Shaw's lucky, he's already crossed that hurdle. All he has to do is put in his resignation and go apply somewhere else if Riley gets on his nerves.

Breathing a sigh of relief, I say, "Okay, thanks."

He puts a hand on the outside of my arm and gives it a squeeze. I can feel the warmth through the thin material of my oversized scrubs. "I'm sorry you didn't see the text about the supply room. I didn't mean for that to get out of control."

Now he's apologizing? Who is this man? "No problem. We got it handled," I stammer, skipping the part about how Tamia showed me there were actually immobilizers in the trauma cart after all.

I still have no idea how I missed them. They are big and orange. That would be like missing an elephant that takes a seat in the ED.

As I walk with Shaw towards the nurses' station, his very presence makes me feel like I'm Superwoman. I straighten my back, holding my head high. I'm with Shaw, after all. And I'm the Chief Resident. He's got my back. The day might have started off a little rocky after nearly losing Snort, but I'm certain he's secured in my apartment, and he'll be there when I get home.

Aren't I?

My surge of confidence evaporates as quickly as it arrives. My shoulders slump. I wish that Donovan had already set up the cameras he was planning on putting in our apartment but hadn't gotten to because of work. With both of us gone so much, he said it makes sense. I mean, we live in Philadelphia, not a small town somewhere. And also, it would be good to know if Mrs. Dixon is rooting through our apartment when we're not home with her extra key. Donovan said he had a set of cameras buried in his boxes somewhere — some sort of a bonus gift from his company. They even came with a year of free surveillance.

I could have used them this morning, that's for sure.

I push the thought of Snort being missing, and more importantly, how the window had gotten open out of my mind, but not before a shudder runs down my spine. It's a full-on terrifying tremor that starts at the back of my neck and runs the whole way down to my tailbone. The idea that someone had been on my fire escape and even worse, had opened my window while I was sleeping, creeps me out. Granted, I could have opened the window in my haze the night before, but it was still creepy. And why would I have done that? I never open the window. My mouth suddenly feels dry. It would have been far less creepy if Donovan had been there, but then again, I wasn't sure where Donovan was, and although he was a big guy, he wasn't built like Shaw, who seemed to be built like a pile of bricks.

Before I have a chance to calm myself down, Tamia gives a low whistle, her fingers pointing towards me and Shaw in a V. "You two. Bay three. Woman fell from a roof."

I frown, looking at Tamia. "She's a jumper?"

"No, she fell. Work accident."

Huh? I shoot a look at Shaw. He frowns but strides towards the woman's room, glancing over his shoulder. "A woman roofer?"

I shrug. "This is Philly. We've got a little bit of everything here." I decide it's a good time to try to be personable. Even though I wasn't sure about Shaw being in charge of the ED, I'm warming up to the idea. "Are you originally from here?"

I ask the question as we walk into the room. Shaw doesn't answer, or more correctly, he doesn't have time to. There's a woman lying on the bed, writhing in pain, groans loud enough that I'm sure everyone can hear them in the hallway. I glance at the tablet to find her name — it's Christine Lasko — and introduce myself, but I'm not sure she hears me. "Christine, I'm Dr. Forbes. I'm here to help you." My pulse quickens. I can tell by the look on her face that she's out of it. Shaw gives me a nod. I take that as his command to run the woman's care. I quickly tug on a pair of gloves and stride to the side of her bed, reaching for my stethoscope. Jasmine is on the other side of the bed, adding a blood pressure cuff and EKG leads. I listen to her lungs. There's something not right. I look at Jasmine. "Let's get an IV started, regular saline. Get her fifty mics of fentanyl for the pain." The microgram dosage is right. I know it. I look at Shaw. "Dr. Shaw, could you please evaluate her lower limbs?"

We normally don't say please in the ED when we are running a trauma case, but I throw it in there for good measure. Shaw's been nice so far. Couldn't hurt, could it?

He doesn't move. It's a silent rebuttal. I feel my stomach knot. Oh, I get it. He's there for backup, not to run the call. I clear my throat and look away, then check her pelvis and both of her legs. No obvious breaks, though she's still on a backboard with her neck immobilized. I double-check her arms. Again, no obvious breaks there either. What is this woman, rubber? I look over at Jasmine who's giving me an encouraging glance. "No obvious breaks, but let's order a full set of images just to make sure we don't miss a hairline fracture somewhere." I look over at Shaw. He gives me a slight nod. I feel a little glow in my chest. *Good one, Mac. Full imaging. Great idea.*

As I look up and check the monitor, I see that Christine's blood pressure is falling fast. I stare at Jasmine. "You have that IV running, right?"

"Yes. It's in." There's something wrong. Very wrong.

I take off my stethoscope and listen to the woman's heart. It's barely beating.

My own heart skips a beat as if in compassion for the woman on the bed. "Her BP is crashing." I look at Shaw, my jaw tightening. I feel the adrenaline dump into my system. This is why I got into emergency medicine, so I can help people like Christine. I love the speed, the pressure of the situation. The reality is that if I don't do something fast, putting the pieces together in the right order, she's gonna die. "Tension pneumothorax."

He takes two quick steps forward, pulls his stethoscope off of his neck and listens to her chest. He gives a nod. "Yep. Procedure?"

"Needle decompression."

I look up. Tamia has joined us. I look at her and then I look at Christine's blood pressure. It's low. Really low. It's dropped to sixty over forty. There's air somehow leaking into the cavity between her lung and her chest wall as a result of the fall. I have to get the extra air out of her chest so that her lung can reinflate again. Otherwise, she's going to suffocate to death, or her heart will stop for lack of oxygen. Either way, it's a bad deal.

"Get me a fourteen-gauge angiocath and the ultrasound. Prep for a needle decompression," I command.

Despite the issues in the last few days and almost losing Snort, I feel like myself again. Jasmine whips around and grabs the ultrasound while Tamia rolls a surgical tray next to Christine's bed. She's stopped writhing for the most part, probably because of the fentanyl, but her face is losing color. It's not a good sign. In one smooth move, Tamia rips open the sterilized equipment tray. I grab a clean set of gloves while Tamia cuts the woman's shirt away from her upper chest and douses it with Betadine, an iodine solution that will sterilize the field. As much as I'd like to have this woman in a hospital gown, we don't have time.

Jasmine hands me the probe for the ultrasound. I squirt some ultrasound gel on the woman's chest and set the ultrasound probe down, looking for the landmarks I need in order to do the decompression. I hear the monitors beep angrily in the background and furrow my eyebrows. When I look up, Christine's blood pressure has dropped even further, now fifty-six over thirty-eight. If I don't do something soon, she's going to code. In the background, I hear a low voice. "Come on, Mac. Do it now."

It's Shaw.

I have no idea why I'm hesitating. I'm a third-year resident, one short step from being in Shaw's shoes. I know this procedure. I've done this procedure.

Setting my jaw, I don't take the time to look at him. With my hands shaking, (Am I that intimidated by Shaw?) I move my fingers down and insert the tip of the needle into the outer layers of skin, then realize by looking at the ultrasound I'm in the wrong spot. I need to be in the second intercostal space in the midclavicular line. I'm not. I withdraw the needle, swallow hard, place the needle again and say, "Advancing," in a loud voice. I try again, but the needle won't penetrate. The beeping of the monitors in the background is driving me crazy. I can't concentrate. I use the back of my hand to wipe sweat off my forehead, then realize my scrub pants are loose. With my luck, I'll lose my drawers right in the middle of treating Christine.

This day is going downhill fast.

I try one more time. I know I can do this. I look down, moving the probe again. Nothing. Everything looks like a blur. My eyes are stinging with tears. I've done this procedure dozens and dozens of times, granted probably only a dozen of them on a human, but on cadavers and practice dummies a lot.

I can feel everyone's eyes on me. Tamia hisses, "Mac. Come on!"

It isn't more than a split second later when I hear Shaw. "Move!" he says in a booming voice. I hold up my hands and step back. He looks at Tamia, holding his hand out. "Ten-gauge."

A ten-gauge needle? That's enormous. How big does he think this pneumothorax is?

I hold the ultrasound and the gel, thinking the least I can do since I couldn't complete the procedure was to put the probe down so that he can figure out where to insert the catheter. I look at the spot where he should insert the catheter, ready to help. There are a few angry prick marks on Christine's chest from where I tried but failed. Without saying anything, Shaw reaches over his shoulder to the tray, grabbing the scissors, cutting even more of her shirt away. Right from the bottle, he dumps a bunch of Betadine, the sheets turning a dark orange as the iodine drips down her side.

Then I see something I've never seen done before.

Holding the needle in his right hand, he uses his left hand and starts a probe down the woman's chest, tracing the anterior axillary position near the fourth and fifth intercostal space. It's close to her armpit, not up near her collarbone, where I tried. I lean forward, watching. I've never seen a needle decompression done like this before. I whisper, "Do you want the ultrasound?"

"No," he barks but doesn't look up.

There's no explanation, just a flat response.

I watch Shaw's hands. They are steady as a rock, not a drop of perspiration on his tanned forehead. He walks his fingers down the woman's side between her breast and her side, his eyes closed. Then his eyes snap open and he plunges the ten-gauge needle into the woman's chest.

"I'm in."

His hands moving so quickly I can barely see what he's doing, he withdraws the needle leaving the catheter in place. There's a brief hiss as the air comes out of Christine's chest cavity. I watch her chest rise. Shaw has his hand out, waiting for gauze and tape to secure the catheter.

Shaw continues to work. I watch the monitor for a second. Christine's blood pressure starts to come up almost immediately, the angry beeping of the monitors slowing down. By the time I look back at Shaw, he's got gauze and tape wrapped around the area where he plunged the needle into the woman's chest.

Shaw steps back, strips off his gloves and orders additional medication and tests. I'm so freaked out by what I've just seen that I don't even pay attention to what he's doing. I make a mental note to check the record later, so I have an idea exactly what he did. It was incredible to watch, so incredible that my own heart is pounding in my chest.

As I follow him out of the trauma bay, I strip my gloves off and toss them in the trash. He starts to walk away but then I stop him, my voice squeaking. "Dr. Shaw?" I say meekly.

He turns around and looks at me, his gaze cool. Is he mad at me? "Yes?"

"I'm sorry I couldn't —"

All of a sudden, I have this memory of one time that Donovan couldn't... ahem, perform. I didn't care that much, but he really seemed bothered at the time. Now, I think I get it. My entire body feels limp.

Shaw just shrugs. I can't tell if it's a shrug of disgust or a shrug because he's like "Whatever."

But I'm so confused by what I saw, it doesn't even really register with me that I might have just now failed yet another test. "How did you do that?"

"What?" The word comes out short and impatient as if he has no idea what I'm talking about.

"The axillary decompression with no ultrasound guidance?"

He shakes his head at me as if I've just asked him for the recipe for a peanut butter and jelly sandwich as if it should be completely obvious. "Mac, the intercostal spaces are in the same spot whether you use the ultrasound or you use your fingers."

"But why such a big needle? And why the axillary approach, rather than midclavicular?" I'd always been taught that the midclavicular line was the easier way to go.

He shrugs again, then gives me a knowing smile. It feels intimate, like it's just the two of us in that moment. I feel my skin heat as he continues. "Just a trick I picked up on a medical mission trip. You'll pick up tricks along the way too." He frowns, looking down the hallway toward the bay where we just were. "Stay close to her. Have radiology double-check all of her scans. We don't want to miss a hairline fracture. Something caused her lung to collapse. Could be a rib fragment." He looks toward the doors that lead out of the Emergency Department. "I'm gonna go grab a sandwich. I'll be back in a few minutes. Have Tamia page me if you need me."

A sandwich? Are you kidding me? I'm still trying to catch my breath. All of a sudden, I imagined Shaw's naked body getting out of bed after a roll between the sheets. Does he get a sandwich then too?

Easy, Mac. Donovan, remember Donovan.

By the time I'm done imagining a post-coital Shaw, he's gone. As I turn away, I still can't believe what I saw. Everything I'd learned so far — from medical school, from the other attendings, from Dr. Riley, they'd all wanted us to use the ultrasound. Said it was the safest way to prevent nicking an artery or some other structure. I mean, yeah, he's right. The intercostal spaces are the same on every person, and he's also right that whether you use the ultrasound or not, you can still find it, but wasn't the ultrasound safer?

And what was with that crazy big needle?

I make a mental note to ask Dr. Riley about the procedure later, then nix that idea. I'm sure that even though I'm genuinely curious, he'd come up with some way to turn it around on me, as though I was criticizing the way that he had trained me.

And I was on thin enough ice with Riley anyway.

As I take two steps towards the nurses' station, I stop and cover my mouth. What if Shaw tells Riley that I was unable to do the needle decompression? I'm a third-year resident, the Chief Resident, after all. If I hope to become an attending soon, I need to be able to do those with confidence.

And I had just failed.

Right in front of Shaw.

17

After what happened with my failed needle decompression, I console myself by wandering down to the cafeteria, but only after giving Tamia a set of hand signals that I was upset and needed a minute and was going to go get coffee. She kinda frowned. I think she's still mad about the Jamir thing, but given the look on my face, I'm sure she knows I need a minute.

And seriously, nothing happened.

As I'm on my way down to the cafeteria, I replay in my head what happened. How had I not been able to get the needle in? Maybe I just needed to apply more pressure? I mean, if people really understood how tough skin, muscle, and bone are, they wouldn't be so surprised when they hear us grunting and groaning during procedures. It's really a workout.

But that's not the reason I failed, is it? I could blame it on the fact that I need to practice, which is probably true, but when am I going to do that? When you're a resident, you have basically two lanes — work and sleep.

As I pass the radiology department, I realize the worst part is that I'd done it right in front of Shaw. Yes, he was handsome, yes, he was new to the floor, but there were other doctors who had floated through, trying to work with Riley. I had always been fine in front of them.

I let the thought roll around in my head as I stroll into the cafeteria, smelling the mixed scents of chicken noodle soup (pretty good), sugary desserts (the frosted cinnamon rolls are fantastic for a crisis eating moment), and coffee brewing. I chew the inside of my lip. There's something about Shaw I can't quite put my finger on, and it's not just that he's stunningly handsome. He moves with a kind of confidence that I haven't seen before. When he gives direction, he's completely intimidating. No one would argue with him. I bet even Riley wouldn't. Randy Riley is like a weird caricature; the strange guy you don't want to leave your kids with. Dr. Jonathan Shaw is like a superhero. All he needs is a cape.

I wince as I make my way past the coffee. Instead of playing damsel in distress, I just ended up looking like a fool.

It's time to recover. I have to get it together. I'm the Chief Resident. Yes, I've had some issues recently, but I have to dust myself off and try again. I decide the best plan is to soothe myself with some food. I pick up a pita sandwich, a Monster energy drink, this time an Ultra Fantasy Ruby Red. While I usually get Pineapple Ice on the day shift, I decide it's time to shake things up. For good measure, I grab two chocolate chip cookies and a chocolate bar to take with me.

The diet of a champion and everyone who's career is falling apart — sugar and caffeine.

For good measure, I take a few bites of the pita sandwich on my way back up to the floor. I didn't need to add a bunch of sugar and caffeine into my system without something there to dampen it. It was bad enough that I screwed up a procedure. The last thing I need to do is have my hands shaking from sugar and caffeine just in case, with my luck, there was another needle decompression that came through the doors.

And it would be just my luck, trust me.

By the time I pass Radiology on the way back, I'm feeling marginally better about myself. I'm not a total failure. I did manage to graduate from medical school. My family is still speaking to me, even if I'm avoiding dealing with Queen Julia like she has a new strain of Ebola. I have a boyfriend and a cat. I even have a job prospect after my residency.

Though it feels like my life is falling apart, I guess it's okay.

I nibble on the edge of one of the cookies as I walk. I chalk up the issue with Bill Palmer's foot to his refusal to take medication, the near miss on Samantha Watkins's diagnosis of leukemia to slow labs, the half-naked episode with Jamir as bad timing, and my inability to do the needle compression with just rookie nerves working with studly Shaw. As I chew my cookie, I feel much better.

I know I'm in total denial, but what else can I do?

I take a bite of my sandwich and stop where I'm standing in the hallway, the liquid burning the back of my throat. My stomach tightens into a knot. There's a little voice inside my head that tells me that something else is going on, like that same feeling you get when someone is watching you, but I push it to the side. I walk a few more steps, waiting for it to subside, but it's still there, in the background. A warning, or something. I'm not sure how to describe it.

I blink and keep moving. I'm sure it's just a lack of sleep.

I hope.

By the time I get back to the Emergency Department, I've eaten half of the pita sandwich. The rest I dump in the trash on the way in, along with the second cookie. As much as I planned on saving the cookie for later, the eerie feeling hasn't left me and now my stomach's upset.

The doors whoosh open. My plan is to drop off my candy bar in my locker for later, but when the doors open, I nearly stop dead in my tracks, sucking in a sharp breath that makes my chest ache. I scurry off the side of the main hallway like a rat when a light is turned on.

None other than Dr. Randy Riley has resurfaced in *his* Emergency Department. He and Shaw are standing off in the corner, Shaw's muscled arms crossed in front of his chest, a concerned look on his face. His eyes keep darting over to the trauma bay where the woman roofer was, Christine something. I see Jasmine going in and out, her eyes dropping to the ground every time she walks out of the room, as if she's afraid that Dr. Riley is going to say something nasty to her. Tamia's the buffer in the situation, her strong presence hovering in the middle of the nurses' station, keeping an eye on the interaction between Dr. Riley and her team of nurses.

Tamia was protective like that. Unlike the nurses, I don't have a backup. I'm out on my own, exposed. Yeah, I have friends from med school, but we've hardly talked since we all went our separate ways after graduating. When you're a resident, it's different. Somehow lonely in a crowd. My legs feel suddenly weak. They aren't talking about me and the failed needle decompression, are they?

Knowing I can't hide forever, I quickly dart for the nurses' station, wondering how long they've been standing there and if Dr. Riley realizes that I've gone to the cafeteria. I pocket the chocolate bar in the back pocket of my scrubs, covering it up with my scrub shirt until I get to the nurses' station, making sure Tamia and the counter are between me and them. A girl's gotta try to run for cover when she can. Watching them from the corner of my eye, I try to pull a quick sleight of hand, pulling the melting chocolate bar out of my pants pocket and stuffing it in a drawer for fear that it's going to leak. I'm imagining the brown stain on the back of my pants already and what everyone might think it is. Happy to have it out of my pants, I hide it under a stack of papers so that, hopefully,

Hudson doesn't find it before I need an injection of sugar later in the shift.

Operation Chocolate Conceal complete, I crack open my Monster drink, take a sip, making an expression that tells everyone I'm seriously considering this new flavor that I am trying. In fact, I am desperately trying to keep from making eye contact with Dr. Riley or Dr. Shaw and at the same time looking serious, as though I'm a Chief Resident getting stoked up for the next round of patients.

A minute later, a scowl on Dr. Riley's face, he moves off with Shaw to the other side of the department, shooting me a look. It's one I'd like to interpret as indigestion, but I'm sure it's actually disgust now that he knows his Chief Resident failed at a simple needle decompression. I pick up a tablet, my stomach churning, and walk toward the bay where Christine is still being treated. The least I can do is to check in on her. After all, Shaw told me to run it. I swallow. I can at least keep doing that, can't I?

Jasmine is standing next to the bed. Christine is awake, sitting up, the catheter still sticking out of her chest. Someone has gotten her off the yellow backboard and removed the orange neck brace the paramedics strapped her into. I frown. "Who said she could come off the backboard?"

Jasmine raises her eyebrows as if that's a really dumb question. "Dr. Shaw."

I feel my face redden. I'd been so freaked out about the needle decompression that I hadn't bothered to tell the nursing staff to take the woman off the backboard and to remove the neck brace from her. I didn't even order a chest X-ray in addition to the rest of the orthopedic panels.

That's mistake #7,322 for me.

I cover my horror with a fake cough and then pull up the X-ray reports. I step to the side of her bed seeing that Shaw took care of ordering the chest X-ray.

Of course he did.

Christine is now awake and seems to be much more clear-headed. "Hi Christine, I'm Dr. Forbes. I'm not sure if you remember, but I was here when you came in."

Christine, with brown hair almost the same color as mine plastered to the side of her head, looks up at me slowly as if she's trying to focus. I know what it is — the pain meds. "I'm sorry, I really don't remember anything." The woman's voice comes out smooth and polite, as though she's well educated.

"Seems like you had a fall off of a roof, huh? Can you tell me how that happened?" I ask as I check her pupillary reflex, shining a light quickly into each of her eyes to see if her pupils contract.

"I already told the other doctor everything, but I guess I can do it again."

So, Shaw had already been in here? I feel my jaw tighten. Now Shaw was taking my case back over? At best, it's embarrassing. At worst, Shaw's lost faith in my ability as a doctor.

Neither option seems good to me.

The woman's voice interrupts my thoughts. "One of our crews was having trouble with an installation a few blocks over on Waterson Street. I was trying to talk to them about it, but they couldn't hear me, so I ended up on the roof. Didn't realize that a big chunk of the wood underneath the roof was rotten. It collapsed underneath my feet and then tossed me off the roof like a rag doll."

"So, you're not actually a roofer?"

"No. I'm not. I work for my dad. It's his business."

I set the tablet down and unlooped my stethoscope from around the back of my neck, listening to her heart and lungs. Everything sounds normal, minus a little rasp on the side where we put the catheter. Correction, where Shaw put the catheter in. I'm not concerned, but given how things are going, I'm going to document it and tell Shaw the minute I get a chance. I feel like I'm already in hot water. No need to do anything that will turn things up to boiling. "That's great that you and your dad can work together." My dad is always trying to get me or Julia to help him with his business. "It's nice to have women in the trades."

"Actually, it's not."

Christine's words startle me. "It's not?"

She closes her eyes and then opens them again. "You know, sometimes men think they know *everything*. They think they're helping, but they're really not." She points at Dr. Shaw and Dr. Riley, who are still standing out on the other side of the nurses' station, watching me. "Like those two jokers out there. They haven't stopped watching since you walked in here. What's the story with that?"

A volcanic level of heat runs to my face. I had no idea that Shaw and Riley were watching me *while* I was in here, or at least not so much that it would be obvious to the patient. "I've got no idea. I'm sure they're just talking about hospital staffing."

Actually, I do have an idea, but I'm not gonna tell her that.

It's because I completely bungled your needle decompression an hour ago and you almost died.

And, oh yeah, there was that part about how I was late to work today too because of Snort's escape.

All I can do is get to work. After giving Christine a once-over again, double-checking all of my results and then double-checking the X-ray results, luckily which had all come back negative, I look at her, and say, "I'm gonna go check with the head of our Emergency Department just to make sure he doesn't want to run any more tests before we send you upstairs, but based on what I'm seeing, it appears that you got really lucky. You did have a collapsed lung, so we will need to keep an eye on that at least overnight, but that will be up to pulmonology. Other than that, it only appears you have some scrapes and bruises." I'm careful to say *appears*. It's up to radiology and orthopedics to make that final determination. "You have no broken bones that radiology has been able to find. I would highly expect though that you're going to be tired and quite sore for the next few days. I'm guessing that orthopedics is gonna wanna take a look at you once you're upstairs as well, but all in all, it's good news."

Christine relaxes noticeably and then closes her eyes. The pain meds again. "Thanks, Doc."

I nearly sigh with her. That expression, the relief I've been able to give her — that's the reason I love my job.

Feeling like I've recovered sufficiently from my bungled start to the day, I dart out of Christine's room, feeling Shaw's and Riley's eyes bore into my back as I walk back to the nurses' station. I keep my eyes locked on my tablet, as if I'm pondering one of the world's secrets, or even just the flow of patients. They are deep in conversation. They really can't still be talking about me, can they? I feel my mind churn. I mean, it was just a needle decompression, that's all. It's not like I have to do those all the time, right?

A lump the size of a grapefruit surges into my throat.

There was Bill Palmer's black foot and Samantha's virus, turned cancer issue, though...

I decide the only logical response to this would be to eat my chocolate. Chocolate solves all the world's problems, doesn't it?

I pretend that I'm fumbling around in the drawer to find a paperclip, then quickly grab my chocolate bar and stick it in the back of my pants pocket again. I know I only have a little bit of time before I'm sure there will be another round of patients that show up. I just need a minute to regroup.

I grab my Monster drink and walk down the hallway, passing Jamir, who's in with another patient. Tamia is nowhere to be found. I'm kind of hoping she's in the break room when I get there. It would be nice to have a friend to talk to.

Well, maybe not. She's still kinda mad at me.

As I push the door open, she's not. The break room's empty. I take another sip of my Monster drink then think about Snort. Usually when I think about Snort when I'm at work, it's a comforting feeling, something to look forward to when I get home.

But it's not the same today.

I rub my chin. All I can think about is the open window. How did it get open? I never leave it open, let alone unlocked? Was I so drunk last night that I forgot that I opened it? I don't particularly remember being that drunk. I mean, yeah, I had a few shots, but just a few.

Geez, maybe I'm not as good with alcohol as I used to be.

The thought leads me back to my original concern. If I didn't open that window and Donovan's out of town, then who did?

The question won't leave me alone — and I'm not sure I want the answer.

18

I try to stop thinking about the fact that the window of my apartment building was mysteriously opened overnight by getting back to work. I blow through three or four more patients. None of them are suffering from anything serious — it's a crying two-year-old with a double ear infection, a man who got a little too aggressive playing pickleball and sprained his wrist, a teenager that cut themselves trying to make dinner for their family and an elderly man that I'm pretty sure has a UTI, a urinary tract infection, which is making him super cranky.

But I'm waiting on the labs to confirm.

And this time I'm going to triple-check them.

Given the fact that I've dug myself into a hole with both Riley and Shaw, I have to do something to redeem myself. My plan? I'm moving even faster than normal. I'm like a whirlwind popping in and out of rooms, handling business like a real Chief Resident.

I'm going to show Riley that he didn't make a mistake putting me in charge. I know Jamir wanted it and he would have been good, sure, but Riley chose me.

And I have to remind him why.

The reality is that if I don't redeem myself, he just might end up making Jamir Chief Resident for the rest of our time at Liberty Hill.

Riley's like that. It's *his* department so he does whatever he wants.

Ugh.

I try to ignore the thought as I head back to the nurses' station. My flurry of guilt-induced activity, paired with the rest of the nurses and the doctors, has cleared out the waiting room and most of the trauma bays. The only thing left to do is to get caught up on charting.

I head to the nurses' station, plop down on one of the rolling chairs and log into the system. I start entering information, still thinking about the open window in my apartment. Every time I think about it, my heart skips a beat. No, not an actual arrhythmia. I ran an EKG on myself a few weeks back. A cardiology resident told me I'm fine. A little bit of sweat starts collecting on my forehead thinking about the window. My mom told me not to rent in a building that had one of those fire escapes. I thought it was an added safety bonus. But no, my mom didn't think that way. She loves me. I know that. She just seems like she's had a hard time showing me that since I went to college. She was relatively sure that some strange person would climb up and peer in my window, stalking me, like something out of one of those crazy movies that plays late at night. I can hear her voice in my head as I'm typing on the computer. "McKenna, I'm not sure this is the smartest idea."

My mom isn't southern — I mean, we're all from Youngstown, Ohio — but she has that way about her where she can criticize you through the prettiest smile.

I love lots of things about my mom, but maybe not that.

I push the thought out of my head, deciding that the next time I'm off, I'm going to stop at the hardware store that's down the block and see if they can cut a dowel for me. I saw on a home improvement show one time where you can jam a wooden dowel between the window and the top of the frame and it will prevent anyone from opening it. Low-cost theft prevention, or in this case, Snort escape prevention. Then I have a brainstorm. I can check on my phone and see if Amazon has something that would work. It would save me from having to make a trip down to the hardware store and deal with the old guys in there, besides the fact that I know myself. As soon as I have a minute off, I'm not going to want to do anything other than take a shower, sit on the couch and sleep.

Not that I get a lot of time off.

Just thinking about it makes me tired. My Monster drink isn't doing as good of a job as normal. Maybe it's the flavor. Maybe I should have stuck to one I already know works. I sigh, looking around the Emergency Department. Everyone has picked up the pace. I glance over the top of the desk and see that there's a new group of people in the waiting room. It's crazy — Liberty Hill's Emergency Department never seems to slow down, or if it does, it only lasts for a few minutes. When I got out of medical school, I thought working in a super busy ED sounded like a great idea. I knew I was lucky. Getting a residency in a busy trauma department was like getting one of Willy Wonka's golden tickets. The thought was that the busier the Emergency Department was the more I'd learn, and I'd be able to get a better job offer.

But after three years of basically non-stop work, I'm not sure I thought through that as thoroughly as I should have. I'm tired. Like bone tired, like I need to sit on a beach somewhere in Mexico for a year or so to recover.

But I can't think that way. Maybe, if I'm lucky, Donovan will show up at the apartment sometime in the next few days.

That will brighten me up, I'm sure.

I close my eyes for a second and sit up straight. I just need to get through the next couple of months — finish my residency, get through Julia's wedding, even if it means holding her hand while she's having her bikini wax done, and then start my new job.

I grimace. The job at Schuylkill Valley Hospital as an attending in their ED isn't mine exactly. At least not yet.

But it will be. All I have to do is finish my residency. I've already agreed to terms with the lady in HR, Monica Albers. I'll be a new attending. Schuylkill Valley isn't quite as busy as Liberty Hill, but it's plenty busy. I know there will still be some supervision, of course, but it won't be the same as residency. I get to work my normal shift, go home like a normal person, and hopefully have a normal life. What normal looks like exactly, I'm not sure. To be honest, I've been on this hamster wheel of studying and working crazy hours for so long now, I don't even know what I'll do. Maybe I'll take up a hobby? Archery? Hiking?

Oh yeah. I live in Philly. That might not be so easy.

I rub the back of my neck, hearing the wheels from a gurney roll down the hallway. Jamir gives me a wave. He's got it. I nod, gratefully.

Then I realize that my whole life basically hinges on whether I can survive the next two months.

The thought sets my heart fluttering. Not my normal heart-skipping-a-beat thing, but a full-fledged flight of birds in my chest. Fighting off the urge to diagnose myself with tachycardia, atrial fibrillation or perhaps even a congenital heart defect, I take a deep breath.

You're just tired, Mac. That's all. There's been a lot on your plate.

And almost losing Snort didn't help.

As I glance at the waiting room again, hearing the buzz of voices, I see Tamia take her index finger and circle it in the air. It's her signal for me to get moving. I give her a nod and then point at the computer. If I don't get some of this charting done,

I'm never going to get home. It's amazing that with all the technology we have, I still have to sit down and finish everything.

Working for a hospital, unfortunately, is sometimes more about getting the bills to the insurance companies than it is about helping people.

But, as much as I don't like it, that's how I get paid.

I get through the chart of the two-year-old with the ear infection, pinging Shaw, who's lurking around here somewhere, to let him know I have cases that are ready for review. I'm sure given the fact that I bungled things so badly with Mr. Palmer and Samantha, not to mention my epic needle decompression fail, that he will be checking everything I do with a fine-toothed comb.

My stomach sinks. Part of me wonders if I deserve it.

I go in to update the chart of the teenage boy, Marcus Hansen, who cut his finger pretty badly while he was trying to chop a cucumber for dinner. Poor kid. All he was trying to do was help. I cleaned it really good and then stitched it up. Only took three stitches. But given the fact that it was a deep cut, I wanna order some antibiotics. Lucky for me, it's the same kind of antibiotic I just ordered for the two-year-old. All I gotta do is do a quick copy-paste and adjust the dosage.

I hold the control button and then hit the Y button, the command to duplicate a prescription and look down at my tablet for a second. All of a sudden, the screen goes black. Like totally black. There's nothing there. I tap the return key and frown, then look up. The computer terminal next to mine is black too. Confusion hits me first, followed by panic. What happened to the system? It's not coming back. I turn around, hearing the wheels on the chair I'm sitting in roll on the tile floor. Hudson, another one of the residents, is behind me. He's a big guy. Looks like he came off a farm with cropped blond hair in the front, the back a little too long. I imagine him with overalls and a John Deere baseball hat on. "Something happened to the computers?"

I shrug. "I don't know. I was just putting in a prescription. All of a sudden, the screen went blank."

Tamia strides over, a panicked look on her face. She knows, just like I do, that we will be paralyzed as an ED if we don't have computers. "Are all the computers down?"

I nod, touching my finger to my lip, silently willing the computer to come back to life. "I think so. I don't know what happened." My voice nearly cracks.

"I'll call tech services," she says.

Tamia to the rescue, I hope. While she's on the phone, I start to panic. What if it takes a long time to get everything running again? I'm gonna look really bad as the Chief Resident if I can't keep the ED running. It could be hours before they get the computers up and running again.

No, I reassure myself. The hospital has their own dedicated tech people. Surely, they'll get us up and going within an hour, maybe two at the most. We can hold on that long.

I hope.

But hope doesn't explain why every screen in the ED went black at the same time.

———

19

The computers are still down.

I stand up, knowing I need to do something, kind of wondering if this is some sort of crazy test Riley is doing. In my mind, I imagine he's gonna come charging down the steps, his tie-of-the-day fluttering, watching and waiting to see how we are going to react.

Which means I've gotta get moving. I'm the Chief Resident, after all. I need to act like one. I tug the tie on my pants tighter, hopefully preventing me from mooning anyone. We have patients who need to be seen. Feeling a surge of confidence, I look at Hudson. "All right, let everybody know we're gonna go old school. I'll get out the clipboards."

Luckily, there's a backup system in place, albeit not a good one. From a drawer in Tamia's desk, I pull out the stack of clipboards that already have forms clipped on them. It's the same information that we would normally enter right on our tablets, just in paper form. I look around, checking the Emergency Department. The good news is, the power is still on, and it looks like our equipment is still working. The big problem is going to be communicating with the lab. We'll have to see if the other departments are also down. I look at Hudson. "The good news is the power is still on. Our equipment should work."

He looks at me, a confused expression on his face. He's a first-year. "What about labs? How do we do those?"

I shake my head. "Kinda depends on if we're the only ones that are down. Outpatient surgery has computers too. We might be able to just run out there and check our lab tests on their computers until ours are back up and running. How about if you walk down there and go see if their's are online?"

By walk, I actually mean run, but this is Hudson. It's like asking a Clydesdale horse to run the Kentucky Derby.

Hudson lumbers off through the Emergency Department. The image of him wearing overalls and disappearing into a field of tall corn pops into my head. How Hudson ended up in Philadelphia at an Emergency Department as busy as Liberty Hill, I'll never know. There isn't one inch of city on him. He's definitely a country boy.

I scan the department, feeling like a general commanding her troops. I'm proud of myself. I've taken charge of the situation. Things are moving forward. I'm just reviewing the paperwork that's on the chart when Shaw hurries to where I'm standing. "Tamia said the computers are down?"

I sniff. He has the same cologne on. I fight the urge to step closer to him. "Yeah. I don't know what happened. I was just working on charting and the screens went black."

Tamia interrupts, her back straight, her tone matter-of-fact. "Tech services are on their way down. They said everybody else in the hospital is operational."

I shrug at Shaw. "I guess that's good news and bad news. I got the clipboards out."

"What are those for?" He frowns.

I keep forgetting he's new. "It's a system Tamia and I set up in case we lose power for some reason or if the computers go down. It's basically a screenshot of what's on our tablets. We can fill it out manually until the computers are back online."

He nods slowly, staring at me with those green eyes of his. "That's pretty good thinking, Mac."

Mac. I like the way he says my name.

As soon as I have the thought, I want to slap myself. *Donovan. Remember, you have Donovan.* There's no reason to jump on the lusting after Shaw train like all the other females that are in his path. I do steal a look at his torso. There has to be a set of stellar abs underneath his scrub shirt. Has to. I bite my lip. I'd like to find out what is under there, but —

"Incoming," Tamia calls.

From the ambulance entrance, I see a gurney hurrying towards us, the wheels clattering on the tile floor. They are moving fast enough that I know this is bad. Really bad. The patient isn't the only one on the bed. There's a paramedic straddling the man, leaning over his chest, giving him chest compressions.

I'm just about to yell bay three when Shaw beats me to it. His voice sounds like a drill sergeant. "Straight to bay three." He looks over his shoulder at me, his green eyes icy. Shaw is all business. "Let's go."

I stride behind him, trying to keep up following the paramedics. As I pass into the trauma bay, I grab a set of gloves, pulling my stethoscope down from behind my neck. Shaw goes to the far side of the bed. I stay on the near side. He calls, "One, two, three," and we slide the patient off onto the hospital bed, the paramedics stepping back as we start our assessment, one of the nurses takes over the compressions.

"What do we have?" Shaw barks.

The female paramedic who has been doing the chest compressions gives the report. "Fifty-two-year-old male was found at home on the floor after complaining of chest pains this morning. When we got there, he was unconscious. We started chest compressions. Tried shocking him in the field but he only held a rhythm for a little bit, lost it as soon as we pulled in here. Started compressions again."

The whole time the woman is speaking, I'm already starting my assessment. Tamia and Jasmine have taken over monitoring the IV and have added an EKG and a blood pressure cuff. I watch as the rhythm shows up on the monitor. Hudson takes a turn with the compressions. Doing them is exhausting. With calls like these, we do a three-minute rotation. I'm checking the monitor, looking at the lurching waves on the EKG. Does he have ST-segment elevation, T-wave inversion or Q-waves. Before I can say anything, I see a change in the monitor. A rapid QRS complex. That's not good. The bottom of his heart — the ventricles — are beating way too fast. Ventricular Tachycardia. "He's in V-tach!"

"Get me a push of Epi." Shaw steps closer to the side of the bed. Tamia pulls a stool from the side of the bay and pushes Hudson out of the way, giving him a break. While they switch out, I pull the crash cart over to the side of his bed while Jasmine puts the manual ventilator over his face and starts squeezing the bag rhythmically. To someone watching us, it might look like we're in complete chaos, but that's not the case.

I told you, that's what I like about medicine. There are rules.

And I'm good at following those rules, most of the time.

The man's shirt is already open, exposing a hairy chest, some of it black and some of it gray. Shaw fists the fabric and rips it apart with a sharp, violent motion, the sound of tearing cloth echoing against the walls. My breath catches hard in my throat — I nearly choke on it — as heat surges up my neck. I glance at Tamia, pulse hammering, praying she can't see the flush in my cheeks. God help me, but all I can think of is how much I want him to do that to me.

Donovan, Mac. Donovan. You already have a boyfriend.

What is wrong with me? I suck in a sharp breath. I'm in the

middle of a code and that's what I'm thinking about? I blink. *Get your head back in the game, Mac.* I press my lips together. There's just something about Shaw that's so raw. He looks up at me, the green of his eyes dark and intense. "Paddles!"

I hand them over, flipping the switch. "Charging to two hundred."

"Charging to two hundred," he repeats.

Tamia steps off the stool and squirts ultrasound gel on the man's chest. Shaw positions the paddles over the man's torso, then waits until I give him a nod. He places the paddles down on the man's skin. "Clear!"

Everyone stands back, their hands up in the air. As Shaw delivers the charge, the man's back arches and then flops back down on the bed like a death throe of a fish on the beach. I watch the monitor, hoping the new rhythm is better. I shake my head. "Still V-tach."

"I'm gonna shock him again," Shaw says.

"Charging," I reply, pressing the button on the machine. "Clear!"

A second later, the man's body convulses again. Shaw straightens, holding the paddles in his hands, watching the monitor. Somehow, I'm managing to watch the monitor and Shaw at the same time. A second later, the monitor gives a satisfied beep. Tamia puts her fingers on the man's neck. "I've got a pulse."

Shaw hands the paddles back to me over the bed. I stow them on the crash cart, then quickly check the man's wrists and ankles for a pulse. "Distal and radial pulses are good."

Without being asked, Tamia slips an oxygen mask over the man's face. Shaw gives a nod. It's like a play where everyone knows their parts. I can feel myself in the flow. My eyes catch his. "Let's call cardiology and interventional radiology. I'm betting this guy has a clogged artery somewhere." He glances at Tamia. "Is his family here?"

Tamia pokes her head out into the waiting room. "Give me a sec. I don't know. I can go check." A minute later, she's back. "The family is here. We also have a big backup in the waiting room."

Shaw gives a sharp nod. "Mac, why don't you stay with this guy for the next few minutes. Keep an eye on his vitals and let me know if anything changes. Hudson, get out on the floor and start clearing cases. I'll go talk to his family and see if we can get cardiology moving."

I suck in a breath to object. Why are I not making this call? I'm the Chief Resident.

Be smart, Mac.

I don't say anything except, "Sure," though I feel a knot in my gut as hard as a rock. One of the nurses can stay with the man. I'm a doctor, after all, not a babysitter. I look away, suddenly feeling the sag of disappointment run through my body. I can't let my ego get in the way of being a team player. Medicine, unless you're Dr. Randy Riley, is a team sport.

I spend the next few minutes with the patient. Now that the crisis is over, I learn his name is Jeff. He's awake, but pretty out of it from the meds. I listen to his heart and lungs a few times, not sure what else to do. They both sound pretty good given what he's been through. I'm just adjusting the oxygen mask on his face when Jeff's wife and two daughters appear at the doorway of the trauma bay.

"Oh my God, Jeff!" the wife cries, running to her husband's side.

The two girls, both teenagers, are built completely differently. One is skinny and tall, and one is shorter and rounder. They stand like statues at the foot of their dad's bed, their arms around each other, tears streaking down their face. The wife, or who I've imagined to be his wife, looks up at me. "Dr. Shaw came and talked to us. He's so nice. Are you Jeff's nurse?"

I grit my teeth. Did you not see the word "physician" on my

ID badge? "No, actually, I'm Dr. Forbes. I'm one of your husband's doctors."

"Oh, I'm so sorry, I just thought —"

I blow it off, trying not to wince, reminding myself that medicine is a team sport. I've heard it before. I straighten. There's no room for ego when you're saving lives. "No problem. In our scrubs, we all look the same." That part is true, but the ego part is nothing but a pure lie we all tell ourselves. "His condition has stabilized. We're waiting on cardiology to come down and do their assessment before we move him upstairs. I'm guessing they are going to want to keep him for a few days and do more tests."

I try to remain as vague as possible. Heart attacks are funny things. Sometimes someone has one of them and they never have any problems again. For other people, it's like opening Pandora's box. Once they have one, then they come more frequently as if the heart muscle has learned a brand-new trick it likes to play on people. Which one this was, I have no idea. And moreover, given the thin ice I'm on with Shaw and Riley, it wasn't my place to talk before the attendings, and cardiology had a chance to make their full evaluation.

"He's going to be okay, isn't he?" The tall daughter asks.

"The good news is, he's stable." *Good job, Mac. That was plenty vague.* "Now if you'll excuse me."

By the time I walk out to the nurses' station, I can see a guy that looks like he's about twelve years old wearing a dark shirt, a matching dark tie, and dark blue pants. In fact, everything about him is dark. His hair, his clothes, even the expression on his face. He's sitting at the computer terminal where I was working when the system went down.

I was so busy with the code that I totally forgot the computers crashed.

I walk over to him, hoping he has good news. The last thing I want to do is document Jeff's care manually. Having the tablet would make it so much easier. I look at Tamia. She points at the guy and then points at me. More hand signals. I guess I'm supposed to go and talk to him? I plop down next to the guy, suddenly tired. "Did you fix it?"

He looks at me, a bored expression on his face. "No, not yet." I frown. Seriously, the guy working on the computer doesn't look any older than the middle schoolers I pass playing baseball on my way home.

Shouldn't you be in pediatric care?

He doesn't say any more, so I try again to strike up a conversation. "I'm Dr. Forbes. I was working on this computer when the system went down."

He barely looks up. "I'm Rudra Bedi from tech services."

I watch as his hands move across the keyboard so fast it's hard to see what he's doing. Somehow, he's managed to get the computer to work again, but it doesn't look like it usually does. The screen is all black with white, blue, and red type plus a lot of funny code on the screen. Rudra, or whatever his name is — I think I call him Rudy because I'm never gonna remember his real name — looks up at me a second later. "We tracked the problem to this terminal. You said you were working on it when the system went down?"

I nod. "Yeah, it was the strangest thing." I scratch the back of my head. As I do, my armpit is exposed. The code has upped the ante on the stink meter to at least a three. I flop my arm back into place, not wanting to offend Rudy. "I was just doing some charting. I went to copy a prescription from one chart to the next and the whole thing went down."

It sounds innocent enough as it comes out of my mouth.

"Yeah, well —"

I furrow my eyebrows. There's something about his tone I don't like. "What does that mean?"

Rudy looks at me, his expression a mix of disappointment and irritation. "I think it's fair to say that *you* did this."

Fair? Me? "What are you talking about? I did what?"

"Crashed the system."

Heat runs to my face. "What?"

My protestations were enough to draw Tamia over. She puts a hand on my shoulder and looks at Rudy. "What did you just say to her?"

That's it, Tamia. Come to my rescue.

Rudy all of a sudden looks bored. "I said that I think Dr. Forbes is the one that crashed the system."

"Come again?" Tamia says, folding her arms in front of her chest.

"You said you were trying to copy a prescription over?"

I nod, sitting up straight. What's the problem with that? I do it all the time. "Yeah, I hit control-Y. I've done it a million times. I think there's something else wrong with the system."

Rudy looks up at me. "Are you sure you didn't hit control-YU?"

I shake my head. "Why would I do that?"

"I don't know. I'm just saying." Rudy goes back to working on the code that's scrolling on the screen.

I can tell by the expression on Rudy's face that he's not actually asking me. He's *accusing* me. Sweat gathers on my forehead. I glance down at the keyboard. The Y and the U *are* right next to each other. I have no idea what that means though. "Wait, I know I didn't do that," I protest, "but if I had, what would happen?"

Part of me wants to glance over at Tamia, but I know what her expression is gonna be like, stern. I keep my eyes glued to Rudy, waiting for him to say something, anything that will make me feel better about the situation.

"Control-YU is what we use to do a factory reset of the entire system."

"A factory reset? What does that mean?"

He shrugs. "It means that by hitting three buttons, you managed to strip the entire system."

My head begins to spin. I suddenly feel dizzy. I feel the breath catch in the back of my throat. "Shouldn't there be a screen that asks if you want to do that? Like one of those permission screens?"

Rudy nods slowly. "Yes, there is."

"Well, I didn't see that."

"I think you blew through the warning."

Are you kidding me right now? I glance at Tamia, feeling the blood drain from my face. I'm not sure what to say. My mouth is dry. I start thinking about all of the thousands of patient records. I mean, where did they go? And who would be so stupid as to make that the command for a complete factory reset?

I whisper, "Can it be fixed?"

Rudy still looks bored. "Yeah, we're working on it. It's gonna take time though. We've got to reload the software and then pull down all of the patient records from the cloud. We'll get you back up and running, but I can't promise it's gonna be today. Could take a while."

Without saying anything more, Rudy gets up and walks calmly away. I look at Tamia, my mouth hanging open. "I didn't do that! There has to be something else that's wrong with the computer."

Tamia looks down at the keyboard. "I don't know what to say, Mac, but the Y and the U are next to each other. Maybe you just slipped up?"

Slipped up? That's a nice way of saying I've now paralyzed the Liberty Hill Emergency Department, one of the busiest in Philadelphia.

I can't take it anymore. I feel tears rising to my eyes, threatening to spill over onto my cheeks, the blood rushing to my face. I can barely breathe. I feel like I've been kicked in the chest by a donkey, not that I would know what that feels like. The only animal I've ever gotten close to is Snort and he was almost lost to the city. I look over to Tamia, unable to talk. I don't know what else to do. I run out of the Emergency Department and bolt for the on-call room. Once inside, I slam the door closed and throw myself down on the bed. My chest is tight, my breath ragged, and I can't stop shaking.

Could this day get any worse?

No sooner do I think it than a cold weight settles in my chest.

What if it does?

20

I 'm by myself in the on-call room curled up on the same rumpled bed I took a nap on yesterday, although it feels like just a few hours ago, the same bed that's right by the spot where Tamia caught me and Jamir doing absolutely nothing while we were half-naked. The sobs come out of my body from a deep place. I feel like my body is going through its own set of earthquakes, every inch of me shaking.

All I keep thinking is, how can I be the one who crashed the entire Emergency Department computer system? I'm not that smart!

Even worse is the guilt I feel. Here I am, collapsed on the bed, crying my eyes out while everyone else is out in the Emergency Department trying to cover for my mistake.

As I think them, the words echo in my head.

My mistake.

How was I supposed to know that if I hit the control the Y and U all at the same time it would factory restart the entire system? I stop crying for a second, wiping my nose on the pillowcase. Actually, I don't even know that *I* did it. Maybe it was something else and Rudy is just trying to come up with an explanation. I don't know the guy, but it seems a very Rudy thing to do. It could have been anyone. Hudson was on a computer at the same time, and I saw Shaw before I went to go do my charting. He was in the break room all by himself working on his tablet. He gave me a funny look as I walked by.

It's a look I can't quite explain.

But no, I guess they just want to take the low-hanging fruit. Once again, I get the blame.

Another round of tears starts. I've now soaked my pillow and part of my scrub shirt, my sinuses completely clogged. As best I can tell, it's about another twenty minutes before anyone else dares to come into the on-call room. My guess is they're playing rock-paper-scissors to see who's going to come in and rescue me. Now, I *could* be an adult and get up, go to the locker room, wash my face put on a new pair of scrubs that might hopefully fit me, and go back to work, but just as I am considering the time it will take to get the swelling to go down in my eyes so I don't completely embarrass myself in front of my colleagues and my patients, the door cracks open. I can tell it's Tamia by the silhouette lighting her up from behind in the hallway. She doesn't say anything, just closes the door and comes and sits on the edge of the bed, but doesn't say anything.

A minute later, she puts her hand on my shoulder and starts rubbing my back. That makes me cry even more. I can feel the salty sting of tears as they run down my face and then taste them in my mouth.

She's a good nurse and even a better friend, even if she is mad at me.

"Are you okay?"

"No," I blubber.

She cocks her head to the side in the darkness. "At least you're being honest."

"I know better than to lie to you," I whimper. At the moment, I sound like a two-year-old. "It makes you mad."

"Correct."

I look at her. All the crying has made my eyes sting. Even in the darkness, I'm sure with her Spidey sense she can tell that my eyes are swollen. "I don't know what they think I did, Tam? I didn't do it! Why would I wanna completely reset the system?"

Tamia stops rubbing my back and shakes her head from side to side. Even in the dim light of the on-call room, I know that look. It's the "It's time to stop the BS" expression. "You might not have meant to do it, Mac, but it happened."

"I know, but I didn't do it." I pause. "At least not on purpose." I wait another beat. "I didn't even know about that control-YU stuff."

"I believe that."

My heart clutches. "Wait. You believe what part?"

She looks away for a second. "Accidents happen, Mac."

At least she believes part of what I'm saying.

I push myself up to an elbow. "I'm guessing you want me to come out and get to work, don't you?"

Tamia doesn't say anything for a second. She folds her hands in her lap and stares down at them.

My mouth goes dry. There's something she hasn't told me yet. I can feel it. "What's happening?"

"I do want you to come back to work, Mac."

"But?"

"Riley wants you to go home."

Stunned, I sit up, throwing my hands in the air. "Why? This was an *accident*. I can wash my face. I'm fine. I can finish my shift." I knew what getting sent home from a shift meant. I was persona non grata — low man on the totem pole.

In other words, in big trouble.

The only other time I'd seen somebody get sent home from

their shift was a gal named Marissa when Jamir and I were first-years. She got the identities of two people mixed up. Nothing bad happened, but Riley sent her home.

We never saw her again.

And I wasn't just getting sent home because I was sick. No one wants a doctor that's sick themselves. No, this is bad. I'm getting sent home because I crashed the entire Emergency Department computer system.

I'm in trouble. Deep.

"He's that mad?"

Tamia nods. "He is. It's going to cost the hospital a lot of money to get everything put back the way that it was."

"I thought that's why we had our own tech services people?"

"Yeah, well apparently, we contract with someone that handles the cloud storage. They're having to rush their team in to get us back up and running."

"I'm screwed, aren't I?"

The realization causes me to flop back down on the bed. Tears start to gather in my eyes again.

Tamia stares at the ceiling. "Yes," she says, using a finger to tuck a strand of my hair behind my ear. It's a gentle move, something like my mom or my sister would do, except my mom and Julia would never do anything like that. My mom would be busy lecturing me or making me feel guilty.

"You're a good doctor, Mac. Riley knows that. But you know how he is. He just has to prove his point."

"Doesn't make me feel any better that he wants to make an example out of me."

Tamia shrugs. "Well, you did crash the computer system."

I open my mouth to object, remembering how many other people were on the hospital's computers and tablets at the same time, but then I close my mouth. The fastest way to get through this is to just take my lumps and be done with it.

I stand up, brushing my enormous scrub pants down my

thighs. I feel like my whole body has gone through a washer and dryer and I've come out a little wrinkled. "All right. You'll call me?"

Tamiastands up next to me, gives me a hug and then walks to the door. "Yeah. I'll call you."

21

I stay in the on-call room for a few more minutes, pacing in front of the bed. I'm trying to figure out how I'm going to make my escape without everyone seeing me and my swollen face. It's embarrassing. I can't even leave the hospital without making a fool of myself.

I take a deep breath in, try to relax my shoulders and strategize.

In order to get out of the hospital I need to go to the locker room first, which is down the hallway and on the left-hand side. It's a one minute walk at best, but right now, it might as well be a ten-mile hike uphill. Once I get changed into my street clothes and grab my bag, I can slip out the side hallway and hit an exit from there and avoid walking right back through the Emergency Department, which is my usual means of entrance and departure. When I'm on good terms with everyone, I like to at least say goodbye.

That's not the case today. I'd rather slip away like something slithering down the drain. I sit back down on the edge of the bed and think some more, trying desperately to remember the moment before the system crashed. If only I could replay what happened.

I stand up, try to get the oversized scrubs to look presentable and smooth my unkempt hair with my fingers. I'm sure at this point I look like I've thrown my entire body into a laundry hamper and lain there for a week. As I touch my hair, I realize it's greasy. Really, really greasy. After my emotional upheaval, I'm definitely at least a five on the stink scale. I feel sticky, as if my entire body has been sweating.

It probably has.

Ignoring my personal hygiene, I tug the drawstring to my scrub pants tighter, grab my stethoscope and slowly open the door to the hallway, trying to get a look without being spotted. I've been in the room long enough that my eyes ache for a second as I adjust to the bright lights. Luckily, I don't see anyone from the Emergency Department, just a bunch of random other hospital employees walking by. I put my head down, pulling my phone out of my pocket and pretend to be looking at it, though the screen is locked. Taking long strides, I make it down to the locker room in record time, pushing the door open. Given that it's the middle of a shift, it's abandoned. At least one thing is going my way. I jog to my locker, open it up and quickly change into my street clothes and grab my backpack. As I pass the mirror, I can see the telltale signs that I've been crying. Not that I have the best complexion anyway, but now it's blotchy, like I'm having an allergic reaction. My brown eyes are rimmed with red. Even my lips are puffy. I sigh. When I get home, Snort and I can commiserate together while I put ice packs on my face. Maybe I'll even get lucky and will be able to find Donovan. I could use him right now.

But in the meantime, I have questions.

As soon as I make it out of the hospital, I feel like I can breathe again. Liberty Hill is beginning to feel like a war zone. Everywhere I turn, there's something going wrong.

I just don't understand it.

Everything was fine, and then...

I push the thought to the back of my mind, not wanting to have another meltdown while I'm trying to get to my car. Outside in the fresh air, my body starts to relax. I feel the sunshine on my chest and shoulders as I walk toward the employee parking lot. I move quickly, keeping my head down. The last thing I want to do is stop and have a conversation with anyone. But like the locker room, the parking lot is pretty desolate given that we're in the middle of a shift and everyone is working.

Except me.

I get in my car, starting it up, blasting the air conditioning, pointing it right at my face, hoping that the cool air will start to depuff my eyes. There has to be someone who can help me, someone who might actually know what happened.

Then I remember.

What about Marshall?

Marshall is a friend of mine. Well, not really a friend, given the fact I can't ever spend any time with him, but he's a guy I met at the hospital. He and I started at the same time. We were in the same orientation group, except we don't work in the same department. Obviously, I'm in the Emergency Department. Marshall, on the other hand, is in security. He's super nice, has basically the same personality as Hudson, very easygoing.

The thing is, he controls all the surveillance cameras in the hospital.

An idea starts to grow in my head. What if I can *see* what happened? What if I'm right and I wasn't the one who crashed the system? Maybe I can prove it and get back on Riley's good side.

Okay, yeah, I need to be reasonable. How about just a better side than where I am now?

All of a sudden, my paranoia reaches a new high. First, data on my patients seems to be different than it should be, the window to my apartment is unexpectedly open, and now someone's accusing me of crashing the entire Emergency Department computer system?

Something's wrong. Really wrong.

I can't wait any longer. At the next stoplight, I send Marshall a quick text. "You around?"

Very Marshall-like, he responds immediately. I imagine it's probably because he spends his day sitting in a dark room watching the security monitors for hours on end. For some reason he thinks it's interesting. I think it's boring.

And maybe a little weird too.

I mean, Marshall sees *everything* that goes on at Liberty Hill. Well, not exactly everything given the fact that there are no cameras in the bathrooms or the locker rooms. Thank God for that. People need to have their privacy to do their business. But everything else, he sees. From the bays in the Emergency Department to the operating rooms to the labor and delivery rooms, Liberty Hill's administration has become so paranoid about lawsuits that they've put cameras nearly everywhere. If you're on the hospital's property, someone's watching.

And that someone is usually Marshall.

"Can you talk?"

I wait for a second for the phone to buzz back but it doesn't. My heart starts to thud in my chest. Did he leave? Go on a break? I grip the wheel harder. I really, really need to talk to him. A second later, my phone starts to ring. I sigh in relief as I look at the screen, then answer as I drive. "Hey, Marshall," I say, trying to sound as casual as humanly possible given the disaster my life is rapidly becoming.

"You okay, Mac?"

His question startles me. I glance at my phone. "Yeah, why?" I try to play the question off. I continue my casual tone.

"You never call me in the middle of the day, and I saw there was some stuff going on in the Emergency Department earlier. I saw you run down the hall to the on-call room."

Oh God, did he see my infantile meltdown?

He continues, "I thought I'd wait and reach out to you after your shift was over."

I squeeze the steering wheel tighter. Geez, he really does see everything.

My chest tightens as I realize Jamir and I were changing our shirts in the on-call room and not in the locker room. A tingle runs down my spine. Marshall, or whoever was manning the cameras that day, has now seen me with my shirt off.

Great.

I'm sure Donovan will love that.

I make a mental note to never, never, never change in the on-call room again and to skip that part of the story when Donovan comes home.

I sniff. I really do miss Donovan.

I wince as I think about my shirtless performance in front of the security cameras, but then realize that maybe it'll work in my favor. Not that I'm exactly well-endowed. Flattish chests run in our family. And really, all he got a look at was my sports bra, but whatever turns you on, right?

"I have a favor to ask?"

"Shoot."

I can tell from the tone of Marshall's voice that he's trying to sound casual but he's actually excited.

"What do you have in mind?"

"There was a little issue in the Emergency Department earlier today. I was wondering if you could help me look into it."

His voice gets serious. "That's kind of my job, given the fact that I'm in security."

Let's be real. Marshall isn't a Navy SEAL, but he's a good

guy. "Those surveillance cameras you have, do you guys keep that video for a while?" I practically hold my breath while I'm waiting for him to answer the question. I can't imagine this is a situation where it's like at a gas station, where they have a bunch of cameras up, but they don't record anything. The hospital wouldn't do that, would they?

"Yeah, we see a lot of what goes on in the hospital, and yes, we keep the images for a year."

A year? That's more than enough time! I just need to see what happened today.

"Do you think you could pull up the video of me working on the charting this morning?" I describe to him what happened. Marshall harumphs when he hears about the accusation. "Dr. Randy Riley. I can't believe he sent you home. Who does he think he is?" He continues conspiratorially, "Man, I have some stories about him. I think he's forgotten we're watching."

It's Marshall's version of a rant.

"I know, I know. The worst, right?" I'm trying really hard not to think about the fact that Randy sent me home and what it could mean for my career. I tell him what Rudy from tech said to me. "I was just wondering if you could take a look and see if you can watch my fingers and see if I actually did hit both keys?" I try to be humble. "You know, because if I actually did, then I want to make sure I apologize to Dr. Riley. I know it's causing the hospital a lot of problems."

I can hear fingers typing in the background. "I can't imagine that you did, Mac. You're too good at what you do. I mean, if I got hurt, I'd want you to be my doctor."

Crush verified. Marshall knows that I have a boyfriend, but it sounds like he's making a play for the replacement team if I ever get rid of Donovan.

"That's so sweet, Marshall," I respond. "No hurry, but could you look into that for me?"

"Yeah, let me see what I can do."

As I hang up the phone, I feel marginally better. At least I'm doing something about my problem. It's far better than just moping around.

Then again, I'm sure I haven't escaped the moping phase.

By the time I get back to my apartment, I'm not so sure that looping Marshall in was the smartest idea. I would love to talk to Donovan about it, but I'm still not sure where he is. And as much as I'd like to call my mom and talk to her, I know that she'll quickly deflect and change the topic to Queen Julia and the upcoming wedding, probably chastising me for not being a better maid of honor. I'm busy running through the options in my head as I climb the stairs to my apartment. As I get to the top of the steps the floor creaks. I shake my head. Could this day get any worse?

Before the thought fully forms in my head, Mrs. Dixon's door creaks open. She pops her head out, wearing a crown of curlers and a flowered housecoat, something I can imagine my great-grandmother wearing, though I never met her. "Mac, what are you doing home in the middle of the day?" She narrows her eyes at me through her thick glasses. "And why does it look like you've been crying?"

There isn't a hint of compassion in her voice, only a tinge of sarcasm, like she's the playground bully and I just got caught in the corner sobbing.

"Allergies," I mumble as I open my door.

I slam the apartment door shut and twist the lock, double-checking the frame to make sure Snort hasn't staged another jailbreak now that he's had a taste of the outside world. My pulse won't settle. Feeling twitchy, I drift from room to room, pausing at every corner, tugging open closet doors as if I actually expect someone to be waiting inside. Maybe I'm losing it. Or maybe, with the way things have been going, it would be crazier not to check.

Satisfied nothing seems to be missing or disturbed, I check my phone for a message from Marshall. It's only been a few minutes. Nothing. How long can it take to look up the footage from this morning?

I toss my phone down and call for Snort. He emerges a second later, his tail curled and the tip of his broad nose in the air, his thick gray coat gleaming as if he's spent the day grooming himself. Jumping up on the couch, he circles once and then finds a spot to lie down, completely ignoring me. After sniffing the air, he gives a little Snort and then begins to groom himself again.

I'd hoped for a little more compassion. Maybe I should have gotten a dog.

As much as I wanna go take a shower, I feel like all the energy has been drained out of my body. Whether it was the cases we had this morning or the fact that I made it into work late, I have no idea. I walk over to the refrigerator, realizing I really haven't had anything to eat yet today. After looking inside, my stomach sinks. I realize that there isn't anything to eat or at least anything that doesn't have green fuzzy mold on it.

I forgot to go shopping again.

I pull out a water bottle and slam the refrigerator door as if blaming it for being empty, then look in the freezer. Still not much, but at least what's in there is edible. I grab a slice of frozen bread and toss it in the toaster. While it's heating up, I walk over to the television and flip it on. Afternoon programming is on the main channels — a smattering of cooking shows, soap operas, and television judges in black robes deciding who is the baby daddy and who isn't.

Wonderful.

A second later I hear the toast pop out of the toaster and smell the warm bread. I dig around in the refrigerator and find a stick of butter and some strawberry jam that doesn't seem to have too much mold growing on it. I smear jam and butter on the bread, enough that I have second thoughts about my cholesterol level and whether I'm going to give myself diabetes, then put the toast on a paper towel. I walk over and sit by Snort. He lifts his nose in the air and gives a little grunt. It's his signal to share what I'm eating.

Yes, I know I'm not supposed to feed my cat people food, but this is a special occasion. My entire life has been shattered. I don't know where my boyfriend is, I've been sent home from work for destroying the computer system, somehow my cat got loose and I've had several missteps at work that are concerning enough that I can only hope that Dr. Randy Riley ties his tie of the day too tight and the restricted blood flow to his brain prevents him from remembering the fact that I've had a really rocky week.

The next thing I know, I find a Hallmark movie about a woman who's been scorned at home — a teacher — who relocates to a small town, the same town where her grandparents grew up. As the story progresses, she falls in love with the man who owns the local hardware store, after she goes in to buy a pair of hinges to replace the ones on her grandfather's front door. Of course, the hinges don't work, so the hardware store owner offers to come out to the house. She's enamored by how kind he is. He of course can't believe how beautiful she is, and they fall in love in a very sweet, gentle way that involves snowflakes, Christmas carols, and lots of neighborhood children who now love her because she is the teacher they always wanted.

Why they are showing a Christmas movie this time of year, I have no idea, but I'm into it.

You know, I've always made fun of people who watch these movies and yet I spend the entire afternoon doing just that. Three movies later with a healthy nap in the middle, I sit up. I rub my face and look at my cell phone. Still nothing from Marshall. As I stretch my arms over my head, I can smell myself. It's not pleasant. I'm pushing the upper limits on the stink scale. It's time for me to go get cleaned up.

I take my time in the shower. After all, where else do I need to go? I use my favorite shampoo and conditioner, shave my legs not once but twice, making sure to do the same for my armpits. It takes the razor blade several passes to get through the caked-on deodorant that I have spackled to my underarms, but a few scrubs, rinses, and shaves later, my armpits are as squeaky clean as the rest of my body. As I step out of the shower, I wrap my hair in a towel and wrap myself in a robe. The nap and the shower have relaxed me. I suddenly have the desire to have a glass of wine. As I open the bathroom door, I see my clothes strewn on the floor, a shirt by the doorway, leggings after that, my bra and underwear near the edge of the bed. Why I didn't take them into the bathroom and toss them into the hamper, I don't know. I guess I'm just disoriented today. I look at them for a second, feeling guilty that I've left them there, but I wave them off. I'll pick them up after I get the wine.

And maybe watch a little more Hallmark.

22

I don't drink wine. Not normally at least. I work so much that drinking is generally not a great idea. Remember the beers and the shots? I still can't figure out how the window to my apartment was open.

But today is a special occasion. After the day I've had, I need something to calm my nerves.

I wander into the small kitchen in my apartment, opening up the refrigerator. Donovan had opened a bottle of wine before he left on his last trip, whenever that was. He is gone so much it is hard to remember. I pull the wine out of the refrigerator, feeling the cool glass under my fingers. I pry the cork off the top of it and take a sniff. It smelled fine, not vinegary at all, but then again, my sinuses are still jacked up from all the crying.

I check the label. A chardonnay. Perfect. I open the cabinet. For some reason, Donovan has put the wine glasses on the top shelf, ones I can barely reach. I stretch on my tiptoes and manage to grab a glass. On the few days Donovan has been in the apartment, he's the one who gets the wine glasses out. With how tall he is and his long arms and legs, reaching things from the top shelf is no big deal. For me, it's a stretch. I set the glass gently on the counter and pour half a glass.

Okay, it's more like three-quarters.

I wander back in front of the television. A new Hallmark movie has started. The early evening offering. Right away, I can see that I'm going to like it. It's about a firefighter. I've all of a sudden become a Hallmark movie addict. Maybe if I get fired from the hospital, I'll become a Hallmark movie influencer or reviewer or something. I find myself wondering if there's a market for that. In my head, I do my own Rotten Tomatoes review. Do Hallmark movies even get Rotten Tomatoes? Could be a niche market. I could have my own YouTube channel. Geez, I might have found myself a brand-new career in the space of one afternoon.

As I stand next to the couch watching the beginning of the movie, I take another couple of sips of wine, the warmth feeling good in my belly. And then it occurs to me why I'm standing here, wearing a robe, drinking wine and watching Hallmark. Riley sent me home. My stomach lurches at the realization.

For how long?

I look at the wine. If I'm supposed to go back to work in the morning, I shouldn't drink more than one glass. But Tamia didn't say that. She just sent me home with no additional information. It was like sending a patient home without discharge orders. My head starts to spin. I grimace. Should I text Riley and ask him if I'm supposed to come in?

I press my lips together. Probably not. It's probably better to just show up. If he wants to send me home again, then he can.

Right?

As I'm getting caught up in the swirl of my thoughts and watching the beginning of the movie standing in my robe with the towel still wrapped around my head, my phone starts to ring. My heart skips a beat. Maybe it's Marshall? Maybe he found out something. Donovan? As I look down, I see the three letters I didn't want to have to deal with at that moment.

M.O.M.

My mother has impeccable timing as usual. I swear she has radar. She always knows when something's up.

For a second, I consider not answering the phone, then I realize if I don't, she will continue to call until she finally reaches me. Grudgingly, I pick up the phone and answer. "Hi, Mom," I say, trying to sound as normal as possible. As I'm waiting for her to respond, I take a big glug of wine. I'm gonna need it.

"Mac. Are you busy?"

Sometimes I wonder if my mom placed surveillance cameras in my apartment when I wasn't looking. "Yeah, I'm busy. You know. Like always."

"Uh-huh. So, I've heard."

Oh.

I wait. I know that tone of voice. Something has gone wrong and I'm about to get the blame.

I run my thumb across the microphone on my phone like I'm running around from place to place. "Mom, I'm super busy right now. Is this something we can talk about later?"

Like later after I have a chance to drink my glass of wine, watch at least one or two more movies and figure out if I'm going to work tomorrow or not?

"I'm sorry, honey, this is something that just can't wait."

My stomach drops. Did something happen to her or my dad? "Okay. This sounds serious. What's going on?" It's very close to my catch phrase I use at work — "What brings you in today?" Non-judgmental, open to conversation, peace-loving — all things I hope that the rest of this conversation reflects.

"I had a conversation with your sister."

You mean Queen Julia? "How is the bride-to-be?"

I'm trying hard to play this off, but the knot in my gut tells me that the proverbial other shoe is about to drop. These are the moments I wish my mom would just get to the point. I can't ever tell if she's trying to prolong the agony or couch the blow. It's like when a patient comes into the Emergency Department. There are days I would much rather deal with an obvious injury or an obvious illness rather than having to dig around and figure out why someone's big toe hurts when they scratch the back of their neck.

Just get to the point, Mom.

"From what I understand, Julia reached out to you about the schedule for the week before the wedding."

"Yes," I say cautiously. You mean the entire week she wants me to take off? That schedule? The indentured servitude I have signed myself up for as her maid of honor? Is that what you mean?

"She's been distraught over the fact that you're not sure you can get home in time."

Distraught. That's pretty strong. Like she's thrown herself on her bed and is crying a river?

Oh no. That was me just a couple of hours ago.

I furrow my eyebrows. "In time? I told her I'm going to come in a day or two before the wedding. I'll be there in time for the wedding for sure."

There's a pause. "I think what I mean is in time to help her do all the things that the maid of honor should do."

The "shoulds" have arrived. "You're referring to the fact that she wants me to take an entire week off of work, which I cannot do because I'm in a residency program that requires me to be here. Is that what we're talking about?"

I regret the sharp tone of my voice the minute the words come out. I take another big sip of wine while I'm waiting for my mother to respond.

This is gonna be bad.

Another pause. "I think that we can have this conversation without sarcasm, don't you, Mac?"

"Sure."

My mother sighs. My stomach drops into my feet. It's the noise she always makes right before she levels the death blow. I don't move, still in my robe with my hair twisted up in a towel, Snort sitting behind me on the couch waiting for me to plop down to drink my wine and watch the next Hallmark movie. He seems very calm.

That makes one of us.

"She's been really thinking and praying about it and has decided that as much as she wants you to be a part of the wedding, she wasn't anticipating your work schedule would be as demanding as it is."

My mouth falls open. I'm in a medical residency program. What did she think I was doing, greeting at Walmart?

Not that there's anything wrong with that. I love the greeters at my Walmart. I'm just making the point that they can get time off.

I can't.

"And because of that, she is going to pass along the maid of honor role and responsibilities to her friend Heather."

I feel my face redden. Heather? Her? That red-haired, twittering pain in the butt friend my sister's had since she was a teenager?

"Are you kidding me? I've spent hours of my precious time off talking to Julia and helping her do whatever I can from Philadelphia. For God's sake, Mom, she asked me to fly in so I could hold her hand while she has a Brazilian wax."

"Mac, I don't think that you understand how important of a day this is to her."

I'm literally about to throw my glass of wine against the wall I'm so mad. "And I don't think you understand how important it is that I finish my residency. Do you know how hard I've worked for this?"

"I do," she pauses like she's chewing on the point, "but your sister just feels this is a once in a lifetime opportunity and that you need to be available." The words come out like she knows she's walking a tightrope.

I plop my glass down on the table so fast that the remaining wine sloshes over the side and dribbles onto my coffee table. "That's just fine, now isn't it? I'll tell you what, she can have Heather be the maid of honor. At this point, she'll be lucky if I even show up for the wedding."

I end the call.

A second later I look down at my phone, my mouth hanging open. I just hung up on my mother. That was probably not the smartest move. I sit down on the couch and use the corner of my robe to sop up the wine on the table then take a swig. I know what will happen next. It's completely predictable. My mom will freak out. My sister will freak out. My dad will end up calling me either tonight or tomorrow because he's a good dad and will give me time to calm down. He will, in a way only he can, smooth things over. He'll tell me my mom and my sister are under a lot of stress and so am I, but we are still a family. I will end up going to my sister's wedding, but I won't be in it.

And somehow, when he says it, it'll sound okay.

I still feel like throwing my wine glass against the wall, but that would waste perfectly good wine. I slug down the rest of it and stomp back into the kitchen, pouring myself another glass and returning to my movie. I'm not sure even Hallmark can fix the mood I'm in now.

I'm just about to sit down on the couch when I hear a knock on my door. If this is Mrs. Dixon, I'm not opening the door, even if her hair is on fire or her head is only hanging on by a string. I walk as quietly as I can, but then the floor squeaks. I grimace. Now Mrs. Dixon knows I'm near the door. I open the door ready to tell her that it's not a good time when I realize she's not the one that knocked.

It's Jonathan Shaw.

He takes one look at me then cocks his head to the side, his eyes glinting. "I guess you weren't expecting company?"

I am completely taken aback. I step back from the door, putting my hand up to my head realizing the towel is still wrapped around my hair. "Oh, no. I wasn't." I laugh nervously. "But come in, please, come in," I stammer.

By now, I'm sure Mrs. Dixon has heard a male voice that's not Donovan's down the hallway. She probably has some sort of camera in the hallway for clocking who's arriving and who's leaving. I close the door behind Jonathan, fighting the urge to check the hallway to see if she's looking. As I close the door and turn toward him, I'm not sure exactly what to do. I feel the blood rush to my face. After all, I'm standing in front of the most handsome man I've ever seen, who just happens to be my boss. And I'm doing it in a robe with nothing on underneath, my hair in a towel. I blink. "Can I get you a glass of wine?"

He smiles, his cute left dimple showing. "Sure."

As I walk to the kitchen, I feel my face redden even more. Was it the wine? Why hadn't I just gotten dressed when I got out of the shower? What is wrong with me?

I stretch up on my tiptoes again and get out another glass, making sure it's not covered in dust. Luckily it isn't. I fill up Jonathan's glass and walk it back over to him, hoping that the wine is actually okay. The two of us clink rims. He takes a sip and then sets his glass down on the table. When I look at him, I realize his normally perfect hair is a little disheveled. He must have seen me staring because he uses his fingers to kind of comb it back in place. "Sorry, my hair must have gotten messed up under my helmet."

"You drive a motorcycle?"

"Yeah. A Yamaha."

I envision Jonathan, I mean Dr. Shaw, on his motorcycle. I know Yamaha motorcycles are super-fast. Donovan always calls them "crotch rockets."

Thinking about it, I'd like to see Jonathan on his crotch rocket.

I feel little beads of sweat starting to gather on my forehead. It's gotta be the wine. "I don't need to remind you to wear a helmet, do I?"

He grins and takes another sip of wine. "No, Doc. I'm good."

I smile back and motion to the chair. My thoughts swirl. I'm starting to feel dizzy. Why is he here? I realize it's not just my forehead sweating. It's my entire torso, down to my thighs. I'm hoping my robe absorbs it and Shaw doesn't see weird droplets of sweat running down my legs. "Do you want to sit down?"

He nods. I sit across from him on the couch next to Snort as if my little gray cat with the smooshed face can keep me from throwing myself at Shaw. In a moment of modesty, I tuck my robe in between my legs so I'm not showing off everything I have. He points to Snort. "Is that your cat?"

Could this be any more awkward? As if I just let a random cat into my apartment for this moment.

I nod. "Yeah. This is Snort."

Jonathan raises an eyebrow. "I'm guessing it's because he has some sort of respiratory issue?"

"Chronic rhinitis." I chuckle.

As Jonathan leans back in the chair, I notice the button-down shirt he has on is open at the collar, three buttons worth. Inside I can see tan skin, the muscles taught and firm underneath it. He looks like he just did four sets of bench press before he came up to my apartment. Maybe he bench pressed his motorcycle.

"I just wanted to come and check on you. It seems like you've had a rough few days."

You think so? "Thanks. I'm okay." I look down at my lap. "I'm sorry. I don't know what's going on with me." I look away thinking about Julia but decide not to tell him.

"We all go through tough times in our residency, Mac. The key thing is that you don't give up."

"Does that mean I should come back to work in the morning?"

Jonathan takes a sip of his wine, then sets it back down on the table. "That part isn't up to me. You need to talk to Dr. Riley about that." He blinks, then stares at me with his green eyes. "You're a good doctor, Mac. Yeah, you need a little more training, but I'm guessing that's because Riley hasn't spent as much time with you as he should have. I'd like to have you back if that means anything."

He wants me back.

I feel a new set of tears rise to my eyes. I quickly count to ten in my head. It's physiologically impossible to cry and count at the same time. Uses different sides of the brain. That's why we always ask people for numbers when they are in the ED. Keeps them calm. I swallow the lump in my throat, attempting to send it back where it came from and look at my lap again. Somehow, I don't think that Riley is going to be as nice about what's been going on as Shaw has been.

Jonathan takes another sip of his wine and then stands up. "Listen, I just wanted to check on you." He scans my robe. I feel heat run to my face. "Sorry if I caught you at a bad time. I really need to be getting home."

I'm half sad that he's leaving already. It was nice to have a regular conversation with a regular person outside of work. It even made me feel kind of bad about asking Marshall to double-check that I hadn't been the one to crash the system. Given the tingling feeling that was running all over my body, I felt even worse for making fun of the other girls who had ooohhed and ahhhhed over Jonathan.

Now I was part of the pack fighting for him.

Donovan, Mac. You have Donovan.

As I walk him to the door, he turns around and looks at me. His expression softened. "It's all going to be okay, Mac," he said, and then he does something I didn't expect.

He hugs me.

Just as he tightens his arms around me, I hear a rattle at the door and then see movement out of the corner of my eye. The door opens.

Donovan.

23

I can feel the color drain from my face. All of a sudden, I feel cool air on my skin. I look down. The belt on my robe has come loose. I grab for the fabric, quickly tying it, my mouth going dry. Did Shaw see my breasts while we were hugging?

Worse yet, does Donovan think Shaw saw my breasts?

Shaw gives Donovan a nod, a quick "Hey," and walks out, closing the door behind him.

Oh God.

"Welcome home!" I manage, holding my arms out, this time my robe tight around my waist. Donovan walks by, his lips set in a thin line. He doesn't even look at me.

Why I expected him to hug me after what he just saw, I have no idea.

Donovan normally takes his bags directly to the extra bedroom to drop them off. He doesn't. He drops them right by the door. Once again, I tug at the belt around my robe, tightening it until it feels like a corset. Donovan eyes up the wine glasses. "I guess you had some company while I was gone."

I try to make words come out of my mouth, but they aren't coming.

Donovan strides through the apartment going to our bedroom. His eyes are nothing more than narrow slits in his head. As he goes through the doorway, I see him stop. My clothes are still on the floor, the bed rumpled and unmade from this morning when I couldn't find Snort. As if the fact that he found Shaw and I together with me half undressed isn't bad enough, now it looks like we just took a romp in the sheets right before he got home. I see the set of his jaw as he strides out of the bedroom. He glares at me. "What's going on here, Mac?"

I reach out for him, but he brushes me away. "Nothing. I had a bad day at work. Shaw came over to see if I'm okay."

"And how much of you did he see?" His tone was sarcastic.

"Nothing!" I lean forward as I yell the word at him as if it will make it more true. And it is true, at least partly, except for when my robe came apart when we were hugging. I feel my skin prickle. What is going on? Why is it every time I turn around, I'm in a jam? I lift both my hands in the air. "I had a long shift. Things didn't go well. Somehow, I managed to mess up the computer system in the Emergency Department so badly that Riley sent me home. I've been trying to call you, but you don't ever answer. I just came in and took a shower like I normally do and —"

Donovan cocks his head to the side. "Let me guess... Shaw came over to treat your issues? How long has this been going on, Mac?"

He doesn't give me a chance to answer.

Donovan turns away for a moment and then back at me. I can see the strain on his face. "I mean, I know I travel a lot, but I've been faithful to you. I thought when I moved in that you understood that I wanted an exclusive relationship."

Even though you've only been home eight days since you moved in? "Yes," I stammer. "I know that. Nothing happened. I've been faithful too!"

Donovan shakes his head, the dark circles under his eyes almost black. "And to think the entire way home all I could think about was spending time with you. I guess you weren't having the same thought, were you?"

I rub at my temples the towel nearly falling off my head.. This is absurd. "Donovan! I'm telling you, nothing happened."

He shakes his head. I know that look. He's already made up his mind.

He glances towards the bedroom and then at the wine glasses. My face reddens again. I understand how it looks. Clothes on the floor, rumpled sheets, wine glasses, my robe hanging open. At this point, I'm so desperate that I'm about to suggest we go to the hospital and I have Hudson do a pelvic exam on me to prove the point. It's a horrifying prospect but I'm desperate. Donovan doesn't give me a chance to offer. "You know those true crime stories you like to watch, Mac?"

I nod, hoping the question leads to some sort of resolution that involves him staying.

"The evidence says that something happened. I gotta go."

I try to grab for Donovan as he passes, but he shrugs his arm away from my grip. He picks up his luggage, opens the door, and then slams it behind him. He disappears as fast as he showed up in the first place. I run to the door and put my hand on the doorknob about to open it and yell after him, but then I realize Mrs. Dixon has probably heard our entire argument through the thin walls. I risk it anyway. I open the door. As I poke my head out, Donovan is turning the corner toward the stairs. "Donovan! Don't leave! Nothing happened. I promise!" I'm half tempted to run after him, but I only have my robe on. It's not like I'm gonna run out in the middle of the street in Philadelphia flashing everyone. I wait for a second in the doorway, hoping he'll turn around and come back. I count to ten, my mouth hanging open, my heart pounding in my chest. Could this day get any worse?

Nothing.

As I turn to go back inside my apartment, feeling the sting of a new set of tears, I hear a little rustle off to my right. I glance that direction. Mrs. Dixon has her head poking out the door. A few whiskers have appeared on her upper lip. All she does is look at me and raise her eyebrows and then she disappears into her apartment, the door clicking closed behind her.

I spin around, groaning, and slam my own door behind me. My hands tremble as I reach for the counter. Wine. I need the wine.

24

I was hoping that given the fact I didn't have to go to work the next morning that perhaps I would be able to sleep in, but I wasn't that lucky.

Dreams of Shaw and Donovan peppered my dreams. After Donovan charged out of the apartment, I tried calling and texting. He wouldn't pick up. I even tried tracking his location, but it became apparent very quickly that he blocked me. I honestly have no idea where he went after we fought. My guess? A hotel. He has enough travel points that he can stay at the Four Seasons for weeks without paying a dime. He probably ordered himself surf and turf, kicked his feet up on the bed and fell asleep. He also has a couple buddies that live in the area, guys that he's spent time running with. They aren't guys we hang out with, which is obvious, I guess, given that he's only spent eight days in the apartment. Maybe he crashed on one of their couches for the night? I have no idea.

I wish I did.

I get up the next morning, wishing I hadn't had more wine. After the fight with Donovan, I managed to finish off the bottle by myself. Not that there was a lot left. It amounted to another two glasses. And I did chug the rest of what Shaw had started drinking too.

So maybe three glasses, plus what I'd had earlier.

I get up and my head is pounding. Whether it's from the extra wine or the nightmare my life had become, I have no idea. I drag myself off to the shower, letting the hot water run over my neck and back. If Donovan had stayed, we could have cuddled in bed, or even something more, which would have been nice given the cruddy day I had yesterday.

But no.

As I get out of the shower and wrap my robe around my body again, the memories of the day before start flooding back. My robe smells faintly like Shaw's cologne. I suck a deep breath in and then remember the horrors of the day before — Snort getting loose, the computer system in the Emergency Department going down, Riley sending me home, the terse conversation with my mom, Shaw showing up. I blink as I remember Donovan walking in on Shaw and I with our arms wrapped around each other, the sound of Donovan slamming the door as he storms out.

It couldn't get worse, could it?

Normally, on the days I don't have to work, I have a plan. I get so few days off — only one a week if I'm lucky — that it usually ends up being a mad dash to try to get my life in order. I try to cram in all the normal, adult things — paying bills, scrolling through social media, buying groceries, doing my laundry.

But this time feels different. I have no idea when or if Riley's going to bring me back. I get dressed, pulling out a pair of leggings and a T-shirt, then dragging a comb through my wet hair. I notice a few more strands than usual seem to be coming out.

Great, now the stress is causing me to lose my hair. Not that it was my greatest feature, but who wants to have a trauma doctor working on them who's so stressed that their hair is falling out?

I wouldn't.

I walk over to my phone, checking to see if any texts have come in. My mind wanders. Tamia? Riley? Donovan? Shaw? My mom? Queen Julia?

Nothing. Not even anything from Jamir or Hudson. I tap the locator app and quickly see my mom and sister pop up but the little wheel by Donovan's name keeps spinning. For all I know, his company called and he's back on a jet again, heading to some other far-off country, away from me. My heart sinks. I really wish that we could talk. I know if I just had a couple minutes with him to explain, that it would all start to make sense.

I glance toward the bedroom. If he'd actually looked, he would have noticed only one side of the bed was a mess. Just mine. The other side was perfectly made, waiting for him. I wish I'd taken a picture of it, proof that nothing happened.

There's no point now, he probably wouldn't believe me anyway.

I put my phone down and turn away, thinking I'll walk over and turn on the television to hear some other voices so the apartment doesn't sound so empty and cavernous. Then I stop. I look back at my phone. Liberty Hill keeps all of the work schedules online. Today would seem a lot better if I knew when I could go back to work. Wondering what Riley was gonna do to me was almost worse than what was going on with Donovan.

Just thinking about Riley in his tie-of-the-day, rubbing his hands together with glee as he determines my fate, makes my stomach start to sour. But being the trooper that I am, I walk back to my phone, open it up and log in to the employee portal for the hospital.

A second later I'm in.

My shoulders relax a little bit. I'm in. At least they haven't revoked my online access. That has to mean something, right? I click on a couple of tabs and then find the schedule for the Emergency Department. I click on my name, checking the list of shifts on the calendar. It usually appears just like the month that we're in with hours blocked out. I narrow my eyes and then cock my head to the side.

There's nothing.

Like literally nothing under my name. The calendar is empty.

I feel my heart clench in my chest. I scroll madly through my phone. I check past months. It shows all my shifts. Did my mess up with the software and the Emergency Department take out the rest of the hospital's scheduling system? If that's the case, then I'm done. Like really done. My hands shaking, I look at another department's schedule, checking on people I know to see when they are working. Furrowing my eyebrows so hard my head starts to hurt, I find Marcus's shifts on the medical surgical floor. His schedule is fine. Same with Marcy over in PT.

I even dig through the cafeteria schedules. They're all there.

Where's mine? It feels like a flock of birds are beating the inside of my chest. I check the ED schedule again. I try to reassure myself, wondering what my dad would say to me right now. I'm so freaked out I can't even think of anything. Maybe it's just the schedules for our department. That's a possibility, right? I pull up the nursing schedule. Uh, oh. Tamia has her shifts scheduled. So do Jamir and Hudson and Shaw. I feel my face pinch, as if all the muscles are tightening all at the same time. I click on my name again. Did I just have the dates set wrong? I reset them and reload the page.

Still nothing.

I've been erased.

I throw my phone down on the couch and pace back and forth, my arms crossed in front of my chest for a second then I start to massage my temple, staring at the floor. My head starts to ache, a dull throbbing behind my left eye. I run through the telltale signs of an aneurysm or a stroke — tingling, weakness on one side of the body, headache, nausea, confusion — as I walk. Yes, to the headache and the nausea. I walk in the bathroom and stare in the mirror. My face seems symmetrical, although I feel like I've lost the feeling on the left side of my face. My right hand is tingling, but then I realize it's been pinched underneath my armpit while I was walking. I take it out from under my armpit and start to shake it.

It would be so embarrassing to show up at work on a gurney. I can hear Riley now, "Forbes! What happened to you?" In my mind's eye, I can see him leaning over me, his buggy eyes calculating risk factors and medications while his tie-of-the-day swings back and forth.

That *cannot* happen.

Get yourself together, Mac.

Completely drained, I walk out of the bathroom and plop down on the couch just in time for Snort to jump on the back of the couch and parade across it like a gymnast on a balance beam, his tail high in the air. I have another moment of panic, glad he didn't slip out when Donovan left. He loves Donovan. He probably would have chased him down the road if he could have.

Then I feel guilty. Did I even check on Snort the night before? I was so busy dealing with my own grief and finishing the wine that I totally forgot about him. He meows loudly as if he can hear what I'm thinking. I sit, staring at him, my mouth hanging open. I blink a couple of times, but I feel like my brain isn't working.

Feed the cat, Mac.

Moving on autopilot, the shock of the fact that I have no shifts scheduled and two months left on my residency to finish, I stand up and go to the kitchen, refilling Snort's water and giving him a scoop of his kibble. He lifts his nose in the air.

Then I smell it. He's apparently left some presents for me in his litter box.

Now my apartment stinks. I've been so upset I hadn't even noticed.

And even better, it involves me walking past Mrs. Dixon's apartment door again.

My entire body feels numb as I find a plastic bag and retrieve the litter shovel, quickly cleaning out Snort's box.

Is this twice in one week with him? It's like everyone is punishing me.

Even Snort.

I stand at the door with the putrid bag of whatever Snort had eaten and digested in my hand. The smell emanating from the bag is horrendous. I look towards the window, desperately wanting to open it up to get fresh air in the apartment, but I don't want to risk Snort getting loose again. I glance down at the bag in my hand. I can't stand here all day. The best thing I can do is get this bag out of my apartment. But I'm frozen by my door. The disposal is going to involve the walk of shame in front of Mrs. Dixon's door after my interaction with Shaw and Donovan storming out the night before.

I grit my teeth. The last thing I wanna do is deal with Mrs. Dixon and her glare. But there's no choice.

I quickly slide my feet into a pair of Donovan's flip-flops. The carpet in the hallway is so nasty I don't want to walk on it barefoot. I open the door slowly, hoping that it doesn't creak. For a second, I'm impressed with my own stealthiness. I manage to get out of the door and close it behind me, checking the corner for Snort before I close it. A sweat breaks out on my forehead. I just didn't lock myself out again, did I? It would be just my luck. I turn the knob.

No. It's unlocked.

Just so I don't second-guess myself, I push the door open a hair, not enough that Snort can get out, but just enough that the lock couldn't prevent me from getting back in. I turn, lowering my chin. I spot the trash door at the other end of the hallway, my eyes laser-focused on it like I'm on some sporty game show where I need to get to the finish line. I start moving slowly, then realize putting on Donovan's flip-flops was probably not my smartest idea. I can't walk normally if I want to be quiet. I have to scoot my feet across the floor so that they're not slapping on my heels, especially given the fact that his shoes are a good three sizes bigger than mine. If I want to walk quickly, I'll sound like I'm shuffling across the floor like I'm wearing cardboard boxes for shoes.

I start skating along, sliding my feet forward on the carpet as quickly as I can, then realize I sound like I'm doing some sort of weird imitation of cross-country skiers in the Olympics, my arms helping me with my progress, the stinky bag swinging at my side.

But I'm being quiet. So, so quiet.

Hopefully Mrs. Dixon doesn't hear me. I make it to the trash receptacle with no issues, dropping the offensive-smelling remains of Snort's dinner down the chute for someone else to suffer with. I turn and start making my way back to my apartment, feeling victorious when I take a step. I knew it was a little too much as soon as I picked my foot up, but there was no saving it. There was a snap of the plastic from the flip-flop on the bottom of my heel. In the empty hallway it echoed like a whip crack. There was no holding back now. I started moving quickly, the shoes going slap, slap, slap on my heels. I make it just past Mrs. Dixon's door when I hear it open.

"Oh, it's you, McKenna."

"Good morning, Mrs. Dixon." I attempt to keep walking, angling for the door, but Mrs. Dixon sticks her head fully out into the hallway. She sniffs the air. "I don't know what's going on in your apartment, but whatever you just threw away stinks. If this keeps up, I might need to call the building superintendent."

"I'm sorry about that," I tried to sound apologetic. "It's just my cat. He ate something that didn't agree with his stomach. It's all cleaned up now."

Mrs. Dixon wrinkles her nose. "Honestly, I can't imagine how your apartment smells."

Would you like to come down for a cup of tea and experience it for yourself? "It'll be fine. I'll open the window and it'll be gone in no time at all." I grit my teeth and try to sound pleasant but I know my voice is strained.

I most certainly am not going to open the window, but Mrs. Dixon doesn't need to know that.

She presses her lips together, pursing them, as though someone suddenly shoved half a lemon in her mouth. "There does seem to be quite a bit of commotion coming from your apartment. Men coming and going all times of the day and night. I thought you worked."

I fight off a groan. This is not what I need right now. You know I work.

Or worked.

A shiver runs down my spine as I think about all the empty days on my residency calendar. "I do, work, that is."

Mrs. Dixon cocked her head to the side. "Strange, because you're home."

I wave her off and keep moving, scooting along in Donovan's shoes as quickly as I can get away. "Yes, right. Late shift. Going in later on."

I grab the doorknob for my apartment and turn it, pushing the door in violently, hoping that Snort isn't standing right behind the door. If he is, I just smashed his already flattened face in.

Luckily, he isn't.

I slam the door behind me and lock it, ignoring Mrs. Dixon and her sharp little eyebrows. Donovan is gone, my career is on the line, and the ache in my chest won't let me breathe. I collapse onto the couch, pressing my face to my knees, feeling smaller than I've ever felt. The apartment is silent, but the quiet presses down on me, heavy and accusing, and I can't shake the sense that something worse is still coming.

25

I flop over on the couch, my chest heaving. I so desperately want to talk to someone, anyone. Well, but not Mrs. Dixon. I can't call my mom. She's up to her eyeballs with bridezilla and it seems that she's taken Julia's side. Even if I could reach her, she's never been one to give me a lot of sympathy. That all seems to be reserved for Julia, even before she was getting married. I could try a couple of old friends from medical school, but we haven't talked in ages. It might seem a little weird to call them and be like, "Oh, hey, my life is falling apart." I could call Marshall. No. He'll get the wrong idea. Before, I'd call Tamia, but I have no idea if she's still mad at me or not.

I cover my face with a pillow. The smell from the litterbox is still lingering, but there's no way I'm opening a window. I glance toward the bedroom, changing my mind. If I have to sit in the stink for one more minute, I just might throw up. I get up, go over to the window and open it just a crack, sticking my nose down in it. I immediately draw a long fresh breath of air. I use my hands to wave it into the room, eyeing up the doorway to the bedroom just in case Snort decides he wants to get out.

But he can't. I've only opened it an inch and there's no way that his skull will fit through the hole. Or at least I think that's the case.

I need to stay nearby while I ventilate to keep an eye on him. I glance toward my closet. Maybe if I keep myself busy that'll help.

I straighten. Maybe there's a bright side to what is going on after all. I've been wanting to clean out and organize my closet. The week before, I'd spent one of my off shifts lying on my couch watching home improvement programs.

This is my opportunity.

If medicine doesn't work out, then maybe I can become one of those professional organizers or something. I throw open the closet doors and look inside. It's just my stuff in the closet, which is good. Although Donovan sleeps in the bed with me when he's home — which as I've established is generally never, he keeps his clothes in the closet in the other bedroom.

I frown, looking over my shoulder. If things are really over, at some point, he's going to have to come back and get those if he's not going to live here anymore.

The thought lands like a rock in my gut. I push the thought away. I can't think about breaking up with Donovan. I'm hoping after he gets some sleep he'll realize that nothing happened between me and Shaw.

I throw myself into my reorganization project, pulling everything out, darting down the hallway as fast as my feet will carry me to get the vacuum cleaner so I can keep an eye on the window. Before I turn the vacuum cleaner on, I stalk around the apartment, trying to figure out where Snort went. I find him curled up in the corner of the couch, sound asleep.

As I walk away, I decide it's kind of offensive. I mean, hear me out on this. Here I am, struggling, my boyfriend walking out on me, my boss sending me home, my family not talking to me, my neighbor keeping her laser focus on my every maneuver, and Snort does what, sleep?

It takes a lot of nerve. Where's his care? His compassion for the person who takes care of him?

Especially after what he did to his litter box.

After a few minutes of digging in, I'm thinking the bright spot in my life right now might be my closet reorganization project. With everything I'm going through, it's oddly satisfying. I vacuum the floor and the corners, even using that little wand thing they include with the vacuum to get every nook and cranny. It's pretty stuck on the machine, so I have to use some muscle to get it off. But it finally comes loose.

Having conquered the vacuum cleaner attachments and the nasty, dirty corners of my closet (Was it dirty like this when I moved in?) I start sorting through my clothes. It's not that I have anything that actually resembles a wardrobe. That would be my sister. Queen Julia is all about the outfits. I'm just lucky if I'm dressed.

And we all know how that went when Donovan showed up and I was in my robe.

I start sorting my clothes into three categories: never wear, sometimes wear, and wear all the time. Sadly, the wear all the time pile is tiny. Anything that is remotely interesting seems to have gone into the never wear and the stuff that doesn't fit me right seems to have gone into the sometimes wear category. I sit and think about what to do with my clothes. It reminds me of how Shaw had the supply room reorganized and I had no idea where anything was.

Yet another horror this week.

I go into the kitchen and grab a trash bag, starting to shove the never-wear clothes into the bag. It's a bunch of dress pants and skirts I wore as a medical student. If I never wear them, why would I even keep them? Then it occurs to me.

I might have to start wearing them if I lose my job.

Just the idea of never walking into the Emergency Department at Liberty Hills again sets my heart thumping. I'm so close to being able to finish my residency. Would Riley really take it away from me just because I hit two wrong keys on the keyboard? Then I think about Marshall. I'd asked him to look into the video footage for me, but I haven't heard back from him yet. Then I feel something that distinctly feels like fingers crawling its way up my spine.

Maybe Riley had gotten to him too.

My paranoia is on full alert, I suddenly blink and see the mess I've made with my closet. The piles of clothes that seemed so neat and organized now look like I'm living in a war zone. My ears start buzzing. I stand up and throw everything back into the closet, slamming the door then stride over to the bed, quickly making it and dragging the vacuum cleaner back out into the hallway. I stuff it in the closet next to a pair of Donovan's winter boots. I see them, thinking about how we used to go for walks in the snow to go get ice cream. I know, it sounds silly, but it was a thing for us, a way of fighting off the winter.

But that was all before he started traveling so much.

And now I'm alone.

I glance at the door out into the hallway. I feel like the walls of my apartment are closing in on me. Everywhere I turn, there's a reminder of either Donovan or work. I've got to get out of here or I'm going to lose my mind. I stride into the kitchen, snagging my cell phone and my keys, and head for the door when I remember that the window is still open. I go slam it shut, loud enough that it wakes up Snort, who lifts his head, then lets it flop back down on the couch as if he could care less that I am spiraling out of control.

I'm telling you, I should have gotten a dog.

I slip my feet into a pair of tennis shoes and head for the door, closing it behind me and locking it, sticking the keys and my cell phone in the side pockets of my leggings. I run down the hallway and head for the steps as I hear Mrs. Dixon's door creak open then close again. My head throbs as I charge down the steps. Why doesn't she mind her own business?

Frantic, I race outside.

As I pass outside, I realize that it's a beautiful morning in Philadelphia. I probably could have used a jacket, though. It's a little chilly, but I decide a brisk walk might be good for me. If I had planned better, I could have gone for a run, but that's Donovan's thing.

Who knows. If he leaves me, I might never run again.

That'll really show him.

I start walking nowhere in particular, my mind reeling. I'm just trying to digest everything that's been happening. I realize after a couple of minutes I'm walking in the direction of Liberty Hill, where everyone that I know in Philadelphia — Tamia, Jamir, Hudson, Shaw — are happily working.

And I'm not.

I turn down a side street and keep going, passing a few touristy shops with plastic Liberty Bells and sunglasses in the windows, a UPS drop off, and a café. I'm sure by now the news of my dismissal has traveled through the hallways. Heck, the women in the cafeteria probably already heard the news about how Riley sent me home.

The worst part? I haven't heard from him.

I shake my head as I walk, thinking. Everything was going fine until a few days ago, the same time when Shaw showed up. But all the stuff that happened wasn't his fault, right? After all, he'd been so nice to come over the night before to comfort me. It wasn't on him that Donovan had shown up and made things awkward.

As I turn another corner, I realize I just want one thing — for things to be the way they were before Shaw showed up. Sure, being in Julia's wedding is a pain, but it's better than not having my mom and Julia talk to me. I want Donovan to be part of my life, even if he's travelling. I want Snort to stay in the apartment where he's safe, and things to go back to the way they were in the Emergency Department. At this point, I would have happily worked every single case on Riley's heels or overnights for the rest of the summer if it meant I could put my scrubs back on and get back to it.

A sinking feeling follows me as I walk. Although I had tried to avoid it, I'm walking in the same direction as the hospital again, like it has some magnetic pull on me.

I stop in the middle of the sidewalk and see Liberty Hill's massive roofline a half a block in front of me. I turn around and go home. I have nowhere else to go.

26

W hen I get back to the apartment twenty minutes later, I realize that a phone call had come in while I was walking. I always keep my phone on vibrate so it doesn't ring while I'm in with a patient, but now I'm so preoccupied by the swirl of thoughts in my head, I didn't even feel it when it went off. I shake my head as I look at the screen, my stomach twisting like a giant fist had it in a grip.

Riley.

As I stare at my phone, I realize I must be in serious trouble. If he called and didn't text me, then something was really going on. I see a little blue circle with a one in the corner hovering over my voicemail. Uh oh. He left a voicemail. I tap on the screen and look at it. Riley not only called but he left a voicemail.

Another twist of the gut.

"Forbes, this is Dr. Randy Riley. I need you to come to the hospital ASAP to meet with me."

That was it. No timeline no other information. No, "I know you've had a hard week and just want to touch base with you about it." My eyes go wide, staring at my work bag. Did he want me to come in for a shift? To talk? I don't know what to do or even what to wear. My head starts to spin. I don't want to look too confident, but at the same time I also don't want to look unprepared.

An unprepared resident was the worst.

The next thought hit me hard: Just over a week ago, I was the Chief Resident. Now, I'd be lucky if I managed to complete my residency.

Maybe that wasn't it? Maybe he just wanted to discuss me being Chief Resident. Sure, I'd screwed up, but not all of it was my fault, was it? I mean, Bill Palmer didn't take his meds. They don't do anyone any good in the bottle. And the rest of it, well, I am still a *resident*, aren't I? I'm entitled to a few mistakes.

My thoughts brightened a bit.

Maybe that was it. Maybe that was the reason that Riley was calling me in. Maybe he was gonna give someone else a shot at the chief resident chair for the next couple of months, give someone else a little leadership training.

Heck, if I got my shifts back, it didn't matter to me what he had me doing.

I run into the bathroom, combing what is left of my hair, which I am now sure is falling out of my head, and pulling it up into a ponytail. I change out of my leggings, sliding into a pair of jeans from the regularly worn pile, grabbing a white tank top, and tossing a light blue cropped cardigan over the top. I study my look in the mirror. It's not great. I switch from jeans to black pants from the rarely worn pile. It's not anything close to what Julia would have worn, but I'm at least wearing clothes that look halfway professional. Having clothes on at all is a bonus after Shaw saw me in my robe and Tamia saw me with my shirt off with Jamir. With the black pants on, I look a little more like I have a life. I straighten my shoulders as I look in the mirror. I mean, with this outfit, I could be going to the market, heading to the airport, or even meeting a friend for coffee.

Not that I have the time or the money for any of that.

I feel a little sadness nip at me. The problem is, I don't look like a doctor anymore. I just look like everyone else.

On my days off, that's okay, but now that my job is on the line, all I want to do is put on a pair of scrubs and get to work.

But that's not an option right now.

Halfway satisfied with my look, I decide at the last second to grab my work bag. I'm absolutely sure that Dr. Riley has no idea what my work bag looks like. For all he knows it's stuffed with heady library books I read on my time off — volumes written by Tolstoy, Hemingway, and Edgar Allan Poe. That's probably the stuff he reads. What's really in my bag? It's stuff Riley doesn't need to know about — my stethoscope, the one my dad bought me when I graduated from medical school, a clean bra and underwear, three different kinds of deodorant to manage the stink meter, breath mints, and three tampons. I try to remain hopeful. You never know, Riley might call me in, give me a long lecture about medical professionalism. I imagine myself sitting and listening patiently as I stare at his tie of the day and nodding as he tells me to go back to work.

Sounds okay.

As I go outside, I consider just walking to the hospital, but then I remember it's supposed to rain later on. If Riley wants me to stay and do a shift, the last thing I want to do is walk home in the pouring down rain. I trot to my car, jump in and get it started, pulling out in traffic, drumming my fingers on the steering wheel. I pass the same stores that I do almost every single day, or have for almost the last three years — Riccardo's tacos, the flower shop Mrs. MacIlvain runs, and this little tiny bookstore called Forester's that I've stopped in a few times at, always wanting to be one of those people that buys books and actually reads them.

But at this stage of my life, I'm not. I prefer sleep.

It doesn't take me long to get to the hospital and drive the ramps of the parking garage to the top floor. I drive extra fast, which means I'm a little nauseated by the time I get to the top, but so be it. As much as part of me wants to circle the lot for a parking spot that's close to the bridge that takes people into the building, I know it's fruitless, especially in the middle of a shift. Everyone will have taken the good spots, the ones right by the doorway to get out quick.

I smile as I get to the top of the parking garage. My luck must be changing because when I get to the top of the parking garage, there's not just one spot, there's an entire line of them, each of them actually close to the steps that lead down to the bridge.

Things are definitely getting better. I can feel it in my bones.

I park the car, jump out, and grab my bag, feeling my swagger return. I mean, who cares if Jamir saw me with my shirt off and Shaw saw me in my robe? It's no big deal and I have a half-decent body. Sure, I could spend a little more time working out and build up some muscle. I resolve right then and there to hit the gym near the hospital, which I have a membership to as part of my residency package at the end of every shift from now on. And people break up with their boyfriends all the time. I'm no different than anyone else.

Whistling under my breath, I trot down the steps and make my way across the bridge that connects the parking garage to the Liberty Hill medical campus. I move on automatic pilot, not even thinking about where I'm walking. I don't need to. After all, I've spent pretty much every waking minute of the last three years of my life holed up in this building. Thinking about it now, I'm kind of wondering why I chose medicine in the first place. I love the outdoors. Working in the medical field isn't exactly something you do where you're outdoors all the time.

I cock my head to the side as I walk, thinking. Perhaps when things are going a little bit better, I'll ask Shaw about his medical mission trip. That needle decompression he did without having to use the ultrasound was pretty cool. I imagine myself rappelling down the side of a cliff to rescue an injured climber, my team above me yelling encouragement and amazed at my bravery. Yeah, I'd like to learn things like that.

But then again, that depends all on what Dr. Randy Riley says.

I won't be going anywhere if I don't finish this residency.

I decide that my best option is to go to his office as opposed to heading down to the Emergency Department. After all, I really don't want to show my face there after what happened the day before. For all I know, the entire place was swarming with tech people. If I show up, there might be lots of points and whispers, "Look! There's the girl that crashed the entire system!" What was I supposed to do? Smile and wave?

No, avoidance was the best tactic.

I head to the fourth floor where Dr. Riley's office is, stepping into the elevator. I take a couple of deep breaths, staring at the toes of my shoes. There is a knot the size of the Grand Canyon in my gut. He surely can't believe that I'd do anything to the computer system on purpose, would he? I mean, it makes my life just as hard as everyone else's.

And based on what happened yesterday, I'm no tech genius.

Then I remember Marshall. What happened to him?

I make my way down the hallway into the administration suite where Dr. Riley has his office, along with a few of the other department heads. As soon as I turn the corner, I can see that his office door is cracked open, his assistant is at her desk, staring at her computer screen. Whether it's a good sign that Riley's in his office or a bad sign, I'm not exactly sure. Has he been waiting for me? My stomach flops. I didn't call him back. Was I supposed to? He just said to come to the hospital, so that's what I did.

I freeze. I mean, it would be super easy to just wait a little bit longer to meet with him, wouldn't it? I pause, looking over my shoulder. He hasn't seen me yet. Maybe I should just go to the cafeteria and get a coffee or something.

Stop stalling, Mac.

I can hear my mother's voice in my ear. She's always been one for taking direct action.

I'm not exactly that way. I prefer to avoid things as much as possible. And meeting with Dr. Randy Riley is something I would prefer to avoid — at all costs.

No, this is a rip-off-the-Band-Aid moment. "Here goes nothing," I mutter under my breath. I walk toward his office door, only to be greeted by the sour expression of his admin, Cynthia. For some reason, I've always thought that they look like brother and sister. She has the same buggy eyes and jowls that he does, and somehow her wardrobe always seems to go with whatever tie he's wearing for the day. Do they coordinate? The thought stuns me. Maybe Cynthia is more clever than I think she is and she's using some sort of subliminal affirmation process to get Randy to promote her. Or maybe she's actually the one in charge and I just haven't figured it out yet.

Sounds like a plot for a new Hallmark movie, except they would both have to be better looking and there would have to be romantic tension.

Eeewww.

I wrinkle my nose at the thought of Randy and Cynthia tangled up. Then I have a thought. Maybe if Randy lets me get back to work, I should start wearing bows in my hair that match his ties.

Cynthia's pinched voice interrupts my thoughts. "Forbes." Yes, she's another one that refuses to use the "doctor" title.

"Hello, Cynthia," I say, feigning a fake smile. "Is Dr. Riley available?"

She sniffs the air as if she can tell I just cleaned Snort's litter box. "I'm not sure. Let me see."

I know darn well he's in his office. His door wouldn't be

cracked open if he wasn't and I don't hear any voices inside. He's probably sitting in there playing with his computer, which is what I think probably does for most of the hours that he's at the hospital. Yeah, he makes a lot of noise about being the head of the department and having so much administrative stuff to do, but every time I see Dr. Riley, he's either creating chaos in the Emergency Department or he's sitting in his office. For all I know, he's watching back-to-back episodes of *Game of Thrones* or playing *Minecraft* on his computer.

But I don't say that out loud. I mean, I'm already on thin ice.

Cynthia holds the phone up to her ear, never taking her eyes off of me as if she has just run into an escaped convict and is calling 911. I hear her say, "Forbes is here," then the echo of the voice in her ear and the voice coming from the office at the same time. It's so silly. His office door is literally three feet from where she's sitting. You'd think she'd get up and just poke her head in to talk to Riley, not call him on his phone.

As Cynthia hangs up the phone, she lifts her nose in the air.

"Dr. Riley will see you now."

Gotta face the firing squad. "Thanks," I mumble.

I walk to Dr. Riley's door slowly, then gently push on it. "Dr. Riley?" I ask, poking my head inside.

"Forbes. About time you got here."

About time? You just called a half hour ago. "I'm sorry to have kept you waiting, Dr. Riley."

I've managed to work in two very respectful Dr. Riley's already. I know I'm winning points here. "You wanted to see me?"

"Yes."

He nods at one of the chairs in front of his desk. I sit down, tucking my bag underneath the seat so he can't see that it's my work bag and not the imaginary volumes of Tolstoy and Hemingway that I want him to think I'm reading. I sit, frozen, like a deer getting spotlighted during hunting season. He hasn't lifted his eyes off of his screen. He's definitely watching something. Reruns of "This Old House?" or maybe reading up on foreign object removal from the anus. (Yeah, we get a fair share of those.) Finally, he blinks, his bulging eyeballs rotating toward me like two little globes, then pushes his glasses up his nose. "Forbes, you've created quite a problem for us."

I shake my head, trying to look dejected. It's not hard. That's exactly how I feel. "I'm so sorry, Dr. Riley. I don't know what to say."

"Well, you better think of something."

As I look up, I'm surprised. Riley is staring at me, his mouth open as if I've just stolen a crown jewel from the king of England.

My mouth goes dry. What's the right answer? "I'm sorry, Dr. Riley. I've been very tired and under a lot of pressure with my sister's wedding."

He grimaces. It's not a terrible grimace. I've seen worse. It's kind of a "I'm the principal and you are the student" vibe. "Being tired is part of the program when you're a resident, Forbes. You know that. You've been with us for three years."

"I know, Dr. Riley. Again, I'm not sure exactly what to say. There's no excuse. What happened yesterday with the computer system was completely accidental. I mean, why would I do that? It just makes my life harder too."

He narrows his eyes at me, which makes him look even more like a frog. I'm waiting for a long, forked tongue to slip out between his lips to eat a fly. "I should hope that's the case. You have no idea what a disaster it is. They finally got it reloaded again this morning. But that means we ran for fourteen hours and eight minutes with no access to our computers. Lives could have been lost, Forbes. Lives. Do you understand that? We have no access to prior medical history, lab results, nothing. There may be issues with billing and charting that could take months to sort out. You've made my job very hard."

I shake my head in disbelief. What he's saying is not exactly true. In fact, it was only the Emergency Department computers that were down. The other floors were okay. They could have brought in a few mobile stations from the other departments, which is, I'm sure, exactly what they did to get by, but I'm not going to disagree with him. He holds my fate in his hands.

I swallow. I'm not sure what to say. My heart pounds in my chest. "Again, Dr. Riley, I'm so very sorry."

What I really want to say is, "Please, can I just have my job back?"

I look up at him. I'm trying. I really am. That has to be at least five very respectful Dr. Riley's. It's helping, isn't it?

As I see the disgusted look on his face, I realize it's not. "I've been reviewing your work performance. You've been slipping, Forbes. I see this once in a while in a resident in my program that's getting ready to finish. You get into the last six months, and you think that you've got it all handled, like you know *everything*." Sarcasm drips from his voice and he throws his hands in the air for a fact.

"I, I don't," I stammer. "I know I don't know everything, Dr. Riley."

"You can tell me that till the cows come home, Forbes, but I've seen it. I know what happens." He seems to settle back in his chair then straightens his yellow polka dot tie as if he's impressed with his own words. "But lucky for you, we've caught this slip at the beginning. Lives were impacted, but we didn't lose anyone. At least not yet..."

The words hung in the air eerily, like cobwebs hanging from the ceiling. I think back to Mr. Palmer and the gal — Samantha Watkins — that I thought had a virus but probably has leukemia. I swear, her blasts were listed at zero, not twenty percent. I'll go to my grave thinking that.

"The question becomes what to do."

Riley continues on with his soliloquy. Why I'm even here in

his office while he's basically talking to himself, I have no idea. Maybe Cynthia is recording it for posterity's sake.

I wait, not sure exactly what else to say. I would hope he knows by now that I didn't crash the Emergency Department computer system on purpose and, as far as the other stuff, every resident makes mistakes.

Breaking news — that's why we're residents.

Riley tents his fingers in front of his chest, doing what I quickly decide is his best impression of Winston Churchill, and studies me for a second. I have the distinct impression that he's been planning this diatribe for the last several hours or maybe has even used it on other people in the past.

He leans forward, staring his buggy eyes into mine. Double eeeewww. "Unfortunately, Forbes, you've left me with no options. You're suspended."

Wait. What?

"Suspended?" I ask. "For how long?"

Riley shrugs. "I haven't decided yet."

My heart pounds in my chest. I think about how there were no shifts listed on the calendar for me. None whatsoever. That would explain it. All of a sudden, I have this vision of Cynthia hunching over her computer happily deleting all of my work shifts, knowing that the axe was about to fall on my scrawny neck even before I did.

"What about my residency?" I manage to stammer.

He shrugs. "I'm still considering what to do about that. It's a shame that all of this had to happen when you're so close to finishing."

Now I feel like he's taunting me. "Please, Dr. Riley, I'll do anything."

He holds a hand up dismissively and looks away. "Honestly, I'm done with you for now. There's nothing that you can do at this moment to make good on the damage that you've caused to this department and to our reputation. I need some time to consider what to do next. You can hold on to your ID for now."

For now? My chest tightens, each beat hammering painfully against my ribs. "Well, okay," I whisper, my voice small. "When are you gonna let me know?"

Suddenly, Riley leaps up from his desk, like someone shot him out of a cannon. I never realized he could move that fast. He juts a finger toward the door. "Get out, Forbes. Just get out."

My eyes widen, my mouth falls open. The room feels unreal, like a warped community theater production where everyone else is in on script and I'm the only one reading the wrong lines. My legs feel like lead as I rise, shoulders slumping, a fresh wave of tears threatening to spill. I grab my bag, barely able to meet his gaze.

"Okay. Thanks, Dr. Riley," I murmur, my voice cracking. I don't know what else to say, don't know how to explain the mess inside me. I just want to disappear.

As I step outside his door, my stomach twists and my pulse races, and somewhere in the back of my mind, a thought lingers: this isn't over.

Not by a long shot.

27

A s I leave Dr. Riley's office, my head is down. I don't even bother to look in Cynthia's direction. I can very well imagine the sneer on her face. I'm sure she's enjoying this. For all I know, she's recorded the whole thing to listen to over and over again. My head is spinning. I've just been *suspended*. This is the kind of thing that might follow me for my whole career. I've heard horror stories about this kind of thing before in med school — about residents that can't finish their education and never work in medicine again. They lose everything. Years of education, lost relationships, sleepless nights, and stress wasted. Riley is exactly the kind of guy that would happily let everyone know that he'd been forced into suspending me for tanking the Emergency Department's computer system and for shoddy work, which isn't true of course.

I walk, feeling every inch of my skin tingle, like I have bugs all over me. I don't really pay any attention to where I'm going until I realize that I've made my way downstairs and I am standing near the Emergency Department room. A shock runs through my body. What am I supposed to do?

I set my jaw. I need backup. Someone has to help me.

Tamia.

As the door whooshes open, she spots me the second that I walk in the doors. I give a head bob toward the break room. She comes out from behind the counter at the nurses' station, moving like a missile locked on a target. Luckily, it seems like everyone else is in a room with patients. From the hum of conversations coming from the other end of the Emergency Department where the waiting room is, it sounds like they have a full load of patients.

That's good.

That means I might be able to sneak a minute with Tamia and then get out of here without being seen or having to talk to anyone else.

Mostly, I don't want to have to deal with their stares and pitying looks.

By the time Tamia joins me in the break room, I've closed all of the blinds and I'm pacing back and forth like I'm a fugitive on the run.

"Where have you been?" she asks, her arms folded across her chest like I missed curfew.

I throw my hands up. "Where have I been?"

"I've been texting you all morning? Didn't you get them?"

I pull my phone out of my bag. Sure enough, there's a whole line of texts from Tamia that I never saw. I groan. "I'm sorry. I had no idea you texted me."

"Yeah, Riley was down here earlier strutting around. Said he was going to meet with you. What happened?"

I look at the ground, my eyes welling up with tears. I can hardly make the words come out. I know she's been mad at me, but I really need a friend right now. "He suspended me."

Her mouth drops open. "What? For how long?"

"He didn't say."

"Are you kidding me?" Tamia's furious. Her hands are

balled into fists. "We're already understaffed. And he's gonna pull you out now? Is it just based on that computer glitch from yesterday?"

The way Tamia said it made me feel slightly better. Unlike Riley's reaction, apparently in her world it wasn't that big of a deal. It kinda made me wonder. Then I remembered how I saw Riley and Shaw talking the other day. I thought it was about me, then I played it off. Now I'm wondering if I was right. "Yeah. And he said my job performance, whatever that means."

"Your job performance?" Her chin drops, her mouth open. "You practically live in this hospital. You have a great reputation." She waves her hand in the air. "Riley wouldn't know his head from a hole in the ground."

Seeing that Tamia is on my side and knowing she's basically the only person I have left, I spill the beans about how Julia kicked me out of the wedding, my mom's not talking to me, and how Donovan found me with Shaw and then walked out.

Her eyes narrow. "Wait, Shaw stopped at your apartment last night?" I nod.

That's what she's worried about? Not Donovan? Not that my live-in, okay sorta live-in boyfriend when he's in town, left me and I don't know where he is?

"How did Shaw find out where you live?"

I shrug. "I don't know. He's an attending. Don't they have access to that kind of information?"

Tamia shakes her head. "No. HR guards all of our personal information like their lives depend on it."

I find that strange. If Shaw didn't get my address from HR, then how did he find me? Really no one else has it, save for Tamia. When I see the rest of the team from the hospital, we are usually out at a bar or a restaurant or something. "Yeah, and he managed to be there just a few minutes before Donovan showed up." I fill in the details about how I had just gotten out of the shower and was wearing nothing but a robe.

Tamia closes her eyes for a second shaking her head. "That's so bad, Mac."

I widen my eyes, then groan. "Not you too, Tam. We didn't *do* anything."

She holds a hand up like a stop sign. "Oh, I believe that. But I can see from Donovan's perspective how he might have thought something happened."

A wave of relief crashes over me. I suck in a breath. "Tam, I *have* to finish this residency. If I don't —"

"You're screwed."

She cut to the chase really fast, fast enough that a huge lump, the size of a grapefruit, has lodged itself in my throat. I nod. "Can you help?"

I really, really hate to ask, but if anybody has power over Dr. Randy Riley, it's Tamia.

Lucky for me, she's my friend. Because at this point, she's all I have left.

28

A fter leaving Tamia, I feel only marginally better. I slip out of the break room and look over my shoulder. Not fifteen feet from me is Shaw. He's standing super close to a surgeon from upstairs, Dr. Lena Harley. She's beautiful, with long dark hair that's the same color as Shaw's, big brown eyes, and a body that could definitely be considered for the *Sports Illustrated* swimsuit cover. Today, she's wearing a low-cut blouse, a maroon skirt that hits just above the knee, and a pair of four-inch pumps that, while I'm not sure how she walks on the slippery floor, definitely do show off a pair of ripped calves.

She definitely hits the gym.

Shaw has half a smile on his face as he's whispering to her. Lena moves in close, listening to whatever he's saying. A smile tugs at the corner of her lips. From the way their bodies are angled, it looks like he could lean in for a kiss at any minute. All of the action stops when Shaw sees me looking at him. He stares at me, as if I'm a stranger, his green eyes suddenly dead. It's creepy enough that it makes the hair on the back of my neck stand up as I walk away. He'd just been in my apartment to so-called console me the night before, and now he's flirting with a surgeon from upstairs? And Tamia's right — how did he get my address?

Something doesn't seem right.

I make my way back to my car, my only solace that Tamia has a full picture of what's going on. I can only hope that she can work her magic with Dr. Riley. I drive back to my apartment, so many thoughts in my head that if you'd asked me what I was thinking I wouldn't be able to tell you. I feel scared, sick to my stomach, anxious, restless, like I'm having a complete mental break. My mind starts to spin even faster. Numbers start to collide in my head. I'm three hundred thousand dollars in debt between medical school and my undergraduate tuition. Every doctor does it — going hundreds of thousands of dollars into debt in order to get the education with the promise that at the other end, they can start to make some of that back, and hopefully quickly.

But not if you don't finish your residency.

I push open the door to my apartment, slamming it before Mrs. Dixon has a chance to stick her head out and stab at me with her latest insult. The next thought hits me like an earthquake. If I don't get my residency back, I have no income.

Within a few seconds, I'm in full-out panic mode.

No money is a huge problem. The bills for my student loans, living expenses, and even food won't take a break.

I'm screwed.

Sweat starts to collect on my forehead. If I'm not a doctor, what am I qualified to do? I'll have to start using my car as an Uber in order to even try to make rent. I mean, I have a little money stashed away that can get me through a few weeks. After all, as a resident, it not like I have a lot of time to go shopping or out with friends.

But it won't last long. Right now, I can't exactly lean on Donovan. If we were on good terms, then he probably would be happy to take over paying the rent for me while I get my life straightened out.

We aren't exactly on good terms. Not at the moment, at least. Frustrated and terrified, I go back to my closet, strip off the sensible-ladies-who-do-errands-outfit and pull on a set of sweats from the pile of clothes that probably should be donated, an oversized pair of stained sweatpants and a giant size T-shirt that hangs over my scrawny shoulders. I throw my work bag into the back of the closet and slam the closet doors. I see Snort scuttle across the floor, the commotion clearly scaring him. I immediately feel bad. It's not his fault that I'm not having a good day. How did things get so bad so fast? Then it hits me.

All of this really did begin when Shaw started in the Emergency Department.

I shake the thought off. I'm being silly. Correlation is not causation. I'm a scientist. I know this and I've gone down this rabbit trail before. Shaw starting and my troubles are nothing more than a coincidence. I stride into the kitchen, getting a bottle of water out of the refrigerator and opening the cabinet next to it. Unlike pretty much every other cabinet in my kitchen, this one is full. It's all of my favorite snacks, the ones that I love to eat when I'm off of work and lounging on the couch.

Or at least the ones I *used* to eat when I was off shift.

Now there's nothing but one long ocean of being off shift in front of me. I feel like I'm drowning in it.

I wipe the tears from my face with a handful of my shirt, then grab a bag of sea salt tortilla chips, a box of Fruit Loops, and a box of lemon cream cookies. I look at my haul and then stuff the Fruit Loops back in the cabinet. You have to be happy to eat Fruit Loops.

And I'm not happy.

I find my way to the couch, flipping TV on, hoping that the

Hallmark Channel is showing another sappy movie I can use to distract myself. Then I realize that if things don't change soon, I'm gonna turn out to be just like Mrs. Dixon, who's busy chronicling the lives of everyone else around her rather than having one of her own. It's a sobering thought as I open the box of lemon cream cookies.

Twenty minutes later, after demolishing the entire box of lemon cream cookies, I lay back on the couch. Funny how during sad moments the only thing I wanna eat are things that are sweet.

Maybe if I can't be a doctor, I can be a food researcher. I wince, brushing powdered sugar from my sweatpants. I'd probably end up gaining like a hundred pounds, Donovan, with his athletic frame, will reject me and I'll die all alone after choking on a spare rib.

I lay back, watching the movie. It's about a dark-haired police officer who looks strikingly like Shaw, and a woman who works for the library. He's apologizing to her, but she can't figure out why.

I've been so busy eating cookies I can't figure out why either.

My eyes are focused on the screen, but I'm barely hearing any of the dialogue. I just keep hearing this voice in the back of my head saying, "Everything was fine until Shaw showed up." That voice has been getting louder and louder over the last few days. My gut is usually right, but Shaw? No. There's no way. He's just the new guy. I can't blame him for my problems, can I?

I frown.

Could it be true?

I mean, someone has to be responsible for my change of luck, right?

I think back to how I saw Riley and Shaw standing so close together talking and staring at me. At the time, I was sure it was just a coincidence. I do a good job. I mean, nothing really went badly until Shaw decided to reorganize the supply closet. But there was that issue with Mr. Palmer and the woman with leukemia, of course, but those were honest mistakes, weren't they? And wasn't it strange how fast Riley decided to retreat to a more administrative position in the Emergency Department, letting Shaw run it? The ED at Liberty Hill was Riley's baby. Giving it up to someone, even as handsome as Shaw, (not that looks have anything to do with it), didn't seem to fit.

Unless there was more to it.

I sit straight up on the couch, moving so fast it almost forces all the lemon cookies up out of my gut and onto the floor. I swallow at the last second, holding them at bay. I grab my phone, quickly Googling Dr. Jonathan Shaw. There's not a lot listed about him, which doesn't surprise me. There are thousands of doctors in Philadelphia and Jonathan Shaw isn't exactly a unique name. In fact, there's not only Dr. Jonathan Shaw that I know that works as a trauma doc, but there's one that's a urologist (eeewww), one that's an orthopedic surgeon (sorta cool), and another one that's an obstetrician. (Another eeewww. What woman wants to go to a male OB?)

After spending about a half an hour digging, I haven't found much. Then I start to wonder. They got buddy-buddy pretty quick. Did Riley and Shaw know each other before they both ended up at Liberty Hill?

It's a good question, I realize, one that I probably would never have asked if I wasn't completely hopped up on sugar and whatever that fake lemon flavor is that I'm sure has like a thousand chemicals in it. If they knew each other previously, that would explain why they seem so comfortable with each other and why they seem like friends. I go on to the Liberty Hill website and pull up Dr. Randy Riley's resume. As expected, it's a good five pages long, including all of the articles and boards he has sat on, and probably, if I looked hard enough, what his favorite color of Jell-O is.

He's just that way.

I pull up Dr. Jonathan Shaw's resume too and start comparing.

The correlation becomes obvious very quickly. They both went to the University of Pittsburgh Medical School. I know that school. Everyone calls it U-Op, like UoP. I shake my head.

Medical school buddies? Is it possible? Were they even there at the same time or is it some "We went to the same school" fraternity kinda thing? They look so different that I think they aren't even close to the same age, but maybe I'm wrong. Maybe Riley just got the short end of the genetic stick like I did.

I check the years on Dr. Riley's resume — he's a lot younger than I think he is, only thirty-seven — and then I start searching for images from UoP's medical school.

I know, I know. I'm grasping at straws here, but what else do I have to do? I've already eaten my entire body weight in lemon cookies. If I don't get my mind busy, I might end up flopping over on the couch into a diabetic coma with all of the sugar I have just consumed. And given the fact that I have no job to go to, research is the next best thing.

What do I know right now? Not much other than they went to the same medical school.

But they do know each other, don't they?

I get up from where I'm sitting on the couch and go into the extra bedroom that still has boxes in it from when Donovan was supposed to move in and grab my laptop. Seeing the boxes makes my heart clutch. I lean toward one of the boxes, running my finger over it. Donovan. I miss him.

But until he reaches back out, there's nothing I can do.

I press my lips together. I have to stay focused. My little research project on the connection between Riley and Shaw is going to require a bigger screen. I sit back down on the couch, brushing another layer of powdered sugar off my sweatpants, and open up the machine. I grab a pillow from the couch and stuff it between the computer and my legs, using it like a little desk. Radiation protection. I'd read the abstract of a study the week before that researchers were beginning to think that the increase in prostate, testicular, and ovarian cancer was from people putting their laptops right on top of their groin while they surfed the Internet.

I haven't even had kids yet. If I don't want my eggs to be fried, a pillow seems like the least that I can do.

As my computer whirs to life, I drum my fingers on my thigh. Where do I start? How do I figure out if the two of them were buddies at UoP?

I try a couple searches that use both of their names, but nothing comes back. I even searched the past records for UoP but can't seem to find anything. That's probably because they are stuck behind some screen that requires a password. I'm just about to get up, frustrated, when I realize that there's one thing I haven't tried.

A reverse image search.

Excited at the prospect, I put their names in the search bar and look under images.

Staring at the screen as the results come back, I grimace. Randy Riley and Jonathan Shaw are not exactly the most unusual names. Why couldn't they have names like Woznitski and Hammerschmidt? The search engine has returned a lot of results from other people named Randy Riley and Jonathan Shaw. I wince. Why would anyone give their child matching initials? Then I remember back to a family that I went to high school with. All of their girls' names began with J. Trying to keep them straight was a nightmare, especially because they all looked like each other, even if they weren't twins.

After hunting for a few minutes, I realize I'm not coming up with anything. The muscles across my back tighten and then I have a brainstorm. I click on the search bar and add the name of their medical school to it. Why I hadn't thought to do that in the first place, I have no idea. That would explain why so many of the results that I came up with were things like car salesman and plumbers.

Now that would be a job for a guy named Randy Riley.

After a couple more failed attempts, I was just about to slam the lid of my computer closed when I see something out of the corner of my eye. Furrowing my eyebrows together, I scroll down, trying to figure out what has caught my attention. It's a group of men all wearing white lab coats from about ten years ago. There's seven of them in the group as best I can tell. I click on the image, trying to make it bigger. I recognize Shaw instantly. I mean, how could I not? The man is stunningly gorgeous. (I feel a little more comfortable admitting that to myself given the fact that Donovan and I are on the outs.) It's crazy to say, but if anything, Jonathan looks better now. In the picture, he had muscles, but he didn't have *muscles*, if you know what I mean.

And standing right next to him is none other than Dr. Randy Riley.

To be fair, Riley looks appreciably better in the picture than he does now. Maybe he's just one of those guys, or maybe it's the fact that he looks like he's packed thirty to forty pounds on his frame since the picture was taken.

Hasn't anyone talked to him about heart disease?

Without the jowls and with a little more hair, Randy actually wasn't bad looking. Not that Riley is the kind of guy I would be interested in and he's definitely not the things that dreams are made of like Shaw, but he's not bad. Maybe a six or a seven out of ten, like me.

Shaw's definitely out of my league looks-wise, but I do know someone he'd be perfect for even though she's already taken.

Queen Julia.

My mind drifts for a minute trying to imagine what kind of children Shaw and my sister Julia would have if they got together. They would be stunning, I'm sure.

And I'd be the homely aunt of their gorgeous kids.

Back to work, Mac.

I stare at the picture for another minute, then read the caption. It says, "New Doctors Hold Fundraiser for Local Library."

I press my lips together. A local library? Then I remember, Jamir and I had done something similar after the end of our first year of residency. The hospitals like to look like good to community members, even if they are mostly concerned about making money.

It was a PR move.

But no matter what the subject of the picture was, it did give me actual evidence that Shaw and Riley knew each other before they ever got to Liberty Hill. That explained Shaw's quick ascension to acting head of the ED, his ability to make decisions like reorganizing the supply closet and also explained why Riley hadn't been skulking around as much as he had before.

My stomach sunk.

I had this feeling that if one of them didn't like me, then the other one probably wouldn't either.

The picture blurred as tears burned my eyes. If both of them had already decided I didn't belong, then what was I even fighting for?

29

This line of thinking took me off into a whole 'nother spiral. Have they been talking about me a lot? More than I suspected? I started sweating. Had Riley decided that he wanted to get rid of me and was making Shaw do his dirty work?

It didn't seem like they had the same feelings about Jamir or Hudson. The two of them seemed to fly under the radar. Maybe this was a boys club thing?

I stand up from where I'm sitting, shoving my computer and my groin protector pillow off to the side. I start pacing, nearly tripping over Snort, who has assumed a curled position underneath the coffee table, my toe nearly catching his paw. He gave a loud yowl and scurried off, glancing back over his leg and sneering at me, clearly seriously offended.

Great, now I've made enemies with my cat.

I guess I'm just glad he's not hurt. The last thing that I need is a big vet bill for a cat with a broken paw, given the fact that I'm not sure I'm ever going to be able to get back to Liberty Hill and finish my residency.

That three hundred thousand in debt looms in my mind, setting off another round of shivers down my spine.

The next thing you know, I'm going to be out on the street homeless.

Whoa, whoa, whoa.

I grab my phone. Everything in me wants to call Donovan, but I've sent him like twenty-five texts, and he still hasn't responded to me. I don't have any idea if he's in the country or has left again. I guess the good news is his stuff is still here. He'll have to come and get it eventually, right? My mind fast forwards to being evicted. I imagine Donovan rolls up in a limo his company has gotten for him. I'm outside packing my car and Snort, dragging a sleeping bag and pillow with me, knowing I'll have to live in my car. Donvan leaves without saying anything. He's on the phone, doing deals all over the world, while I can't even buy enough gas to get back to Youngstown.

I blink, trying to bring myself back to reality. There's really only one person I have left to turn to. I'm on thin ice with Tamia, Marshall is at work, and Donovan is nowhere to be found. I'm all alone. It's a desperate move, one I spend a minute weighing in my mind. But then again, I have no choice.

Mom.

I dial, my hand shaking as I hold the phone up to my ear. One ring. Two.

"Hello?"

My stomach tightens. Mom didn't answer her phone. "Hey, Jules."

Never in my wildest imagination did I expect that Queen Julia would be answering my mother's phone. My heart pounds in my chest. The last interaction I had with her was about the weeklong Brazilian wax-athon she wanted me to attend.

"I'll get Mom."

That's it? No, "Hey Mac, how are you doing?" or "What's

new with you? Any cool cases recently?" Not even a question about Donovan.

Why am I not surprised?

"Honey?" my mom's voice comes on the line.

I sigh in relief. "Mom?"

"It's the middle of the day. Is everything all right?"

Moms always know.

I throw myself down on the couch and grab my groin protecting pillow, holding it close to my chest. At the moment, there's nothing that I want more than to be at home. I want to be sitting in the kitchen where my mom can make me tea and hand me a box of tissues as I cry my eyes out. I snuffle. "No, it's not."

I quickly recount the story of what happened with the computer system, skipping the part about Mr. Palmer, Samantha the leukemia patient, and the storage room debacle. I don't even attempt to describe my failed needle decompression.

Mom didn't need to know all of it, did she?

"And they suspended you for that? How could they think you did that?"

See, someone's on my side.

I cry even harder. "I don't know. I didn't do it, Mom!"

I go on to explain how I was just trying to copy one prescription that I was using into another patient's file and now the tech person blamed me.

My mother's voice got tight. "They need to look into that. Seems like the computer shouldn't do that."

That's right, Mom, you tell 'em.

"I just don't know what I'm going to do," I whine and then the conversation shifts. All of a sudden, my mom sounds distant. I think I can hear her whispering in the background, but I'm not sure. "Mom?"

"I'm here."

But she's not. Whatever connection we had, it's gone. "Is there something going on?" It's close to my catch phrase from work, but it feels awkward using it on my mom. There are butterflies in my stomach all of a sudden.

There's a pause. "It's just Julia. She needs my help with something for the wedding."

The wedding. Again.

I fight off a groan by swallowing hard. Even when I need her, my mom is overrun by the stupid wedding. I try to be a good sister, putting my sadness off to the side. "Is everything okay with her?" I asked tentatively. "She picked up your phone. Didn't sound all that happy to hear my voice if you know what I mean."

In my mind I imagine her walking out to her sunroom to get a little distance from Queen Julia's radar-level hearing. My mom lowers her voice. "She's just under a lot of stress, Mac."

Stress? Are you kidding me? I cut people open, stitch them up, shove needles into their arms, tubes down their throats, and even break their ribs trying to save their lives. What could possibly be *that* stressful about a wedding of all things?

I don't say that, though I really want to. "What's the problem now?"

"It's the florist," she says quietly. "Julia wanted to have her bouquet filled with white phalaenopsis orchids, but they can't find them. They're talking about having to substitute in another variety of orchid."

Orchidgate. Someone call the FBI. It has to be a vast conspiracy to prevent Queen Julia from having the wedding of her dreams.

"Mom, they're just flowers. That's it. No one will even notice."

My mother's voice stiffens. "It's a lot more than that, McKenna. I know you don't understand, but perhaps someday you will. She just needs some time and space. She's still dealing with the disappointment that you're not going to be able to come in a week ahead."

Oh, for God's sake.

I fight off the urge to say, "What happened to the new maid of honor, Heather?" Instead, I go with, "I'm disappointed, too. I really wanted to be there for her."

It's not a *total* lie.

After hanging up with my mom, I realize I don't feel any better. If anything, I feel worse. Mom has gotten completely sucked into the black hole that's Queen Julia's wedding. She doesn't have any time or sympathy left for me. What am I, just an afterthought?

The thought hits me like a runaway train.

That's exactly how I feel. I feel like I'm everybody's afterthought. Tamia hasn't gotten back to me, neither has Marshall after looking at the security footage. Donovan won't respond to my calls, and I'm away from the hospital so I don't have any contact with Jamir, Hudson, Jasmine or any of the other staff. And given the zero texts or calls I've gotten from anyone, I'm clearly persona non grata at this point.

Riley, or even more likely his lackey, Cynthia, probably put a bounty out on my head.

The revelation that no one has put me first leads me to a whole new round of tears. How sad is it when even your own mother doesn't have time for you? I throw my phone down and curl up on my side on the couch, the pillow I was holding now half covering my face and the other half covering my chest. Sobs rack my body. I'm all alone, I'm buried in debt, and I have no idea how I'm going to get myself out of the problem that I'm in. It feels like this is being done to me, like I'm the one at the center of a conspiracy, not Jules and her flowers. Everything was going so smoothly and then all of a sudden, it's like my world started crashing down around my head.

I'm too hysterical to even get up and get tissues. I blubber into the pillow for another minute or two and then sit up. There are so many tears running down my face they're dropping onto my T-shirt, leaving a wet stain. I wipe the snot from my nose right on the couch. What do I care? I'm probably going to get evicted from my apartment anyway. I won't have any place to take my old couch. The next tenant can take advantage of my snot-crusted pillows.

Just as a new round of sobs arrives, my phone rings. Startled, I look at it, hoping it's my mom or Donovan or Tamia — anybody who could offer me a little comfort.

But it's not.

It's a number from Schuylkill Valley Hospital.

Panic rises in the back of my throat. I need to answer this call, don't I? Am I going to sound like I was crying? I swallow, trying to get the mucus to go down my throat and then tap on the screen of my phone. "Hello?" I attempt to sound cheery.

"Dr. Forbes?"

"Yes, this is she." I know darn well who's on the other end of the line. I'm trying to give myself a second to gather my wits about me.

"Hey, Dr. Forbes, this is Monica Albers over at Schuylkill Valley Hospital. I'm not sure if you remember me. I —"

Darn sure I do. You work for the HR department.

"— work for the Human Resources department, and I just wanted to touch base with you about your pending job offer."

I furrow my eyebrows, using the back of my hand to wipe the dripping boogers away from the bottom of my nose. Why is she calling? I still have two more months on my residency. Maybe it's about my college records? They asked for those. Had they gotten there? Or the references? My medical school advisor, Dr. Nottingham, had said she'd send her form. Maybe she didn't?

"Yes, sure, Monica. Sorry, I'm a little congested. Allergies."

I'm not sure exactly what to say at this point. Monica's voice sounds strained. My heart skips a beat in my chest.

"No problem." There's a pause. "I, um," Monica stops talking again as if she's searching for the words. "I'm sorry, Dr. Forbes, this is an uncomfortable phone call to make."

Uncomfortable? What's she talking about? "I'm sorry, Monica. I don't understand."

Monica clears her throat like she's about to start giving a prepared speech. "Dr. Forbes, I'm sorry to say that it has come to our attention that you have recently been suspended from your residency over at Liberty Hill."

Oh.

"As much as we want to be able to offer you the open attending trauma physician position in our Emergency Department, this suspension has cast a poor light on your application."

I didn't give her a chance to finish. "Wait. What are you saying?"

There was a pause. "We're not rescinding your job offer just yet, but the head of Human Resources is a little concerned if you know what I mean."

So am I. "It's all a misunderstanding. Dr. Riley — he thought that I crashed the Emergency Department computer system —"

Monica interrupts. "I don't want to know exactly what happened. It's better that way, Dr. Forbes."

I stand up, running my hand through the back of my hair, my eyes wide. My heart is pounding so hard that I feel like I just sprinted around the block. I'm suspended, I have no income and now what, my only job offer is about to disappear into thin air?

"I'm calling to let you know that we're going to take your application from active to pending until the issue can be resolved."

I start to stammer. I'm not above begging at this point. "Monica, I *really* need this job. It's not a big deal. I promise. What can I do? Is there anything I can do to make this better?"

Monica lowers her voice. "Listen, I shouldn't be saying this, Dr. Forbes, but I like you. I think you'd be good for our hospital. The suspension is a real problem. A big one."

The thundering in my chest continues on. My heart is pounding so hard it feels like I am standing on the track during the Kentucky Derby. "I'll do anything. Please!" The idea of more than a quarter of a million dollars of debt looming over my head is making me desperate. This has been the worst week of my life. How had things turned badly so fast? A week or so before, I was happily working in the Emergency Department. Ok, maybe not happily, but I was at least at work. Now I have a huge mess on my hands.

Monica lowers her voice even more. "If you can get this resolved quickly, then I can move your application back to active and as soon as you finish your residency the position will be yours. But this has to happen fast. Really fast, so it looks like it was just a misunderstanding. I know that working in the Emergency Department can be high stress and sometimes mistakes are made."

Wait. It sounded like Monica knew more than she was letting on. And the timing was highly suspect. I had literally just been suspended. How had she heard so fast? Did she know about what happened with Mr. Palmer and Samantha Watkins? Was she referring to medical mistakes or the computer system?

Where was she getting all this information anyway?

She continued. "Hopefully you can work things out. Sometimes personalities clash. In my experience it's best to just get things sorted out as quickly as possible."

"Um, okay," I say, realizing that probably the last person that Riley wants to see at this moment is me. And yet that's exactly what Monica is asking me to do. I blink. "Monica, can I ask you a question?"

"Sure."

"How did you guys find out about my suspension so fast? It literally just happened."

In my desperation, I'm getting bold.

There was a telling pause at the other end of the line. I had the sense that there was a lot that Monica wasn't telling me. "For as many doctors as there are, Dr. Forbes, it's a small community. Word gets out. Watch what you say and do. People notice."

As we hang up, I can't help but think she's giving me a warning.

30

I didn't leave my apartment for the rest of the day. Using some of my precious, what I am sure to be dwindling funds, I order Indian food from the place down the street. I probably should have walked down to get it, but given how swollen my face is, I decide to splurge on delivery.

Crazy how quickly things change when you don't have a job.

When I go to the door to grab the food, I notice Mrs. Dixon stick her head out into the hallway. I grimace. She just can't leave me alone, can she? I fight the urge to stick my tongue out at her — it would have been so satisfying, but then again, she's the one that has my extra key. I manage a gentle glare instead.

I'm hoping it sends the message that she's being a nuisance.

She probably knows that, though.

I plop down on the couch, deciding to eat my food right out of the bag. Normally, I'd at least get a plate. If Donovan was here, I might have even set the small table in my kitchen.

But tonight, I'm alone, my chest aching in a weirdly hollow way. I feel my life tipping off the edge of a cliff.

Am I about to lose everything?

As I chew a piece of garlic naan, I sniff my armpit. I'm surprisingly smelly — back to a four, I think. I lift a single shoulder. I don't care. It's not like I'm going anywhere. From inside the bag, I dig a set of plastic silverware from the bottom of the bag, ripping open the cellophane holding it together. With a flimsy plastic fork, I dig juicy tandoori chicken out of the container, stuffing my face. There's enough food in the bag to feed three people even though I only ordered for myself. That was one of the things I liked about the little Indian place around the corner — the guy that ran it — Mr. Lawani — always gave me extra. Usually, I saved it and could make two or three meals out of it.

But not tonight.

As I chew, I change the channel on the television. Hallmark movies just weren't doing it. I end up watching some old war movie, one that I was sure my dad would have approved of. I thought for a second about calling him, but in order to get him on the phone, I'd have to go through Mom. And in order to get to Mom I'd probably have to go through Queen Julia again, who seemed like she was monitoring Mom's phone like she was part of some super-secret spy agency like the NSA. And what exactly would my dad say to me anyway? I can almost hear the disappointed silence on the other end of the phone. The undercurrent of the conversation would be palpable. He wouldn't say it out loud, but I know he would be thinking that I should have stayed in Youngstown like he told me. He never wanted me to go to Philly. Doesn't trust big cities or the people in them. He might even be secretly glad that things weren't working out so that I could come home. Not that he didn't want me to be a physician, he just liked to have his family close by.

I sit on the couch for hours then finally drag myself off to bed. I toss and turn for a while and then, as I roll over for what I think is the hundredth time, I think I see a shadow crossing in front of my window. My eyes pop open, every muscle in my body tense. I sit straight up in bed. Was there someone on the fire escape? I watch for a second, my mouth dry and my stomach aching from all of the food I'd consumed. My eyes are so swollen and bleary from crying that I can't even focus well enough to make out what I think I'm seeing.

This can't be happening, can it? Is there really someone on my fire escape?

After a minute of sitting there, I'm sure I'm just imagining things. I feel Snort jump up on the bed and curl up near my feet. Aren't animals better at perceiving these things than humans? Is that true of cats or is Snort just getting close to the window in case it happens to magically pop open?

I am losing my mind. I'm sure of it. I'm gonna end up in the Liberty Hill ED talking to myself and drooling. Shaw is gonna look at me, shake his head and send me to the psych ward on a three-day hold. Riley will strut around saying he predicted it, and only Tamia and Hudson will come and visit me.

My throat nearly closes. I have to get it together. I mumble to myself, "Go back to sleep."

Easier said than done.

No matter what I do, I keep waking up. It seems like every hour on the hour I feel like I hear something scraping or moving on the fire escape. It's driving me crazy. Am I losing my mind? I get up and slowly walk towards the window, wanting to see if anyone is out there, but afraid that if they see me, then I'll have to do something.

And I don't know what to do. I'm not sure Donovan would either.

My mind flickers. An image of Shaw, his muscles, cut jaw, and tanned skin pops into my head. I bet he would. He probably learned a thing or two when he was on his medical mission trip. He probably carries some sort of knife in his belt or knows how to turn a straw into a deadly weapon.

He seems like that kind of guy.

When I finally fall asleep, I start having dreams that are, I'm sure are fueled by my tears and the mix of strange foods I've eaten — Donovan's head plastered on Shaw's body and Shaw's head plastered on Donovan's body. I toss and turn enough that I'm sure I'm going to need to see a chiropractor.

Snort, who must have left at some time during the night, jumps up on the bed hard enough that it scares me and then walks away making his little noises. I know what he wants. Food. Had I even remembered to feed him the night before?

As I sit up on the edge of the bed, my head drooping toward my chest, I feel like I have a hangover. I have no idea what time it is, but it's still dark. Really dark. My nose is congested, my eyes feel puffy, and the back of my throat is sore like I've had heartburn all night. As I stand up, my stomach lurches. I stumble toward the bathroom, tripping over a shoe that I left out after my failed attempt to clean the closet. As I make my way toward the toilet, I stop and look in the mirror.

The damage is worse than I think.

There are black circles under my eyes, the rim underneath my nostrils bright red. My brown eyes, not nearly as big as Queen Julia's blue ones, seem small and shrunken. I notice the skin on my hands. It's still red and chapped from the allergic reaction I've been having to the hand sanitizer at work. I decide to splash a little cold water on my face.

I guess that's one bonus to being suspended. Maybe my hands won't look like I've dipped them in beet juice.

Overall, the way I look isn't much different than this kid that used to get taunted when I was in elementary school. He was constantly sniffling and blowing his nose — he had a case of constant allergies. I always felt sorry for him. After all, even in elementary school, Julia was the one that got all the attention. I had a few friends, but yep, I was the one who always got picked last for kickball.

And here I am again.

It doesn't seem like anyone is feeling sorry for me.

As I dry my face, I see a dark shadow cross in front of the bathroom door. I shriek and jump out of the way, only to realize it's Snort. "Are you kidding me?"

He looks at me like I'm losing my mind.

As I'm about to lean over to pick him up, I stop, feeling every muscle in my body tense. I look out of the bathroom toward the window. Listening, I'm sure I hear scraping from the fire escape. My heart pounds in my chest. What am I supposed to do? It's not like I'm a black belt or anything. If somebody tries to break in here, I could try some crazy Jackie Chan move from one of the films that Donovan loves so much, but coordination isn't exactly my thing.

No, if someone is actually trying to break into my apartment, I'm going to have to make a run for it. The breath catches in my throat. I visualize myself running out of the apartment for dear life, ending up at Mrs. Dixon's door, pounding on it furiously, looking over my shoulder with my eyes wide as the assailant charges at me. Mrs. Dixon never opens her door, fully absorbed in a Jerry Springer rerun. She finds my body the next morning slumped and bloody in a pile on her doorstep. Of course, she feels guilty. But she was asleep, right?

Okay, maybe I'm just being dramatic, but I'm absolutely sure I hear something outside. I tiptoe back to my bed, thinking that's the safest place for me to be. Then I remember my bed is right next to the window.

Maybe that's not the best move after all.

Sufficiently freaked out, I snatch my pillow off the bed and tiptoe out of the room, careful not to turn any lights on. If there is someone on the fire escape, then they've already seen the bathroom light go on and off. At least if I can make it out of the bedroom onto the couch, I have a straight shot for the door if someone decides to break in. Trying to be clever, I even close the bedroom door, knowing that it creaks. I tiptoe my way out to the couch and throw my body down on it, trying to fluff up the pillow underneath my head. I spend the next five or six minutes wrestling with the pillow, trying to get the lumps out of it. If anyone was watching me, they'd just shake their head. I look like I'm in the middle of a WWE fight with a very small, lumpy opponent. I make a mental note to buy some new pillows.

Then I freeze.

I've been suspended. I'm not making any money right now, so no new pillows. Headaches for the rest of my life, plus complete financial ruin are on the horizon.

The thought of not being able to buy myself a new pillow sets me off into another fit of tears, as if my eyes weren't already swollen enough. I toss and turn, too scared and freaked out by the noises on the fire escape to get up and get tissues. I text Donovan, sending an SOS, a crying emoji, and a 911, holding my breath and waiting to see if the little bubbles will pop up. As I check the time, I realize it's eight minutes after three in the morning. Donovan's a heavy sleeper. Unless he's in another time zone, he won't get this text until the morning.

I pull the thin blanket that Donovan and I use for watching movies together from the top of the couch over my body. Curled in a fetal position, I use it to wipe my nose and eyes. I try to tell myself that things will work out. My dad always says, "It'll come out in the wash."

I pull the blanket tighter, but the sound on the fire escape doesn't stop — this time it's louder, closer, like someone testing the window.

Maybe it's just the pipes, or the wind, or my nerves finally breaking — but deep down I know I'm not imagining this.

31

W ell, good news. I survived.

I wake up as the sunshine streams through the windows in my apartment, still on the couch. It takes a second to get my eyes to open. They feel glued shut by a collection of salty crud in the corners of my eyes. I guess I should be happy I can see at all. Pressing on my eyelids using my fingertips, they feel squishy.

I'm gonna need a lot of ice.

As my vision clears, I see the bedroom door. It's still closed. Good news. My attacker didn't make it through my formidable defense. I sit up on the edge of the couch and run my fingers through my hair. Not only is it greasy, but I can feel something caked in it. As I tug it a few strands I realize snot from my crying fit the night before is now crusted my hair. I can't help but laugh out loud. Yes, I sound a little crazy, but I have this visual of showing up for Queen Julia's wedding looking just like I do now.

That would be a sight. Queen Julia might actually pass out at the horror.

I decide the next logical thing to do would be to take a shower. I mean, no one can make reasonable decisions about their future with boogers caked in their hair, right? I go to the bedroom door, hoping that no one is lurking inside. I go to the window and look out, making sure no one is sitting there waiting for me. It's empty. I'm about to turn away, when my eye catches something.

There are some marks on the black paint.

I stand and stare for a full minute. My heart starts to pound in my chest like thunder. I narrow my eyes, wondering if through their swollen state I'm just not focusing well. As I study them a bit more, I realize I'm not seeing things.

There are marks on the fire escape.

First, I think they are from Snort's escape, but they are long, like something has been dragged across the black painted metal. The marks aren't down to the metal itself, just along the surface.

Part of me wants to open the window and investigate, but there's another part of me that just wants to pretend they aren't there.

I go with the latter, telling myself it's entirely possible someone from a floor above me has been using the fire escape.

It's nothing, I'm sure.

Except, I'm not so sure...

I realize that unless I'm going to open the window and go out and look, there's very little I can do. I don't want to chance opening it, for fear that Snort will escape again. With my luck, I'll somehow get locked out, then have to go down the fire escape and beg Mrs. Dixon for the extra key to my apartment again.

I need to think. Maybe a shower will clear my mind.

Twenty minutes later, after scrubbing my body from head to toe, washing my hair twice to get the grease and snot out of it, I emerge from the bathroom feeling halfway normal.

Let me tell you, halfway is generous.

I go to the kitchen, popping two Advil then deciding to add a third to hopefully deal with the pounding headache I have. I grab a bag of peas from the freezer and a bottle of water. I plop down on the couch and apply the cold peas to my eyes, hoping that it will reduce the swelling enough that I'll be able to see better. While I was in the shower, I went through my options in terms of what to do about my suspension. Honestly, they're pretty limited. I can do nothing or call Riley. I remember what Monica said the day before. My attending position is hanging in the balance.

Call Riley it is.

Given how bad things are, I'm not above begging. I mean, begging isn't all that bad, is it?

I pick up my phone to call him and then realize I better have a game plan — some sort of a presentation. If Donovan was here, he'd know exactly what to say. Then again, he's in sales. He sells enormous, expensive software systems to high-powered people and governments all over the world. He knows how to talk to people.

I'm not persuasive like he is. After all, what do I have, just my catchphrases? Not sure that approaching Riley with "What brings you in today?" is gonna do the trick.

I pick up my phone and check it. Still nothing from Donovan. I frown. I open up my text app. Was I just imagining that I sent him an SOS text last night? I mean, how embarrassing. My stomach drops when I see it. Yes, I even included the loudly crying face emoji.

Yes, I want to get back with Donovan, but I don't want to appear desperate.

But the truth is, I am.

I'm desperate for everything to go back to the way it was — my crazy hectic schedule at Liberty Hill, watching Tamia's hand signals to tell me what's coming next and help me deal with the likes of Riley, the exhaustion, the night shifts, all of it. Heck, I'll even deal with Queen Julia and all of her Brazilian wax trauma if it meant that things could go back to the way they were.

Just the thought of it makes me sniffle again. I start repeating in my head, *I will not cry, I will not cry, I will not cry.*

It helps. A little.

What I need is a plan. I need a plan to get back to work and to figure out how and why all of this is happening. A chill runs down the back of my spine. I can't help but think that there's more here than I'm seeing. Too much of this has happened all at once. It's almost like someone engineered it. My stomach clenches.

Did they?

I get up and start to pace. But why? Why come after me? I'm nobody. I'm just a resident. Yeah, I'm the Chief Resident — or I was — but it's not like it means anything. I think about Jamir. He wouldn't set me up, would he? I shake my head. That's not like Jamir. Yeah, I know he wanted to be Chief Resident, but he's not the kind that would actually do anything. Could it be someone who doesn't like that I'm with Donovan? It's not like he's super-hot or anything. I mean, Donovan's okay, but he doesn't look like Shaw.

Shaw.

Everything fell apart when he arrived.

But what could he have against me?

I shake my head. No. That can't make sense. That's all just a coincidence. I'm sure of it. He hasn't even been in Philly that long — maybe a month or so? That's definitely not enough time to hate someone enough to destroy their life.

I stop, holding my hands up in the air like stop signs. I need to quit this ridiculous analysis. It's just a coincidence. All of it. I need to just focus on what I can do, which is get back on track with work.

More specifically, with Riley. He holds the key to my future in his hands.

I need a plan. I walk into the kitchen, grabbing a pen and a piece of paper. Maybe if I write myself a little script it'll help. I scrawl out a few lines and scratch them out. I mean, how do you gracefully beg for your job back? After a few minutes of brainstorming, I realize there's only one thing to do.

Grovel.

If groveling means getting me out of three hundred thousand dollars in debt and getting me back on the road to being a physician, then so be it.

Satisfied with my new, morally degrading plan, I run into the bathroom and gargle with some mouthwash of Donovan's that I think might have expired, but it doesn't matter. As I do, I realize that Riley can't smell my breath, but maybe the alcohol, which is burning the back of my throat, will help clear some of the residual hysterical mucus from my vocal cords.

Then I remember that mouthwash doesn't actually reach the vocal cords. That's good. I'm thinking like a physician again.

I dial Riley's number, all prepared to leave him a message. I'm going to say something witty like, "Well, *Dr.* Riley, I'm sure you're with a patient," making sure to use "Dr. Riley" liberally, or even better, using my best professional tone, "Dr. Riley, this is Dr. McKenna Forbes. Please call me at your earliest convenience."

But, of course, that didn't work.

He picks up.

"Forbes."

For some reason, Riley sounds out of breath. I mean, it doesn't surprise me. That extra thirty, actually, probably closer to forty pounds that Riley is carrying is probably putting strain on his heart.

My mind flickers. I wonder what his angiogram would look like?

I stop myself, realizing he's waiting for me to answer. "Dr. Riley," I stammer. "I was just going to leave you a message —"

"Well, you got me. What do you want?"

Rude. Exactly what I was expecting unfortunately. "I was wondering if we could talk about my residency."

"There's nothing to talk about," he huffs. "You're suspended."

This is my opportunity to sell him. I try to think about what Donovan would say. Nothing is coming up, so I go for a distraction to buy myself some time. "You sound out of breath. Are you all right?"

There's a pause. My question seems to have gotten his attention. "I've got a waiting room filled with patients and a bus accident on the way in. Multiple casualties and my Chief Resident is nowhere to be found."

I pause, pressing my lips together. Now whose fault is that? "I'm sorry, sir, I can imagine that's putting some strain on the department."

"You don't say." His voice sounds sarcastic, the same way it did when I was a first-year and handed him a tube for a catheter instead of a tube for an intubation in the middle of a code. The rest of the staff didn't let me live that down for weeks. Everywhere I went, I found that catheter tube — in my locker, in the pocket of my lab coat, even in my bag.

Haven't really liked inserting catheters ever since then.

"I could come in and give you a hand," I say gently. After all, I have only been suspended for a day.

There's silence then a grunt. "All right. If I wasn't so buried with administrative work and demands from the board, then I'd make you suffer a little longer, Forbes. You can come back. But not until tomorrow. You have clinic duty until further notice. I'll have Tamia put you back on the schedule."

Inwardly I groan, but I adopt the tone of Queen Julia

cheering at one of our high school football games. "Great! I'll be in first thing tomorrow. Thank you, Dr. Riley!"

He hangs up without saying anything. I offer a silent prayer of thanks. I think I read somewhere that faith grows during tough times.

If faith really does grow in trials, then by the end of this, I'll either be a saint — or I won't survive long enough to find out.

32

The next day can't come soon enough. I spend the rest of the day doing all the things that I would normally do on my day off — buying groceries, cleaning, and doing laundry, which is additionally challenging because of my failed closet organizational project. I can't seem to figure out what's clean and what's not, so I end up washing all of my clothes and then piling them back into the closet. I check my phone obsessively to see if Donovan has responded after my embarrassing text. I even look up ways to retrieve a text after it has been sent, but there's no point. Too much time has gone by. I'm just gonna have to suck it up and pretend I'm not totally desperate. I text Marshall, but don't hear anything back. I have a paranoid moment that my phone isn't working. Is that why Donovan and Marshall aren't getting back to me? Then I get an updated schedule for the wedding texted to me from Queen Julia and realize that, unfortunately, all is well tech-wise.

I spend a little more time on the computer obsessing over how Riley and Shaw know each other, then clean out my work bag, emptying it of wrappers, half-used deodorant, and a tampon wrapper. As I do, I decide that it's a fresh start tomorrow. Feeling energized by the chance Dr. Riley has given me, I even lay out my clothes for the morning, just like I did on my very first day of residency.

You never know, this might end up being something great. Maybe this is my chance to start a redemption cycle.

With any luck, I'll be back in the ED trauma area in a day or two, Julia will cool off and Donovan will come back, bringing me flowers and wine, telling me he misses me and how sorry he is he never responded to my text.

Yeah, I might be thinking a little too positively, but you never know.

Completely exhausted after all the drama with Riley, Donovan, and the fire escape, I sleep better than I did the night before. I wake up once sure that there's another shadow on the fire escape, but I turn over on my lumpy pillow — two new ones are on the way from Amazon now that my job has gotten restored — and ignore the threat. Whatever it is, I don't care anymore. I manage to get a decent night's sleep. I even wake up early, jump in the shower and take the time to dry my hair neatly and put it into a ponytail before I go to work, dabbing a little makeup on. The circles under my eyes still look like vast caverns, but they look markedly better with a little mascara and concealer.

When I get to Liberty Hill, I get changed into my scrubs and go out onto the floor. I know that Riley wants me in the clinic, but at least I can say hi to everyone, right?

But the reception isn't exactly as warm as I would have hoped.

Tamia narrows her eyes at me. "You're supposed to be in snot and vomit, aren't you?"

That's the name we call the clinic.

I blink. Wow. I forgot how fast news travels in the ED. "Not even a welcome back?" The last time I saw her, she was so friendly. What gives?

"Maybe you should go say hi to *Jamir* first."

Clearly, Tamia still isn't sure that nothing happened between me and Jamir. She's a slow-burn kind of person — it takes her a while to react to things. And now she's reacting. Could the timing be any worse? The last thing I need is to be on the outs with Tamia.

"Jamir?" I stammer. "No, I don't need to say hello to him." I realize as the words come out of my mouth, it doesn't sound the way I intended. It sounds like he and I talk all the time, like maybe he was hanging out at my apartment last night or something.

Which he wasn't.

"I mean," I try to correct the damage as I see her narrow her eyes. "I just saw him a couple of days ago when I was here. I need to get to work. I don't have time to socialize. I need to text Donovan before my shift starts." It's a total lie. Donovan hasn't responded to me at all, but Tamia doesn't need to know that. She just needs to be clear that I don't have designs on Jamir. And I don't. I promise.

Tamia's lips thin. I've talked myself out of a hole, but just barely.

Worried that things are going to get even worse the longer I stay, I turn on my heel, giving Hudson a wave from across the E D. He, unlike Tamia, gives me a grin. I walk quickly towards the clinic.

The clinic at Liberty Hill is attached to the main trauma area. It's the place where we funnel people who have less serious illnesses — people who would normally be seen by their primary care doctor or those that might seek out an urgent care. The idea behind it is that we can move people in and out of there faster or slower depending on the load in the Emergency Department, triaging the most critical cases so we can keep the bays open. But most people don't know that. If we're busy in the trauma area, then they might have to wait longer as we move staff over to help with more catastrophic injuries. But that said, the clinic does try to get people in and out as quickly as possible.

I started in snot and vomit when I was a first-year resident. Riley likes to throw people in there while they get their bearings. It makes sense, I suppose.

Why? Because that's pretty much all you see. There's an occasional broken bone or rash, but for the most part it's a lot of sinus infections, bronchitis, influenza, gastrointestinal viruses — all the delightful symptoms that involve tons of bodily fluids.

Honestly, it's boring work.

As I get into the clinic, I drop my bag behind the nurses' station. It's a miniature version of the one that we have in the trauma area with only two computer terminals. There's a nurse sitting behind one of them, a woman I don't know well — her name is Rebecca. She's been there for years. She looks up at me and then narrows her eyes.

Like I said, news travels fast.

I check in with the charge nurse. She's no Tamia, but she's nice enough. Her name is Margaret. She has silvery gray hair that she wears in a knot behind the back of her neck, a pair of glasses always on the top of her head. She's somewhat of a legend at Liberty Hill. Spends a lot of time breaking in residents. While I know her, I haven't spent a lot of time with her. Unlike a lot of the other residents who spent almost their entire first year with Margaret, I got moved over to the trauma bays after about a month of my residency. That's how I know Tamia so much better.

Margaret nods slowly. "Well, if it isn't our little tech wizard. When I didn't see you here yesterday, I was absolutely sure that you had accepted a programming position with Microsoft."

I shake my head. "Very funny."

I glance down at Rebecca, who seems to be staring at the

computer longer than she should. "I guess the computer system still isn't working that well?"

As the words come out of my mouth, I already feel guilty. I don't know why no one believes me. I didn't do what they said I did. I'm not that smart, and no one is that unlucky.

It has to be something else.

"No," Margaret shakes her head definitively. "But that's okay. We'll manage. It's just running slow, that's all."

At least that was good news. I glance out into the waiting room. Per usual, there's a lineup of fairly miserable-looking people waiting. When I look back at Margaret, she's staring at me. "You ready to get started? Dr. Malowski is already in with a patient."

"Absolutely." As the words come out of my mouth, I'm never been so sure of anything in my life. I have to prove to Riley that it was a good decision to bring me back. I grab a tablet from the nurses' station and look over my shoulder just in time to see Shaw staring at me from the doorway between the trauma unit and the clinic. He stares a little longer than I would have guessed he would, his look a mix of surprise and something I can't place but makes me instantly uncomfortable. It's not the kind of stare that's like, "Wow! Forbes is back!"

No, it's something else, but I can't place it.

He moves off before I have a chance to stop and wave. Margaret glances at me, looks at the doorway where Shaw had been standing, then back at me. "Everything okay?"

I nod, slowly, feeling my stomach tighten into a knot. Is it? I look up at her. "Great. I'm heading to room one."

After an hour, I'd cleared rooms one, five, three and almost seven. Seven needed to go for an X-ray which was something that the clinic didn't handle in-house. Patients in the clinic had to go upstairs to get their films done. I stop back at the nurses' station, setting my tablet down. Margaret gave me an appreciative nod. "You're on a roll this morning, Dr. Forbes. You got those cleared out pretty fast."

It's such a good feeling.

I suck in a deep breath, straightening, trying hard not to giggle. "Yeah, they weren't too complicated though. You know, just the normal clinic stuff."

In fact, it had been two sinus infections and a double ear infection. It took me longer to hear their symptoms than to do the diagnosis. They all required the same prescription for antibiotics. Instead of trying to copy and paste them — I had learned the hard way that could land me in trouble — I actually recreated all of the prescriptions in each file.

Safety first.

A couple more hours go by. I've now dealt with a dislocated finger, a sprained ankle, a baby that looks like he has Rotavirus, and stitched up a little girl who went head-first into the hearth of her family's fireplace, cutting her head open.

Margaret looks at me. "Have you grabbed your lunch yet?"

Lunch? "Um, no." Why is she asking me about food? I'm used to grabbing whatever I can scavenge or begging for a cafeteria run. What's going on here?

She scans the waiting room. It's quiet. "All right. Why don't you head out? Take half an hour and get some food in you. We still have the rest of the afternoon to crank through."

Wow.

I'd forgotten that in the clinic, the docs actually get a lunch break. Usually, the trauma room at Liberty Hill is too busy for us to eat while we are on our shifts.

Maybe there was an upside to being back in the clinic.

It was something to consider.

On my way down to the cafeteria, I stop outside of the clinic door and take a picture of myself with the clinic logo in the background with a smile on my face. Not an enormous smile, but a grateful one, or at least that's what I was going for. I quickly text it over to Monica Albers at Schuylkill Valley Hospital. "I'm back at work!"

Her response comes a second later. She sends a thumbs up. A wave of relief turns to anxiety. What does the thumbs up mean? Do I still have my job at Schuylkill Valley?

I decide that's a problem for another day.

33

A half hour for a lunch seemed like an incredible luxury after working in the trauma unit for so long. I can count the times I've gotten to sit down for lunch and actually eat a meal in the last year on one hand.

To be more accurate, probably two fingers.

I make my way down to the cafeteria, walking at a brisk pace, but not the normal breakneck pace that I usually have to go in order to quickly grab a Monster Energy drink and then head back to work.

I actually get to sit this time.

I take my time choosing my lunch. After all, I'm a *physician* in the hospital. I should set a good example, right? I straighten my shoulders a little bit and pick out a salad with grilled chicken, and a bottle of water. I look at the chips, protein bars, candy, and lift my nose just like Snort does when he's annoyed with me. Rejecting the processed snacks, I grab an apple and head to the checkout.

As I wait, I realize maybe one day of suspension was good for me. I mean, the closet makeover was a complete failure, but maybe finishing up my residency in the clinic isn't so bad. I mean sure, I'll miss out on all the really cool calls, getting a chance to perfect my techniques, but then again, if it means I get to sit down for lunch every day for the next two months.

That can't be bad, right?

As I go to the checkout, I see a couple of people moving slowly toward the cashiers. Feeling crafty, I angle for the second checkout line. I flash my badge, scan my items, and quickly sit down at a table. A nervous flutter runs through my stomach. What am I actually supposed to do other than eat? I'm so used to eating on the run that I'm not even sure what it looks like to sit down and take my time enjoying a meal.

Enjoying might be a little bit of a stretch. I'm eating at the hospital cafeteria after all.

I take a bite of the salad after pouring a generous amount of ranch dressing on it. Everything tastes better with ranch. I stab a bite that's the size of four normal bites, stuff it in my mouth and try not to choke.

Like I said, it's been a while since I've been able to sit and eat while I'm at work.

The next few bites go much better. I slow down and make them a more reasonable size. It's less of an opportunity for anyone to have to practice the Heimlich maneuver on me, though if you're going to choke, I can promise you, the best place to do it is in a hospital cafeteria.

While I'm sitting, I pull up my phone. It seems like the only reasonable thing to do. There are quite a few people sitting by themselves, but I don't know any of them and I'm not the kind of person that's going to go and plop down and say, "Hey! I'm Mac. Who are you?"

No.

I decide while I'm sitting there that I need to do something to entertain myself. I restart my Internet search about Shaw and Riley again. Now that I know that Shaw and Riley went to medical school together, things make a little more sense. But I feel like there's still something I'm missing. The way that Shaw was staring at me that morning has rattled me. I shrug it off for a second. Maybe Riley put him up to it. Maybe he didn't know I was coming back. Maybe they're just hazing me a little bit on my way out the door. Medical training is nothing if not a mind game. Tamia taught me that. Honestly, I had wished I knew that when I started medical school.

And I'm just having a little fun. Just trying to entertain myself.

I scan the pictures again, looking at Shaw and Riley all buddy-buddy when they were in school. Then I find a few more pictures, another crowd of guys hanging around them. Another guy appears in the picture. He's built like Shaw — thick with wide shoulders and skin the same color as Tamia's. Actually, they look so similar that I kind of wonder if it's Tamia's brother, but there are no names underneath the pictures that I found. I take another bite of my salad and look up at the ceiling. Does Tamia even have a brother? It occurs to me that I don't know. We're usually so busy just dealing with whatever is in front of us that it's hard to know much more about anyone else unless you're out with them after work.

Given how exhausted all of us are at the end of a shift, that happens only rarely.

To be fair, Tamia doesn't know that much about my family. She knows about Queen Julia but that's about it. Like I said, it's not normal for us to talk about our families. It's kind of a practical thing. There's not really time to comment on your mom's dry Sunday roast when you're busy doing chest compressions because someone's in the middle of a major coronary event.

As I finish my lunch, I turn off my phone and drop off my tray. My hands empty, I pull out my phone again and stare at the screen as I head through the doorway back toward an afternoon of fun in snot and vomit. I sigh, wishing that Donovan would text me back. I check his location. It finally pops up. Looks like he's at the office here in Philly.

My spirits brighten. He's letting me see where he is. I guess that's a slight improvement.

I'm just weighing whether I should text him again or not when I run smack dab into someone. I look up, realizing I feel like I hit a brick wall.

It's Shaw.

He has a half-amused, half-irritated look on his face.

"Oops," I mumble.

"Dr. Forbes. Good to see you back at work."

"Thanks," I say, trying to sound cheerful. Our last couple of encounters have been awkward. First at my apartment, then seeing him stare at me a couple of times. I wait for him to move out of the way so I can get back to work. He doesn't. "How are you doing?"

"Okay."

His expression softens. "Sorry about what happened the other night with your boyfriend. Those kinds of things can put a real strain on a relationship."

I furrow my eyebrows. What is he saying? "We're fine. No big deal." I lie.

"Good," Shaw says slowly as if he knows the truth. "I'm glad to hear that my visit didn't cause you guys to break up or anything."

I look at him, my mouth hanging down. Something about what he's saying is really strange. I shake my head. "Donovan and I trust each other. He travels a lot, so he has to trust me. And I'm around people all day long. It's not like I'm home writing novels or something."

Shaw nods slowly, his eyes searching my face as if he's looking right through me. "Right. Well, nice to see you, Dr. Forbes."

As I walk back to snot and vomit, I glance over my shoulder

at Shaw. He's disappeared into the cafeteria, probably to get some sort of a he-man lunch that involves a lot of raw meat. For a second, I imagine him going to the hot food counter and requesting something like six turkey legs to eat for lunch. He seems like the kind of guy that would do that and then go into the break room and bust out a hundred push-ups before he goes to his next patient. I keep walking. I need to focus on work. I can't get swept up with Shaw.

Focus, Mac.

The second I get back to the clinic, Margaret points at me frantically, jabbing a finger in the air. "Riley needs you in trauma."

Riley. Needs. Me.

Music to my ears.

Tamia, although she's not completely happy to see me, does look slightly relieved when I run in, quickly shrugging out of my lab coat and draping it on one of the chairs. She points and waves, then signals five. It's the code for hurry up and get to bay five."

Happy to oblige.

By the time I run into the room, spray some of the stinging hand sanitizer on my hands, rub it in and pull on a pair of gloves, the patient on the bed is in full arrest. Hudson is leaning over the patient, a middle-aged man with a belly that looks very similar to Riley's, pumping up and down on his chest. Beads of sweat are dripping off of his face. My adrenaline kicks in immediately. Riley's standing near the foot of the bed, watching the monitors. Jasmine is standing at the head of the bed, rhythmically squeezing a BVM, bag-ventilator-mask, to force air into the man's lungs. "Where do you need me?"

Riley looks over his shoulder and gives me a nod. "Forbes. Glad you joined us. We need to intubate this guy. Do it."

You don't have to ask me twice.

I stride over to the top of the bed and drop the head so it's lower than horizontal. Jasmine hands me the laryngoscope. I glance up at her. "Meds are in?" She nods. I figured as much. If Riley was ready for me to do the vent as soon as I walk in, he was probably just about to do it himself. I insert the scope, get a visual of the man's vocal cords and push, watching the scope descend into the man's trachea.

"Tube," I say matter of factly.

Jasmine hands me an endotracheal tube. I feed it down into his throat through the hole in the scope then quickly pull the stylet out. I hold out my hand out for the bag. I attach it quickly and Jasmine takes over while I whip the stethoscope off the back of my neck, stick the buds into my ears and lay the bell on the man's chest. I replace it on the back of my neck and look up at Dr. Riley. "Good breath sounds bilaterally."

Hudson feels the man's wrist. "We've got a pulse."

Riley looks over his shoulder as he walks out of the room. "Good work, Forbes. You can stay here."

I fight the urge to pump my fist and jump up and down. Instead, I go for the laid-back response. "Okay, thanks, Dr. Riley."

I'm back.

34

T hings start to come together a little bit quicker than I anticipated. I knew Riley was going to put me back on traumas. It was only a matter of time. If anyone knows how short staffed the trauma wing is, I do.

I'm the Chief Resident, after all.

Later on that afternoon, I'm standing at the nurses' station, trying to thaw the tension between me and Tamia, when a man wearing a suit walks in. He's carrying a briefcase and has short dark hair and ebony skin. He comes directly to the nurses' station as if he's on a mission.

"I'm Jackson Soto. I'm with Pharmacol Medical Devices. I was wondering if I could talk to the head of your department? I heard that you're interested in some of our newest blood coagulation dressings."

Tamia starts to respond. Our normal policy is to tell them to make an appointment with Dr. Riley, but I hold my hand up. "Hi Jackson, I'm Dr. Forbes."

He looks confused. "I was hoping to get to talk to the chief of the department."

I know how Dr. Riley is. Unless he actually invited a

medical device salesperson to come to Liberty Hill, he wasn't going to have any use for them. I can take care of it, you know, get something off of his plate and build a relationship with a device company rep in the meantime. Maybe get some information and pass it along? I know it's a little abnormal, but maybe it's a way to win a few points? "You know, I think Dr. Riley is involved in some administrative meetings this afternoon. How about if you walk me through what you guys have, and I'll pass things on. I'm the Chief Resident here."

I'd seen Dr. Riley disappear a little while earlier, mumbling something under his breath about too many meetings. Maybe he'd appreciate it if I took the initiative to handle this for him.

Then again, maybe not, but it was worth the shot.

Truth be told, the meetings are probably the reason that he wants me to stay in the first place. By now, he's probably back up in his office plotting his next strategic move to climb the Liberty Hill ladder with Cynthia and watching more reruns on his computer. "Why don't we head over there." I point to one of the small conference rooms we keep for talking to patients and their families. "Would you like some coffee?"

Hospitality is a gift, right?

Jackson nods. Even his dark skin looks pale. "Yeah. It's been that kind of day. I'd love to have a cup of coffee. Liberty Hill's finest, right?"

That might be stretching things.

"How do you take it?"

"One sugar, two creamers."

I go into the break room, pour him a cup — luckily someone has been nice enough to make a fresh pot — add the sugar and quickly pull the really good creamer that we have out of the refrigerator. Before dumping it in, I check the label. Still good. Hasn't expired yet. Popping a cap on the coffee so that I don't accidentally spill it, I march straight across the width of the ED and meet Jackson in the conference room. He's already made himself at home, sitting in one of the upholstered chairs, opening his briefcase and laying out a replica of a human arm plus a few different prepackaged bandages. I hand him the coffee. "Here you go," I say, sliding the coffee across the table and sitting across from him.

"Thanks." He stops for a second, pulls the lid off of the coffee and takes a sip, then another. "That's good. You weren't lying. You guys do have good coffee."

I look at Jackson for a second. He looks like he was just about to say something when his eyes open wide. His hand goes to his throat. I can hear him wheeze, as if the breath won't get to his lungs. I stand up, nearly knocking the chair over, staring at him. "Are you okay?"

He shakes his head no. He holds his wrist out. There's a bracelet on it. I flip it over. He's allergic to nuts. Something has given him a horrible reaction. I hear him try to suck in a breath, his face paling. His body topples to the floor with a thud.

I run to the door. "I need some help in here! Bring me an EpiPen!"

A second later, Tamia appears at the door, seeing the man lying on the ground, with me hovering over him. "He's got a peanut allergy." She hands me the EpiPen. I pull the cap off, not taking the time to put gloves on or cut his pants. I jam the cylinder against his leg and push the stopper. Nothing happens.

"It's not working! I need EpiPen, now."

As I look at Jackson, I can see his lips and tongue have already swollen nearly double their normal size. We have just seconds before his throat completely closes.

Tamia disappears. She comes back a second later, "Here!" She says, thrusts a bottle of epinephrine and a syringe at me.

While I'm drawing down the epinephrine, my hands are shaking. I look up at her. "Get Shaw. I've never seen an allergic reaction as bad as this one before."

She nods, without saying anything. I pull out a half a CC of epinephrine from the bottle and jam it through Jackson's pants into his quad muscle. He's still out cold. Shaw appears at the door a second later, his face stony. "What happened?"

From where he's standing, I know that Shaw can't see Jackson's face. He's fallen off his chair, so his head is facing the door. Shaw stares at me, his look accusing. "What did you do?"

"I tried the EpePen. It failed. Just injected half a CCs of epinephrine but it's not working."

Tamia appears at the door a second later and kneels down in front of the man, applying a blue BVM to the man's face and starts blowing air into his lungs. "I'm not sure anything is getting through. The epi's not working."

I see a flicker of concern on Shaw's face. "How much did you give him?"

"Half."

He shakes his head. "For a guy this size, you probably have to do at least one or one and a half."

Epinephrine is a serious drug. I wince. "More than one? Isn't that going to cause arrhythmia?" I know that too much epinephrine, which is basically the same as speed, can stimulate the heart so much that it can force it out of rhythm. The last thing I want to do is to force his heart out of rhythm.

But Shaw is the attending.

I draw down another half of epinephrine and inject it into the man's leg. I stand up, darting out of the room. Shaw yells behind me. "Where are you going, Forbes?"

"To get the crash cart!"

As I run down the hallway I skid to a stop, sending a quick text and then grabbing the crash cart and coming right back. I run down the hallway pushing it as fast as I can without running into anyone or risking the expensive equipment on board, the wheels rattling.

When I get back, Tamia still has the bag over Jackson's face. Shaw is still standing over the man watching him. All of a sudden, I see Jackson's foot move. That's good news. Maybe we won't need the crash cart after all. I leave it in the hallway and stand in the doorway, letting Shaw take the lead. The last thing I want to do is to get suspended again. Shaw moves from Jackson's feet to his waist, taking a knee on the ground. All of a sudden, I see his face twist as if he's seeing something he never expected. Just then, Jackson wakes up. His eyes open and he pushes the mask off his face. I step close to them, watching the interaction. Jackson starts to sit up, staring at Shaw. "Shaw? Is that you?"

Shaw's head snaps back. His lips part for a second then he clamps his mouth closed. "Yes, my name is Dr. Shaw. You had an allergic reaction."

"Darn it, Shaw. I know." Jackson shakes his head from side to side and licks his lips. "How are you here?"

Shaw tries to stand up, but I can see the man is fixated on him. He grabs Shaw's arm. "Seriously, *how* are you here?"

Shaw shakes his head. I can see him glancing at me and Tamia. I feel someone behind me. It's Riley, who has now taken up the entire doorway. I step out of the way but stay in the room. "What do you mean? I work here. I'm an attending. Maybe you should lie down. I think you are confused."

Jackson scowls. "Man, why are you acting like this? We served together. I thought you were still locked up."

My eyes become bigger and buggier than Dr. Riley's.

Shaw tries to move away, but Jackson still has a grip on his arm. Shaw shakes his head like a dog trying to dry itself. "No, I'm sorry, you're mistaken. You must be thinking of my brother, Ryan. I'm Jonathan."

By now the man is sitting straight up looking at Shaw. I hear a commotion in the hallway. Jackson grabs for Shaw's sleeve and pushes it back. There's a long scar that runs down Shaw's forearm that I'd never noticed before, probably because he always wore long sleeves. Now I know why.

Shaw had something to hide.

Jackson starts to laugh. "Yeah, I knew you were pulling my leg, Ryan. We were together when you got that scar. Remember when we were in Kandahar? That was some crazy stuff. But that's the night you got yourself in trouble."

Doctor Riley frowns. "Trouble? What are we talking about?"

Shaw stands straight up, his face paling. "Nothing, Dr. Riley. I think that this gentleman has me confused for someone else. Probably just that extra epinephrine we had to give him to revive him."

Jackson scrambled to his feet and sat in the chair again. "No, I don't have you confused, Ryan. You in trouble or something?" His eyes widen. "You aren't supposed to be here?"

Just then, I see a man put a hand on Riley's shoulder and move him out of the doorway of the conference room, blocking Shaw's escape. He's wearing a green pullover and green fatigue pants. Behind him are two enormous men in full fatigues, both of them with pistols on their hips. I stand back, plastering myself against the wall, watching the interaction. Tamia joins me, then grabs my hand, our fingers interlaced. My heart is pounding in my chest. Something is going on. Something terrible. The man who stands in the doorway has a name tag that reads Padilla. He has a square jaw that's even sharper than Shaw's and by the looks of him, he does the same workout Shaw does. He stares at Shaw. "You thought you could hide for from us forever, huh, Sergeant?" Padilla glances over his shoulder. "Take him into custody."

Shaw tries to bolt for the door, but Padilla takes a step toward Shaw, hooking his arm into his grip, and then the two men in fatigues take over. They quickly wrestle Shaw up against the wall, handcuffing him. As they turn him around, he's irate, fighting them with everything he has, his body thrashing every single direction, the veins in his neck sticking out. He starts in on the man in the doorway. "How did you find me?"

"We've been watching you, Shaw. Just waiting for the right time to come and get you."

As they turned him toward the hallway, he looks at me, his eyes filled with fury. "This is because of you! It's all your fault!"

I shake my head, my stomach in a tiny knot. I feel Tamia step between me and Shaw, protecting me. My body starts to shake.

Me? What did I do?

35

The next few minutes were a blur. Tamia, Riley, Jackson, and I slipped out of the room as Padilla and his guys were dealing with Shaw.

And let me tell you, they have a problem on their hands.

Shaw, wrestling and fighting every inch of the way out of the hospital is finally dragged outside by the two men who I quickly learn are military police. We got Jackson into a wheelchair and got him situated in one of the bays, where we could continue to monitor him for any side effects of the allergic reaction. I stand in the hallway for a second, staring at the doorway where Shaw had been taken. Riley stops and looks at me, putting a hand on my shoulder. "Are you okay, Mac?"

Mac.

It's the first time in three years he's used my first name.

I blink. Am I? "I think so, Dr. Riley."

"If you need to take a little break, that's okay. If not, maybe you can go check on the patient with the allergic reaction. Jackson. I need to figure out what exactly just happened with Dr. Shaw. The ED is yours."

Was Riley actually being nice to me? Did he just turn over the ED to me? "Of course, Dr. Riley."

I start down the hallway. Turning into Jackson's room, I see he's already hooked up to the EKG, and a blood pressure cuff. Tamia had taken over Jackson's care personally. The two of them were so similar looking they could have been brother and sister. I checked the man's vitals, and had Tamia start an IV and hang a bag of saline. Looking at the monitor, he doesn't seem any worse for wear. "Jackson, I'm sorry about all of that. And I'm sorry about your allergic reaction. I'm really glad that you wear that bracelet and that you were here when it happened."

He shakes his head. "This happens to me every now and again. The creamer must have been processed on the same machines they use to process nuts. Why they do that, I have no idea. It doesn't take too much to throw me into a full-blown fit."

A "fit" is not exactly what I would call anaphylactic shock, but if that's what he wants to call it, that's fine with me.

I nod at him. "I'm gonna double check your care with Dr. Riley, but Tamia's gonna get you started on some fluids and we're going to monitor your blood pressure and your heart for a couple hours here in the ED because we loaded you up pretty good with epinephrine. Just want to make sure you don't have any long-lasting effects from the allergic reaction. Sound okay?"

He nods. "I've been through this before." He looks towards the doorway where I can still hear Shaw shouting from the ambulance bay. I won't repeat what he's saying but let me just offer that I've never quite heard that amount of swearing out of anyone before.

Jackson shakes his head. "Well, maybe not exactly this."

I stand back for a second. "I have to ask you, what was that all about?"

Jackson's expression is suddenly sad and far away. "I don't know. I haven't seen Shaw in years. He and I served in

Kandahar together. We were in the Green Berets together. He was our chief medic. We went through some crazy stuff. But then something happened to him. His brother died and then he went AWOL, and nobody was ever able to find him again. After that, there were some nasty rumors."

"Nasty rumors?" I ask, suddenly curious. "About what?"

Jackson sighs. "Well, let's just say that the Army doesn't take kindly to people stealing their technology and selling it on the black market. Last I heard, Shaw was being held at a military prison. Then I heard he escaped."

"Escaped?" A shiver ran down my spine.

Jackson nodded. "That's one bad dude. He was great to be in the military with. Tons of skills, no conscience." Jackson paused, his expression grave. "That's someone you want on your side. Now that he's out of the military, he's as dangerous as they get."

36

I 'm not surprised by what Jackson said.

I didn't say anything, but I'd figured it out already.

Before I leave for the day, I head upstairs and check on Jackson Soto one more time. We decided to send him upstairs overnight as a precaution after all. He's resting comfortably. I've called in a favor from the head of our immunology department to do a full workup on him. There are some new therapies that could retrain his system to not react. He'll be fine.

I change into my street clothes and grab my bag. As I head out of the hospital at the end of my shift, I give Tamia a hug. Things are just fine between us. I whisper to her, "I'm gonna see Donovan tonight." I'm on my way to pick up celebratory takeout.

She pushes away from me, holding on to the outside of both of my arms, a big grin on her face. "That's great, Mac. I hope you're able to relax a little bit. Today was over at the top."

She's right. All in all, it's been a crazy day.

But a really good one.

I'm about to respond when I see Tamia look at someone or

something behind me. Still a little paranoid given what's been happening, I glance over my shoulder, then start to giggle. Jamir is waiting for her at the nurses' station. "Looks like you might have a nice night too."

She raises her eyebrows. "It's just a drink. But we'll see."

I walk out of the hospital feeling a lightness in my footsteps I hadn't felt in a while. Or at least since Shaw had started. I walk to my car and drive around the corner to pick up the Indian food. Chicken Tikka Masala for me and an order of Tandoori Chicken with extra naan for Donovan.

He's a runner so he can afford the extra carbs.

The man at the Indian place, Mr. Lawani, packed my bag with extra food and extra sauce. Honestly, the bag is so heavy I have no idea what he put in there. "For you and your tall boyfriend." He chuckles and then gives me a wink. "A little extra surprise for the two of you."

Not sure I'm ready for another surprise. Seems like I've had enough chaos lately.

As I drive toward my apartment, I think back to the last couple of hours. It had been a whirlwind, probably the craziest shift I'd ever had as a resident. The entire ED was nearly silent as Shaw fought his way out of the hospital, dragged off by Padilla and his men. We all stood huddled at the nurses' station until Riley gently reminded us that medicine doesn't wait.

And then, we did what we'd been trained to do.

Got back to work.

I'd checked in with Dr. Riley as I ended my shift. He didn't have long to talk or check my cases. He had to go. His phone was ringing off the hook. From what I could gather, it sounded like he was getting called to an emergency board meeting after what had happened to Shaw.

Like I said, it was a crazy shift.

But I wasn't entirely surprised with the way things turned out.

I knew there was something up with Shaw. Like I told you before, everything in my life was pretty good until he arrived in the Emergency Department. I'd catch him every now and again looking at me funny as if he was sizing me up.

And then I started to put things together.

The so-called mistakes that Shaw tried to get me into trouble with were mostly real — at least one of the three of them. Mr. Palmer had refused to fill his prescriptions. That was the reason his foot had become so septic so fast. Luckily, the doctors upstairs in the orthopedic unit were able to save it with some aggressive antibiotics and wound care. I researched the needle decompression stunt I saw Shaw pull. The large bore needle and the axillary placement is a classic field trauma technique. And the gal that I thought had a virus, but that Shaw was sure had leukemia, Samantha Watkins, ended up being just fine. A negative biopsy revealed that there's no cancer in her body anywhere. Later on, a so-called "technical glitch" was exposed that had changed her blast count from zero percent to twenty percent.

That's when I became suspicious.

For as tired as I was, I knew that her blasts read zero. I'd also seen Shaw playing with his tablet right before he came in to point out my mistake. There is a way — if you know what you are doing with the computer system — to alter the lab results. It's kind of complicated. You'd have to get into the admin panel, create a secondary account, or steal a login of one of the lab techs and then go in and manually change the result.

The good news is that other than Samantha getting quite the scare, her health is nothing short of perfect now that she's through the virus. She and I had coffee last week — she reached out to me when the news broke about Shaw — and we discovered we have a lot in common. She wanted to hear all about what had happened to me, and I spent the first half hour apologizing profusely, until she told me to shut up.

Yeah, Sam's pretty cool like that.

And the drama with the storage room? That one took me by surprise. Remember my buddy Marshall in the security office? Not only had he discovered that Shaw was the one who had crashed the computer system, but Marshall found video that Shaw had also taken the splints out of the trauma cart right before he asked the overnight nursing staff to rearrange the supply room.

All of it was meant to trip me up.

And it did.

But then things got really crazy when Snort disappeared. When he reappeared and I closed the window, I told the story to Mrs. Dixon. She's actually kinda nice when you stop to talk to her. She commented that you could never be too careful and called her grandson, who works for the Philadelphia Police Department. Using her stellar people skills, Mrs. Dixon managed to convince her grandson to go up to my fire escape and dust the window for prints. Mrs. Dixon is always concerned about Peeping Toms.

I got a call from her grandson the next morning, a great guy named Gerald, saying that they had retrieved fingerprints and that they were running them. He saw the scrapes in the paint just like I did and although he couldn't tell me who'd been on the fire escape, he was pretty sure someone had. He said he'd let me know what they found out, told me to keep something jammed in the window to keep it from being pried open again, but I never heard back from him.

My guess? Shaw was the one on the fire escape. And when Gerald ran his fingerprints, that's what set off the alarm bells with the Army.

Gerald told me when they submit fingerprints, it goes to all of the databases — local, state, and federal.

The Army is federal, after all.

Even without Gerald, it wasn't like I hadn't figured out most of this on my own. During my suspension, I'd spent a good chunk of the day going through pictures. Not only did I find pictures of Shaw and Riley together, but I found pictures of Shaw and Jackson Soto, the pharmaceutical guy, together. Jonathan and Jackson had been friends in college. From what I could tell, Jackson had toyed with a career in medicine and then decided to enlist in the Army. As luck would have it, Jackson ended up in the same Green Beret unit as the twin brother to his friend Jonathan, which is where Ryan and Jackson met.

And then there was the real kicker, the thing that tied it all up into one neat bow for me.

I found a picture of Ryan Shaw and his identical twin, Jonathan, together.

See, the Shaw that I was working with was actually Ryan Shaw. His brother Jonathan had died in a climbing accident. He was the one that had been pictured with Riley. Ryan and Riley had gone to medical school together. That would be the real Jonathan. The Jonathan that had gone to medical school.

Ryan Shaw, the one that had been posing as Dr. Jonathan Shaw in the Liberty Hill Emergency Department, was already in the military and was deployed with Jackson Soto. That's where Ryan had gotten his medical training.

When Jonathan Shaw, the actual doctor, had died, Ryan had already run from the military and was hiding in Philadelphia. He quickly adopted his brother's identity and got to work. After all, who could tell them apart? They were identical. Ryan, posing as Jonathan, had worked at a variety of different hospitals in the area, jumping from job to job until he finally landed at Liberty Hill.

While it was hard to figure out that Shaw was a twin, it wasn't too hard to figure out who the pharmaceutical guy was. He didn't advertise his military background, but Donovan, with his contacts in government, was able to run the photo for me and get me an identity. Lo and behold, Jackson worked for a medical device firm. Even better, they had new products that were perfect for an Emergency Department, and he was local to Philly. Donovan, through his contacts, had even been able to figure out that the man had a peanut allergy.

Turns out, Donovan might be more dangerous than I thought he was.

There's an old saying that it only takes a spark to start a fire.

In this case, I lit a bomb.

(I'm grinning from ear-to-ear thinking about it.)

Marshall, my friend in the security office, has a couple buddies who are Army Reserve. To be honest, I wasn't sure who I could trust except for Donovan, but Marshall has always been good to me. When I let him know my concerns about Dr. Shaw, he was more than happy, working in his capacity as hospital security of course, to let them know that we were concerned about the identity of Dr. Shaw. So, when I ran out to get the crash cart to have it ready for Jackson, I sent Marshall a quick text. All it said was "Now!"

He'd been watching the entire scene unfold from his office.

After reaching out to the Army, Marshall had coordinated with Padilla and his team. Given Shaw's background as a Green Beret and his lethal training, the Army preferred to retrieve Shaw themselves rather than trusting that to the undertrained hospital security staff. Guys like Marshall might be able to handle drunks and domestics, but even Philly PD wasn't trained to deal with someone like Shaw, who could quickly take out people with the flick of his wrist.

Like Jackson said, Shaw's a scary guy.

Really scary.

And now, according to Marshall's buddies in the Army, Shaw is going to be spending a lot of time in a maximum-security military prison.

I do feel bad about causing Jackson to have a reaction. In

the military, he'd be considered collateral damage. And to be honest, the EpiPen didn't fail. I just needed help. I needed to get Shaw into the room so that the two of them could see each other. We needed to confirm his identity. I had no idea about the scar. That was just an extra bonus.

Can I tell you how excited and scared I was when Jackson pulled back Shaw's sleeve and exposed it?

Icing on the cake.

The one thing it took a little time for me to figure out was why. After all, like I said, I'm a very average-looking, third-year trauma resident in Philadelphia. There's nothing outstanding about me at all. When Shaw was dragged out of the Emergency Department, he kept shouting at me that it was all my fault. For people like Tamia, Dr. Riley, Hudson, and Jamir, they might not understand and chalk it up to him being crazy.

That's fine with me.

But after doing a little digging with Donovan's help, I know exactly why he said that.

When Ryan Shaw, the one I'd been working with, made his way back from overseas, he was still AWOL from the Army. He'd holed up with an ex-Army buddy on the outskirts of Philadelphia. The guy was another vet — somebody who had seen just as much action as Ryan had.

Except, unlike Ryan Shaw, this vet had PTSD. And Ryan's buddy — a guy named Ben Montgomery — had developed a poor coping system for his trauma. Drugs.

One night after a deeply traumatic evening, Ben decided to take more drugs than usual. When Ryan had found him, he was unconscious. Ryan, with his Green Beret medical knowledge, gave him Narcan and then rushed him to the hospital. They ended up at Philadelphia Main, or that's at least what we call it. It's the largest metropolitan hospital in the area. A team of doctors worked on Ben for nearly two hours. A resident who had just finished her first year was asked to place the intubation tube under the supervision of one of the attendings. Everyone thought that the tube was in the right spot, but it wasn't. It was a failed intubation. She placed the tube into the esophagus instead of the trachea and no one, in the chaos of Philly Main's ED, realized it in time. Everyone assumed it had been placed correctly and then had been drawn away by a slew of ambulance runs that arrived all at once.

Everything looked fine until about five minutes later when the attending passed by the room and noticed that Ben's vitals were dropping off a cliff. Ryan Shaw had been sitting in the waiting room hoping for good news about his friend.

There wasn't any.

The misplaced endotracheal tube, which sent air into his stomach and not his lungs, ended up giving Ben a bad case of hypoxia — which means brain death. No oxygen means no fuel for the brain. Ben lasted on life support for another two hours and then passed away.

How did I figure this out? I know the other resident. She now works at her father's store, helping out.

How do I know her?

Because her name is McKayla Forbes.

Uh huh.

Shaw's not the only one that's a twin.

I am too.

And McKayla Forbes is my sister.

I'm sorry that her mistake killed his friend.

But it wasn't *my* mistake.

EPILOGUE

Two months later, I walked down the aisle wearing a pale lavender satin gown, carrying a bouquet of white flowers just ahead of my sister. Heather, my sister's annoying friend, and I ended up being co-maids of honor.

Honestly, I could care less, except that I'm secretly glad I'm walking just ahead of Heather.

That's a win for the good guys.

I pass Donovan, who's bought a new suit for the occasion. He had it custom-fitted in London when he was there last and he looks good.

Real good.

The music plays softly, and I try to walk at the rhythm that my sister wants me to. The rehearsal dinner the night before had been a nightmare — Queen Julia running around alternately looking calm and freaked out all at the same time, her wedding planner looking at least ten years older than the last time that I saw her.

And all I could do was laugh.

I managed to get home early for the wedding. Not a week

early, but early enough that I was able to be on hand for the dreaded Brazilian wax. I just held Julia's hand while she cried. I didn't bother to look at exactly what they were doing. Waxing the nether regions was a procedure I just didn't need to learn.

I suffered through the mandatory manicures and pedicures, only spending a few minutes wondering about the overall cleanliness and the amount of bacteria that might be in the salon that Julia had decided to use, sat through the half a dozen speeches at the rehearsal dinner at Boardman Hills Country Club, where Julia's fiancé's parents were members. The only people that looked more annoyed than I felt were the serving staff who clearly just wanted to go home.

Apparently, they had dealt with one bride too many that summer.

Perhaps Queen Julia had pushed them over the edge.

I even managed to make it through the sleepover at my mother's house the night before the wedding, leaving Donovan in a very nice hotel all by himself. I would have much rather been snuggling with him than sleeping on my mother's couch, but Julia, well, she required a lot of attention. It almost got to the point when I wanted to order a tranquilizer for her just so that the rest of us could get some peace and quiet, but then again, I don't have privileges in Ohio.

So back to the wedding.

McKayla, my twin, went down the aisle ahead of us with her daughter, and my niece, Lily. She's beautiful and blonde. After McKayla's failed intubation, she decided that medicine wasn't for her. Our parents were actually thrilled. They weren't thrilled about the fact that she'd invested in four years of medical school, which she wouldn't be using, but they were happy to have her home. She reconnected with a high school boyfriend after a couple of weeks, managed to get herself pregnant, and Lily was born. Now, she was using her medical knowledge to raise her family. Lily is blonde like Julia with big blue eyes, and we all enjoy spoiling her rotten.

Another high maintenance Forbes in the making.

As I make my way up to the altar and stand off to the side, fluffing Julia's train, making sure the acres and acres of white silk taffeta is extended behind her like she's royalty, I look back at Donovan. He lifts his chin ever so slightly. The night that he stormed out on me was the night that he said everything changed for him. It wasn't that he ever believed anything happened between me and Shaw.

I didn't know it at the time, but that wasn't it at all.

While I was busy freaking out about losing him, he was having the same experience. When he saw me with another man, he decided that he couldn't be without me ever again. We were both scared at the same time.

Isn't that so cute?

Now Julia is not the only one with a ring on her hand, except for the fact that Donovan and I are planning a very quiet, very private wedding the next time that he goes to Thailand. No family, no flowers, no taffeta, and no Brazilian wax.

Wait, well maybe a Brazilian wax.

In fact, our trip is only a few weeks away. We're squeezing it between when I start as an attending at Schuylkill Valley Hospital and when Donovan heads off for another round of travel through Asia. We're looking at houses on the outskirts of Philly with a nice yard that's close to the airport for Donovan. Who knows, maybe we will even get a dog. I think Snort could use a canine companion.

He'd really hate that, don't you think?

Looking at Julia and her fiancé become husband and wife, I realize that if Shaw hadn't targeted me, then Donovan might never have figured out that he couldn't live without me. And now I'm about to become Mrs. Donovan Keller.

...fter I'm married, I'll always be Mac.
...u see me at the hospital, Dr. McKenna Forbes.

To join my exclusive reader list and be the first to get updates on new books and sales, giveaways and releases, click here! I'll send you a prequel to the next series FREE!

Made in the USA
Middletown, DE
20 January 2026

27378057R00159